dead behind
the eyes

Brock Car

Prairie W
Milt

Dead Behind the Eyes

Copyright © 2014 by S.K. Car.

Published by Prairie Wind Publishing
1709 Saint Mary's Bay Drive
Milton, Florida 32583

ISBN: 978-0-9836761-6-4

Publisher's Note: This is a work of fiction. Names, characters, places, and incidents are a product of the author's imagination. Locales and public names are sometimes used for atmospheric purposes. Any resemblance to actual people, living or dead, or to businesses, companies, events, institutions, or locales is completely coincidental.

Printed in the United States of America
First Edition: June 2014
10 9 8 7 6 5 4 3 2 1

For My Daughters,

One I loved and lost and the
two who healed my broken heart
Rebecca Ruth, Mallory Ann and Sally Rose Car

dead behind
the eyes

PROLOGUE

Max Riley straightened his tie before bounding up the stairs of the corporate jet—two steps at a time. He felt every bit as good as he looked. Being declared, "golden" by the cardiologist at his Monday morning physical made for the beginning of a most excellent week. When Max stepped into the cabin the other passengers erupted with applause. His modest laugh gave a momentary glimpse of the shy boy he once was. Holding up his hands to quiet the adulation, he beamed.

"With apologies to Lou Gehrig, 'Today, I consider myself the luckiest man on the face of the earth.' *You* know The Board has just named me CEO but *I* know the privilege of leading this company is thanks in no small part to the support of all of you. Next to the day I married Trish and the births of my three children, this is the most remarkable day of my life. Thank you one and all."

"Now, if you'll bear with me, I know we're all anxious to get home to our families but I'm waiting for some papers to be delivered before we can take off. So kick back and enjoy some refreshments and we'll be in the air as soon as possible."

After the papers were delivered and the courier left the plane, Max signaled the pilot to take off.

Max slid the door closed that separated the two front seat passengers from the rest of the cabin. He lit the forbidden cigar and poured the Absinthe as was his daily ritual. He knocked it back in three quick gulps then doused his cigar in the empty glass. Soon he would be home with Trish and the kids. He splashed Old Spice aftershave in his hands and slapped his cheeks. Then he applied a generous handful to his genitals. His wife loved the smell of Old Spice. It was the only fragrance she liked. It was the smell of the man she adored.

Max's head began to spin. The Absinthe was doing its job. Suddenly his heart began to beat intensely and erratically. That was odd, Max thought. If he hadn't been pronounced "golden" by the doctor, it might have been cause for concern. That was Max's final thought before falling into a deep, alcohol-induced sleep.

Moments later, Max Riley, the luckiest man on the face of the earth, was dead.

Chapter 1

Friday, 5:00 am

Her husband had gone crazy. Trish Riley laid in bed watching Max's chest rise and fall and prayed today would be the day the old Max came back to her.

The three Riley teens were sleeping when Max's alarm clock sounded. Trish had been up for an hour. With freshly brushed teeth, new make-up, and nothing else on, she slipped her trim, athletic body back into bed and cuddled up to her husband.

"The coffee is perking and so am I," she whispered into Max's ear. "I think we've got time for a little eye-opener."

Max rolled over and began his usual sixty seconds of foreplay. "I'll do anything you want. Anything," Trish whispered.

But Max didn't want anything new. He wasn't in the mood to make the effort. Certainly not with Trish. He maneuvered himself into his wife of twenty years and began fantasizing to speed things up. He was anxious to get to the office, especially today.

By 5:15, Max was patting Trish on her bare butt. "Thanks for the nice surprise. Now I've got to get in the shower and get to work."

Trish kissed Max on the back of his neck as he steadied himself on the edge of their bed. She slipped into her short, purple silk kimono and headed for the kitchen. When Max walked in, Trish was sipping a cup of coffee, seated across from the fruit plate she had prepared for him. Her kimono had slipped off one shoulder to reveal milky white skin dotted with freckles. Her short, reddish brown hair was full and tossed. Against the backlighting of the kitchen window, her freckled face took on the soft glow of a woman half her age.

"You look nice this morning. Got big plans for the day?" Max asked without waiting for an answer. He looked at his watch and announced that he had to get going and wouldn't have time for breakfast.

Trish followed him to the door. As Max headed out, something made him stop. He turned to Trish and asked, "You know, you deserve a whole lot better than me. Why do you stay?"

"Because I love you. Until death do us part, remember?"

Max smiled at Trish. A smile filled with pity.

Trish closed the door. She heard the morning sounds of her three children getting out of bed.

"Good morning," she yelled up the stairs. "I'm making pancakes. Better hurry."

Trish began preparing the batter. She made exactly fifty strokes around the inside of the bowl with the old wooden spoon. As she looked at Max's uneaten fruit plate, a familiar feeling of sadness washed over her.

Chapter 2

Friday, 6:15 am

John Wellman stared at the report on his desk and felt sick to his stomach. He couldn't believe his eyes. To add insult to injury, it was clear that while the report contained information that was shocking to him, it was apparently common knowledge. John had been accused of being naïve, and the accusation stung. He resisted the tag, but maybe they were right. Being naïve was probably costing him his job, and now it felt like it was costing him his self-respect.

John was a dying breed and a bit of an enigma, even to those who knew him best. The company newspaper once described him as a compassionate Renaissance man who just happened to be CEO of Great Western Communications. He loved his job, his family, and his life. There was not a greedy bone in his body. But at the age of fifty-seven, his thirty-four years with the company was coming to an end. He was not leaving of his own accord. Like most executives who elected an early retirement to "pursue other opportunities," he was leaving with a not so gentle shove.

Three weeks after the breakup of the old Bell System, John was appointed CEO of Great Western, one of the Baby Bells as they came to be collectively known. He had been president of the company under the old Bell System, so it came as no surprise that he would remain as president of the newly formed Great Western. John's intellect and soft-spoken Jimmy Stewart manner made him as popular with the board of directors as it did with the employees. But times were changing. Taking risks, branching out into maverick, unrelated business ventures, and making money—lots of money—trumped any values that got in the way.

In his years at the helm of Great Western, John never hit his revenue targets. That's not to say Great Western wasn't profitable. It was extremely profitable. But when it was a part of the old Bell System, Great Western never met the inflated revenue goals set by its parent, AT&T. The idea of "reworking" the numbers to make goal, never occurred to John. When the Chief Financial Officer, Dave Crease, suggested they go back and "massage" the numbers, John was stupefied.

"John, how do you think the other companies make their numbers? We are the only operating company that consistently misses our revenue target. And *you* are the only company president who doesn't massage his numbers. If I may be blunt, failure to recognize that reflects poorly on all of us," Dave explained.

"Massage the numbers?" John looked straight through his numbers man. He knew exactly where this was going and he didn't like it. "You've certainly got a way with words, Dave. And by making 'all of us' look bad, I expect you mean that if the numbers don't look the way the big guns want them to look, then the guy in charge of the numbers won't look good."

Dave chose not to respond directly to the jab. Was his self-interest so obvious? "With all due respect, John, you're being naïve. Every corporation in America makes numbers say what their shareholders and board of directors want them—no, *need* them—to say."

"Dave, there's more to Great Western then our enviable profit margin—and we do have one. Our customer service ratings and safety records are unsurpassed. Our marks as a good employer and corporate citizen can't be matched. There are more ways to measure a company's success than simply how fat the bottom line is."

"I'm not disagreeing with you, John," Dave insisted. "But, I'm not the guy calling the shots. The board may applaud your safety record and how you're the only guy in the system to make his EEOC numbers, but believe me, they couldn't care less about such things. All they care about is the inflated millions we're not making. This is going to cost you, and very likely me, our jobs. Please don't shoot the messenger. You need to hear the truth."

John looked out the window, hands thrust deeply into his pinstriped trouser pockets. He felt like an eight-year-old schoolboy being scolded in front of the entire class. His athletic, six-foot four-inch frame was tanned and handsome. When he was in college, friends teased that he looked like the Arrow Collar and Cuffs Man. He wondered if anyone younger than him would even know what that meant. His teeth were straight and white and his expressive blue eyes conveyed a range of emotions without uttering a word. His chiseled good looks and thick dark hair, perfectly silvered at the temples, only added to his imposing presence.

As he looked at the distant landscape, he pondered the mighty Missouri River, twenty-one stories below. From John's perspective it looked more like a lifeless earthworm than a powerful force of nature. The metaphoric insignificance of one man's life was not lost on him. John nodded slowly and turned back to Dave. He heard the truth in Dave's words but was not ready to reconsider what he had to do.

"I appreciate your candor, Dave, I really do. But we're not changing the numbers. I consider myself trusting and optimistic, but naïve is probably a more apt description. After all, at the ripe old age of fifty-seven, I'm a bit of a fossil in this post-divestiture environment. But telling the truth is always the right thing to do. And I still intend to do what's right."

Great Western Communication continued to earn millions in profits. It provided well paying jobs for 40,000 employees across sixteen states and made significant contributions to the communities it served.

But the profits were never enough to satisfy the executive board members who insisted GWC's stock should outperform the other Baby Bells. It was all about the money. And so John was on his way out. Dave Crease's cautionary conversation was never far from John's mind. He took his termination personally and was deeply hurt. But the sting of that hurt paled compared to the pain he was feeling this morning. His best friend had betrayed his trust. John re-read the report for the fifth time. With each reading it stung a bit less. It no longer made him want to cry. Now, it just made him want to kill somebody.

Chapter 3

6:30 am

Max Riley flashed his company ID card at the security guard as he headed for the elevator. "Good morning, Robert, got big plans for the weekend? "

"I leave that up to the wife," Robert smiled. Forty-thousand employees and Max never failed to address Robert by name. Max knew that greeting employees by name did more to lift their spirits than extra cash in the paycheck ever could. When it came to producing a charming smile and engaging the employees of Great Western, nobody was more skilled than Max. That one small gesture upped his likeability quotient and gave him a mound of undeserved respect.

Max got off the executive elevator on the twenty-first floor. He looked to the left and saw that the curtained glass door and windows to the office of his boss and best friend were closed and the lights on. Max thought it was a little early for Wellman to be in but it did not deter him from walking around the jungle of potted palms and into his own office. As he approached his office he could see that his lights were on and the door closed. Max smiled.

He could smell her before he opened the door. Her signature perfume was sexy and earthy. The light, spicy aroma meant if it rubbed off on Max, it didn't make him smell too girly. He appreciated that.

Max entered his office and locked the door behind him.

"Nice bulge." Leah laughed. "Did you wake up with that? Doesn't your wife ever take care of you?"

"As a matter of fact, she took care of me about an hour ago. But I saved some seconds for you," Max smirked.

"I suppose that should bother me, but it doesn't. I love that you can never get enough. I think it's sexy...you're sexy." Leah knew she should be hurt to think that Max had just made love to his wife, but she wasn't. This morning it even turned her on.

"I see that Wellman is already in," Max cautioned. "We'd better hop on it...so to speak." When Max was thinking with his penis, there was never room in his pants to think about the incredible risk he was taking.

He eased down in the swivel chair behind his imposing desk and dropped his trousers in one well-practiced motion. Leah's short, tight skirt did not move as she positioned herself on Max's lap.

Both were facing the door in case there was a knock.

"My God, you're wet," Max panted.

"I knew we wouldn't have time for foreplay so I got started while I was waiting for you," Leah moaned.

Max was getting close when his phone rang. He picked it up while Leah continued her rhythmic movement.

"Max Riley," he barked into the phone.

"Dad, it's me, Tim."

"What do you need, son?"

"It's mom. She's crying really hard and she won't tell us what's wrong."

"I'll call you right back."

Max hung up the phone and bit his lip as he came into Leah. His timing, for a change, was perfect.

"Wow." Leah breathed.

"Yeah. Wow."

Chapter 4

John Wellman brushed past Leah as she waited for the elevator.

"Good Morning, Mr. Wellman," she cooed.

Wellman looked through Leah with uncharacteristic scorn.

"Good Morning, Leah. What brings you to the executive floor at this hour of the morning?"

"Oh, just dropping off some reports that Wayne asked me to deliver," she lied.

"I see. Say, will you ask Wayne to give me a call this morning?"

"Sure."

"It's important."

Leah's stomach was in her throat and there was a burning, screaming sensation in her ears. Something bad was about to happen.

Max stood at the window, his back to the open door. With the Missouri River in the distance and cars starting to fill the streets below, Max wondered why everyday life seemed so surreal to him. He could not define how he was feeling, but he didn't like it. Was he just unhappy? Depressed? Bored? Empty? Yes, that's how he felt, empty. But why? Everything was falling into place. He should be on top of the world.

John knocked on the door jam. "Got a few minutes?"

"Of course!"

John sat down and planted both feet firmly on the floor. His body language was casual and open yet empowered.

"Max, this is tough for me to say, so I'll just lay my cards on the table. You are aware that when we conclude any executive search for an outside hire, we always do an extensive background check. To protect the company from a potential lawsuit, I couldn't show preferential treatment when hiring our next CEO. So, I hired Buddy Drake to investigate you. He very quickly discovered what a lot of people—not me—but apparently a lot of people already know. Your affair with Leah came as a terrible shock and personal disappointment to me."

"Now just hold on," Max interrupted. "You're not asking me to believe that you were legally obligated to snoop into my personal life. My private relationships are none of your business."

John's reply was measured and direct. There was a tone in his voice that was unfamiliar to Max— forceful and intimidating. "You will not put me on the defensive. You will stand there and listen to what I have to say. And then we will fix this mess you've made. If you don't, I promise you will never be president of Great Western.

"At the top of our list of corporate values is honesty. Yet here you are, living a lie. Buddy tells me that over the past few months, you have become increasingly indiscreet. Apparently, I'm one of the few employees at Great Western unaware of your behavior. You have lost their respect, and that is critical in leading this company.

"On a personal note, next to my wife and sons, you are the most important relationship I have. Now I feel like our friendship is a lie. And if I feel that way, how must your family feel? How could you be so unspeakably cruel to Trish and the kids? I paid Buddy a lot of money for what he admitted was very little work. Apparently you're not wasting much time covering your tracks. He tells me that Trish and the kids have known about you and Leah for months, but that satisfying your libido is more important to you than your family's happiness."

Max looked at the floor and shook his head. His

shoulders were slumped and he spoke softly, with a catch in his throat.

"You're right. You're right about everything. I've wanted to talk to you about this for a long time. But, I was too ashamed. I have tried to break it off with Leah. But I just can't stay away from her. John, I'm in love with her. More to the point, I'm addicted to her. It's true that Trish and the kids know. I've begged Trish for a divorce, but she won't even consider it. This thing is tearing me up. I'll do whatever you say. Just tell me what to do. Where Leah is concerned, I'm unable to make rational decisions."

"Max, you might not be able to change how you think or how you feel, but you can change your behavior. And that's exactly what I'm going to help you do. I'll be meeting with Wayne Winston later today. I will arrange for him to offer Leah a job — a downgrade — in our Connecticut office. We have an opening there for an office manager. It's an office that you will never have a need to visit. If she won't take the job, she'll be terminated. Her job here will be eliminated. We're 'right-sizing' Wayne's department. You will apologize to your family and beg their forgiveness. You will live the rest of your life in a way that is worthy of their forgiveness and trust."

Max looked relieved. "John, I am sincerely sorry. You are the best friend I've ever had, and I've let you down. This thing with Leah has got such a hold on me; I won't be able to do this on my own. As long as Leah is here, I won't be able to stay away from her. Thank you for taking control of this. You can't imagine what a relief this is. I won't let you down. But you've got to get her out of here. She's like heroin to me."

Chapter 5

Max's thoughts were interrupted by the ringing of his cell phone. He could hear the panic in Leah's voice.

"I ran into John Wellman at the elevator after I left your office. He has summoned Wayne. Do you know what this is about?"

"I have no idea."

"This may sound crazy, but I think he knows about us," Leah whispered.

"I think he does, too. Maybe we'd better cool it for awhile."

Wayne Winston walked into John Wellman's office filled with expectation. Finally, he thought, his day had come. Wayne had been on the corporate "hot list" since his early days at the phone company. Once a hot shot was identified as a rising star, it was almost impossible to screw up. Wayne knew a private audience with John Wellman had to mean he was about to climb another rung on the corporate ladder. He had been asked to sit in on three executive level meetings in the last month. To be personally summoned to

Wellman's office was a good sign. A very good sign.

"Thanks for coming up," John said as he shook Wayne's hand.

"Of course."

"I'll get right to the point. I want Leah Beaulay out of Omaha. You will inform her today that her position in your organization is being eliminated. Your department is being 'right-sized'. There is a position you can offer her in our Connecticut office. It will be a downgrade, but we will pay her relocation expenses and not cut her salary. If she isn't interested, she's gone."

"Unless she can find another position within the company here in Omaha," Wayne quickly added. "That's outlined in the HR right-sizing plan. Leah is an excellent employee and I know she won't want to relocate. You know, her husband works for the company, too, and he's here in Omaha."

"That woman has a husband?" John asked. "I didn't know that. But it changes nothing. Staying in Omaha is not an option. She either goes to Connecticut or she's out. Frankly, I'd be happy to see her leave the company altogether."

Wayne wasn't one to disagree with his superiors, but this was different. "John, I hate like hell to do this. Leah is a wonderful person and she's made a huge contribution to my department. Can you enlighten me a little as to exactly why she's being fired?"

"She's not being fired. It is part of our right-sizing effort. Believe me, Wayne, that's all you want or need to know."

Chapter 6

This wasn't going to be easy. Wayne and Leah's own affair had ended over a year ago. He sometimes wondered if she had ended their affair for another man, but she assured him that was not the case.

"I can't do this to your wife," Leah insisted. "I feel terrible about this. You have a family and I don't want to hurt them."

Wayne loved that about Leah. He was sure she had feelings for him, yet she was too decent to continue their affair. He wasn't surprised when Leah broke it off. He couldn't believe someone with her astounding beauty could be interested in him. He would never have been able to pull the plug, so it was just as well that Leah did. He was happy when the office rumor mill shifted the focus from Wayne to Max. Even after their romantic relationship ended, there were half a dozen times when Leah and Wayne were on the road and ended up in bed together. He asked Leah if the rumors about her involvement with Max were true. She was incredulous.

"Is that what people are saying? You know I'm not a slut. I hope you came to my defense."

Wayne believed her.

Despite the passage of time and rumors that Leah had moved on to Max, Wayne couldn't shake his feelings for her. Transferring her would be painful but Wellman had spoken and he knew it was her career or his.

Leah stormed out of Wayne's office and immediately called Max on his cell phone.

"I'm being transferred? Demoted? You must have known about this. Why didn't you tell me? You're not going to let this happen, are you?"

"I learned about this five minutes before you did. I can't talk to you about it now, but just go along with it. I'll see what I can do once Wellman retires."

"You'll see what you can do? Are you kidding? Believe it or not, my career is as important to me as yours is to you. I'm not going to let this happen without a fight. Trust me, this will be a whole lot easier on everyone if you turn this around today."

"This is Wellman's doing. I can't defy him. Not just now. We've already destroyed my marriage; it would be stupid for both of us to destroy my career. Just be patient. I can't defy Wellman and be the next CEO. You don't want to cost us that, do you?"

"Forget it, Max. This relationship has been all about you long enough. I'm through being the victim."

Max was caught off guard by Leah's reaction. She had never made demands on him.

"Calm down. You're going to take that job in Connecticut and you'll take your husband with you. Once I'm president, everything will be different. Until then, you are not to contact me or even acknowledge me if we happen to cross paths.

"If and when I can see you, I will. But I'll be the one to make it happen. And it will happen. Until then, don't bother me. It has to be this way." Max hung up the phone before Leah could catch her breath.

"Don't bother me? Don't *bother* me?" Leah repeated out loud. "You have no idea who you are dealing with."

Chapter 7

Peter Anderson wanted Leah to take his last name when they married but she refused. Beaulay was a prominent name in the Choctaw community and Leah refused to abandon her Native American heritage. Peter suspected that Leah's newfound interest in her history had more to do with the company's commitment to advancing women and minorities and less to do with ethnic pride. But he didn't put up much of a fuss. She had enthusiastically agreed to marry him, and he couldn't believe his good fortune. Sure, he'd heard the gossip linking Leah to one man or another. He confronted her once but she denied the rumors. "They're just jealous," she said. "Every time a beautiful woman gets a promotion it has to be because she's screwing the boss, right?" Peter never really doubted her. He knew she was right.

That was six years ago. Peter, easily the best looking man at Great Western, had married Leah, the most striking beauty of any corporation. The sizeable trust fund his grandmother had set up for him made him even more attractive to her. In the early years of their marriage friends often commented that he and Leah would make the most beautiful babies. But as the years passed, and no babies came, the comments ceased.

Leah had her tubes tied (something she failed to mention to Peter) soon after she divorced her first husband. She knew that having a child would "seal the deal" should she and Peter ever divorce, but it wasn't worth it. The last thing she wanted was more children. Peter was so focused on his career and his beautiful new wife that he never raised the issue of children. When Leah's children from her first marriage visited, she enjoyed them but was always ready to return them to their dad and stepmother. She and Peter enjoyed their freedom.

Leah concocted a plausible transfer story to share with her husband. She explained that the move to Connecticut, while it looked like a demotion, was anything but. "I'll be getting important cross-training in the corporate finance department. They are grooming me for a director's position. I'll be representing the company in Washington, D.C. and on Wall Street. This could be good for your career, as well as mine."

Peter suggested that maybe they should think about starting a family, instead. Leah wouldn't have to move. Peter could easily support them if she wanted to quit working altogether.

Leah interrupted. "That's not even up for discussion. You don't want children any more than I do. Let's not do something stupid so you can control my career."

Peter knew when to fold 'em. He would remain in Omaha while Leah moved to Connecticut. They would make sure to spend at least every other weekend together. Without children in the way, this could work.

"I just worry that some guy will steal you away from me. Every man you meet is going to fall in love with you, just like I did. I'm not going to lose you, am I?"

Leah sat on Peter's lap and kissed him on the forehead.

"You have nothing to worry about. I promise you. There is no one in Connecticut who could take me from you. Besides, you know what they say: absence makes the heart grow fonder."

Leah didn't delude herself. She knew her sexual relationships within the company had been largely responsible for her rise to middle management. She worked hard—but so did the rest of the employees. Most mid-level managers had MBA's. She hadn't even finished college. No, she recognized what her real talents were and she didn't feel guilty about using them. She had screwed her way up the ladder, eventually reaching Wayne, and finally Max. She couldn't screw any higher than that. She could complain about things all she wanted, but she knew that she could never match her salary or position outside the company.

Chapter 8

L eah had been on the new job less than a month when her boss called and told her she would be attending a meeting in Denver. The finance directors of some of the old Baby Bells were convening to network and share success stories and he wanted her there. She was flattered. This would be great exposure.

Minutes after Leah hung up the phone, her private cell phone rang. It was Max.

Employees at Great Western had long suspected that there was some sort of executive eavesdropping privilege that allowed their bosses to listen in on telephones within the company. How else could executives know such details about employees? The notion was routinely denied, but few employees bought that denial. Leah knew it was true. Max confessed to as much when he gave her a secure Sprint cell phone that the company had no access to.

"Damn, I miss you," Max began. "I'm the reason you're flying out to Denver if you hadn't already figured that out. I'll meet you at the company condo. I'll call you later with the details. Not a word to anyone. If anyone finds out, this could ruin everything we've worked so hard for. But I can't wait any longer. This is killing me."

"I miss you too," Leah whispered. "I can't wait to get my hands on you. Call me when you know more." Leah hung up the phone and smiled. But she felt nothing.

Chapter 9

The Gulfstream IV was filled to capacity as it headed to Denver for the board meeting that would confirm what everyone already knew: Max Riley would be the next president and CEO of Great Western Communications.

James Beck, head pilot for the company, was flying the left seat that day. But his co-pilot, Brad Wilson, would be doing most of the flying. James (he never allowed anyone to call him Jim) scheduled himself to fly only when the biggest of big shots were on board. GWC owned six corporate jets. The Gulfstream was the largest and best in the fleet. Max Riley considered it his personal jet and had it outfitted to meet his unique need for privacy.

James had flown so little in the past few years that he had lost his touch. But when they pulled out the big jet for Max Riley and John Wellman, James made certain he was in the pilot's seat. He had grown tired of the act of piloting. But he wasn't about to miss an opportunity to kiss some presidential ass.

James always looked like he just walked off the pages of *GQ*. He was tall and fit, thanks to running seven miles every day. His suits fit him to perfection and no matter how many hours he sat in the pilot's seat, they never wrinkled. He could have passed for the president of any Fortune 500 company. James stood at the bottom of the stairs to greet the passengers as they boarded the jet.

The Wellman's arrived first. James helped Mrs. Wellman into her seat. Five minutes later, the Riley children piled out of the corporate van and started unloading duffle bags, skis, and ski boots. Max's mother-in-law, Ruth O'Kiefe, her arms loaded with books and magazines, stepped out into Corporate Vice President Claudia Sullivan's waiting hands.

"Be careful of these old knees," Ruth cautioned as she gingerly stepped out of the van." Despite a thirty-eight year age difference, Ruth and Claudia Sullivan were the closest of friends. Ruth frequently joined Max, Trish and her grandkids on ski trips to Aspen, but not this year. It wasn't her recent seventieth birthday that slowed her down. It was the unexpected diagnosis of osteoporosis. She refused to believe she even had the disease since she was athletic and tall and exhibited no symptoms. Still, the diagnosis spooked her and she didn't want to risk breaking a bone.

Claudia hadn't seen Ruth since the lavish Christmas party Max and Trish hosted for company officers each year in their home. The entire Riley family looked different today. They seemed happier, much happier. At Christmas Trish appeared distant and disconnected. The children had not treated Claudia with their usual spontaneity and warmth. That night she observed what it must be like for children to live in a home where divorce was a better solution than an unhappy marriage. Claudia attempted to discuss her concerns with Ruth without repeating the rumors she'd heard about Max and Leah.

She cautiously approached her old friend. "What's up with the kids? They've lost their sparkle. They seem emotionless, kind of like they're dead behind the eyes. I don't mean to butt in, but are they okay?"

"Yes, I know exactly what you mean, but they'll be fine. Kids are resilient." Ruth then quickly changed the subject.

Claudia was an unlikely vice president. Her peers marveled that she had climbed so high on the corporate ladder at such a young age. At thirty-two, she was nothing like the other ambitious officers. She brightened any room she entered. Her shoulder length, thick blonde hair was usually twisted and clamped on top of her head for the office. Her bright blue eyes held just a trace of makeup. At five feet, nine inches, she glided into a room and heads turned. She looked more like a college junior than a corporate officer. Claudia was bright and a natural when it came to writing and public speaking. She worked harder than anyone on her staff. She was outspoken and candid without being gossipy. She was a little too witty and far too authentic to be taken seriously. So when she was tapped to become vice president of public relations, everyone was surprised, especially—Sumner Jackson. The entire PR department expected Sumner to get the job, and he was livid when a lightweight like Claudia was awarded what he felt was his entitlement. But John Wellman and Claudia clicked. She had the ear of the next generation of Great Western employees. She was his conscience and his guide and it was his choice alone that she should head up the public relations department.

When Wellman asked her if she knew about Leah and Max, she told him she had been hearing the rumors for months but didn't want to believe them.

"Does Trish know? Does Ruth?" John asked.

"Ruth and I have remained close friends all these years because we have an understanding that we don't discuss the company or Max. But yes, I think everybody in the Riley house knows what's going on to one degree or another. And all of them, especially the kids, are clearly miserable."

Claudia boarded the plane and sat next to Ruth. The two front seats were reserved for Max. And being on time was not one of Max's virtues. Claudia took a stack of papers from her briefcase and started to read. Ten minutes into her reading, Ruth nudged Claudia and nodded for her to look out the window. John smiled and nudged his wife, Phyllis. Korey Riley looked out the window and squeezed her sister Katy's hand. Tim Riley looked past his sisters and smiled. Looking very much in love and walking hand-in-hand to the waiting plane were Trish and Max Riley.

Max popped his head into the cabin while Trish passed a box of warm Krispy Kreme doughnuts to Tim. "Everybody strapped in?" Max asked. "Let's fly."

Max slid the door closed that separated the two front seat passengers from the rest of the cabin. James stepped into the cockpit and closed the door. James and Brad put their headphones on and James flipped on the "listen" switch he had secretly installed. He could now eavesdrop on the personal conversations of every passenger seated on the jet while Brad took instructions from the control tower.

"The best thing about catching a ride on the company jet is not wasting an hour going through security," Claudia said to John.

"Funny you should mention that. It's the lack of security on private planes that keeps me up nights. I called for, and approved, a very in-depth plan for improving security as it relates to corporate air travel. Don't be lulled into thinking that we're not vulnerable —*extremely vulnerable.* I approved the plan months ago and I haven't seen one item implemented. I guess James figures that he doesn't need to waste his time working on an assignment for a lame duck like me."

Exactly, James thought.

You can learn a lot about people by observing what they read on airplanes. Ruth picked up P.D. James', *The Murder Room.* She loved the detail of a good British mystery. They challenged her more than most American works. She loved the descriptions, the development of the characters, and the many possibilities that made for great whodunits. She learned long ago to take notes from the very beginning so she could keep all the characters straight. She enjoyed the way the author imparted wisdom without being preachy and how she revealed the events in her characters' lives that ultimately led them to murder. Ruth nestled into her seat like a mother hen about to lay a prize-winning egg.

Phyllis Wellman began to write notes to her sons. She lamented how computers were robbing people of the joy of reading and re-reading a personal handwritten letter. One evening Phyllis was looking for a recipe and came across a recipe for tuttie frutti written in her grandmother's hand. She could almost feel her presence. From that point on, Phyllis vowed to write at least one note or letter to someone every week.

John moved the *Wall Street Journal* aside and picked up *USA Today*. He had evolved beyond wanting to impress others by reading The Journal. He liked his news light and simple.

Claudia went back to her stack of papers. She never did buy into that phony corporate show of working on the plane. If she wasn't studying for her private investigator's licensing test, she would have been doing the crossword puzzle in the back of *People*. Her feelings, today, were all over the map. She felt excited, nervous, silly, and ultimately a sense of peace with her decision to leave the tedium of being an overpaid PR hack at Great Western for the life of a self-employed private investigator.

Chapter 10

When the jet landed in Denver, a small fleet of company cars was on hand to disperse its occupants. Max hugged his children and gave Trish more than a cursory kiss as the driver loaded the van for Aspen. Skis, poles, boots, luggage—it was a tight fit.

Ruth gave her son-in-law a hug and whispered in his ear, "Thank you. And I don't mean just for the lift."

Max knew exactly what Ruth meant. He loved his mother-in-law and knew his infidelities hurt her as much as they did Trish and the kids. It was obvious that she knew more than she let on, and Max appreciated how she minded her own business. He squeezed her again and gave her a knowing pat on the back.

Claudia and Ruth shared a car to downtown Denver. Neither was scheduled to return to Omaha on the company plane. Ruth would visit her sister in Englewood and Claudia would attend the board meeting and visit the Denver PR staff before returning to Omaha via United. There wouldn't be room for her on the company jet, anyway. The board meeting would confirm new officers and they would bump Claudia in a heartbeat for a chance to fly on the Gulfstream and get some coveted face-time with Max. Claudia looked forward to freeing herself from the many ridiculous nuisances of the corporate class system. Everything from the size and shape of your office wastebasket to what seat you took on the company Gulfstream was determined by rank. Flying commercial would be a small price to pay.

Max climbed into the front seat of the SUV next to Quentin Saunders, his personal driver when in Denver. Quentin was anything but corporate looking. A handsome African American with wide, sparkling eyes the color of amber, he was the only Great Western employee with shoulder-length dreadlocks. Very Rastafarian.

"How's it going, Max?"

"Excellent." Max smiled as he gave Quentin a warm two-handed handshake. "I hope you've ordered up some good powder for my wife and kids. They're on their way to Aspen."

"They won't be disappointed," Quentin laughed. "I was just in Keystone this weekend. You ought to join them."

"I'd like to, but somebody in the family has to work to pay for all this."

"I hear you, boss. I hear you," nodded Quentin as he eased over to the right hand lane towards the posh new corporate headquarters that recently laid-off employees rightfully suspected their lost salaries helped subsidize.

"Oh, Quentin, you need to get over into the left lane. We have to swing by the company condo.

"I thought you were staying at The Marriott this time," Quentin said as he cut back into the left lane.

"I am. I just need to check on something there. I'd

like you to wait for me. I should only be twenty or thirty minutes."

Quentin nodded as he stared straight ahead, not wanting to catch Max's eye. Earlier that day, he had dropped another employee off at the condo. Leah Beaulay.

Chapter 11

Leah was looking out at the mountains, her back to the door, when Max walked in. She was wearing a form-fitting, red, raw silk suit jacket and pencil-thin black skirt. Her black stiletto heels showed off her toned, bare, olive-colored legs. Her dark hair glistened in the sunlight that backlit her perfect body.

"God, you take my breath away," Max said. In the weeks they had been apart, Max had a difficult time forming a picture of Leah in his mind. Her beauty still astounded him.

"Well, catch your breath and tell me why I'm here. What was so important that I had to fly halfway across the country before the sun came up?"

"You have to ask? You're here because I thought I'd die if I didn't see you."

Max walked over to the window, lifted Leah up and sat her on the deep windowsill. He tore open her jacket to expose her firm, bare breasts. Not a single button popped off the expensive, well-made suit. He buried his face in her breasts and breathed her in as if he was starved for oxygen. Picking her up from the sill he carried her to the bedroom. When he finally caught his breath, he lifted her skirt and finished what he had come to do.

"That didn't take long," Leah announced. The relationship hadn't changed. There was never any time for foreplay or small talk. "I'm going crazy in Connecticut. You've got to get me out of there. If I can't work in Omaha, move me to Denver. I'll do anything."

"Just be patient," Max said. "I don't like it when you make demands. It doesn't become you. If I can make something happen for you in Denver, you know I will. But it's not going to happen anytime soon."

"*If* you can do something for me?" Leah repeated. "Do you really think I'll fly across the country every time you feel like getting laid? When you tell me you love me, do you mean it at all? "

"You know I do. Let me grab a quick shower and we'll discuss this when I get out. I can't go to the board meeting smelling like we just made love or Wellman will have me fired before I get his job."

Max gave Leah a quick kiss and squeezed her bare butt a little too hard before jumping out of bed.

"You know, lover boy, I'd hate to have to hire somebody to whack you. And I don't mean that in a good way," Leah smiled.

Max was in the shower and Leah was sitting topless on the bed watching "*Judge Judy*", when she heard the key turn in the outside door. She ran into the bathroom. "Max! Somebody's here."

"Well, get dressed," Max barked.

Too late.

Leah turned back into the bedroom to find pilot, James Beck, and co-pilot, Brad Wilson, overnight bags in hand.

James didn't even attempt to hide his disgust from Leah. "We've got the condo reserved for the next two days. What are you doing here?"

He hadn't heard Max in the bathroom. When the bathroom door opened, James' and Brad's jaws dropped in unison. Max didn't miss a beat.

"Wait outside in the outer hallway," Max snapped. "I'll be there in a minute."

Outside James and Brad waited.

"What have we stepped in?" Brad asked.

"I think we've just picked up a little job security," James replied.

The five-minute wait felt like an hour. Max finally emerged, dressed in a fresh shirt, red-and-white striped tie, and $1,500 black power suit. James waited for Max to begin groveling for their silence and loyalty. He felt smug in the thought that he suddenly had the upper hand and would be indispensable. If the board decided to discuss cutting back the flight department, James knew he and Brad would be safe. Blackmail tasted sweet.

Max looked James square in the eye. "James, part of the security plan you failed to implement included securing this condominium, did it not?"

"Yes sir, it did."

"I support John Wellman one hundred percent

and I share his frustration with you for not following through. My life could have been at risk here. Anyone could have waltzed in just now."

James couldn't imagine where Max was going with this. And he had never been scolded like a child in front of a subordinate.

"As part of the right-sizing of the flight department, you will each receive a handsome early retirement package and two years severance pay. You will be expected to sign a non-disclosure statement. If you discuss anything about the company, including what you 'think' you might have seen here today, you will forfeit your severance pay. Do you understand?"

Before either could respond, Max continued, "The papers will be in order and waiting for your signatures when we return to Omaha. I expect you both to be at the airport for the return flight."

Chapter 12

Claudia looked around the boardroom and was struck by what a crap shoot success in the corporate world was. She knew the personal biographies of all the players—board members and Great Western officers—by heart. If they were lucky enough to rise to a position of vice president and were fired or resigned, they thought it was their birthright to move into another position at another company with equal prestige and an even more obscene salary. And they were right. Every move brought a bigger salary and more stock options.

But when lower or middle managers were laid-off, they spent months looking for employment and most had to settle for a lesser position and lower pay. The snobbery repulsed Claudia. At best it was dumb luck. And at worst, it was a not so subtle caste system. Either way, it made Claudia uncomfortable.

Shortly after her own promotion to vice president she heard herself referring to the company as "we". Prior to the promotion, she had always referred to it as "they". The day she caught herself using the "we" pronoun was the day she knew she had to get out before she became one of "them".

She listened carefully to what the officers and soon-to-be officers said and did. She knew she was smarter than most of them and that she could easily compete in their arena. But she also knew that she would never get the chance. Feminists were calling human relations and public relations "female ghettos". Those were the only departments where women had any chance of rising to the top. But the "special writing skills and artistic talents" of those women were never considered for top level, meaningful, officer positions.

As she took her seat, for once she didn't feel anxious or bitter. Absent was the ever-present knot in her stomach. She was resigning at the conclusion of the meeting, and she felt both excited and at peace with her decision.

Claudia's friends, and especially her husband Jake, thought she was crazy to walk away from such a fat paycheck. Jake, an undercover narcotics detective, was not happy with Claudia's decision and they argued about it daily. He liked the money and the prestige. Part of his attraction to Claudia was her paycheck and her title. They made her a novelty as a cop's wife and his friends envied him.

Years ago she told him, "I think a good job should be fun, socially relevant, and pay well. My jobs within the company have been fun and I've certainly been well compensated. But those days are over.

"My job pays well. Period. It's not enjoyable, anymore. And it's not like I'm keeping the world safe for dial tone. I'm wasting my life."

This was an argument they had repeated every night for the last year. Claudia worried that quitting her job might jeopardize her marriage but she finally decided if her job was such a big cornerstone in her marriage, then it wasn't built on much to begin with.

Claudia had been an employee of Great Western for ten years, working her way through and up the public relations department. Her career began as a writer on the company magazine. She moved through a series of lateral assignments including trade journal contact, media relations, and advertising manager. Her first significant promotion was to executive director of advertising and accounting. When Claudia was first offered the promotion, she declined. "Words are my business, not numbers. I love the creative process. I'm good at what I do. The budget job will kill me. I can't even balance my checkbook and you want me to keep tabs on a sixty million dollar advertising budget?"

After turning down the promotion three times, Claudia reluctantly accepted. It meant a $20,000 raise and would help Great Western make its EEOC target for a level within the company that few women reached.

"You won't be in the budget job forever," her boss insisted. "Besides, it will give you great exposure to the power positions in the company—the money men. We PR types don't get much respect. You'll have a chance to get some cross training in a more visible and valued area. This will be a huge boost for your career."

The numbers job turned out to be nothing like Claudia had expected—it was worse. The problem was, she was really good at it and that kept her there. But this was the assignment that brought her close to John Wellman and that was its own reward. Before long, Wellman created a new officer position for her and moved her onto the twenty-first floor in the office next to his. He never gave a speech or walked into a union meeting without first consulting Claudia. She was the last person he saw before he went on camera. She told him when to button his suit coat and what color and length of socks to wear. Once off camera, he went directly to Claudia for her critique.

The men (and all but two officers and one board member were men) at the top of the food chain always treated Claudia well. They knew she wasn't a threat and she had no hidden agenda. They genuinely enjoyed her engaging personality.

But today, the big wigs had no time for Claudia. They were there to be seen by those who could advance their careers. They liked her, but she didn't possess the star power they sought.

She made her way over to the coffee and breakfast bar where Sumner Jackson was examining the fruit tray. Claudia and Sumner had been friends until she was promoted ahead of him. Now he never missed an opportunity to stab her in the back.

"Say 'thank you' Sumner," Claudia chided.

"Thank you for what?"

"By the end of the day, I will be single-handedly responsible for advancing your career."

"Oh really? How are you going to do that? Are you going to hand over your job, which we both know should have been mine to begin with?"

As Claudia opened her mouth to tell Sumner that was exactly what she was going to do, he caught Max's eye and pushed past her to get to him.

The letter of resignation Claudia had prepared included a glowing recommendation for Sumner. Claudia asked herself what on earth had possessed her to take the high road and recommend this pissant who had undermined her so many times. Before she took her seat, she tore up the letter and tucked the pieces into her purse. Her resignation would have to be a verbal one. Sumner would probably get her job, anyway. But he would have to do it without her recommendation.

Chapter 13

T he board meeting came off without a hitch. Every item on the agenda made the attendees smile. While the company made a comfortable profit, it did not hit the inflated target the board had set. But they were confident that their aggressive new CEO would fix that. Max Riley knew how to get results.

As he reviewed expense-cutting efforts, Max volunteered that he was reducing the flight department by half and selling three of the jets. He had already made some significant changes in staff. John Wellman looked puzzled. Pleased, but puzzled. Wellman was not cut out to be a hatchet man and he knew it. In a few hours, the unenviable task of putting loyal employees out of work would no longer be his responsibility. While Wellman agonized over each layoff, Max could eliminate an entire department without batting an eye. "I'm doing them a favor," Max once told his secretary. "It's just business. The quicker the cuts, the faster the pain goes away. These people need to get on with their lives."

When Wellman stood to announce that he was retiring, many in the room feigned surprise. When he voiced his enthusiastic support of Max Riley, heads nodded in affirmation. This was the main event. Everyone knew that the purpose of this board meeting was to pass the torch.

Claudia felt isolated by her sadness. John looked like a great weight had been lifted from his shoulders.

But she knew it had been a long, painful process to get to that sense of relief. She also grieved for the dedicated employees who would begin losing their jobs in record numbers. John's retirement would speed up that process and increase the number of layoffs. She remembered an earlier board meeting where John attempted to explain that naming the new Denver arena after Great Western would cost the company over one hundred mid-level managers' salaries. The board didn't care. The prestige of their name on an arena did something for their egos, and if it cost a handful of jobs, so be it. It came as no surprise to Claudia that in the boardroom today, only she felt the loss in John's departure.

As John sat down, Claudia dialed her secretary's number with the go-ahead to release the news to the employees. John had presented a rough draft of the correspondence to Claudia for her usual input. She didn't change a word.

To All Employees of Great Western Communications:

After thirty-four years with the Bell System and now Great Western Communications, I will be retiring effective February 1.

I have loved every day of my job here. It never really felt like work, due in no small part to the wonderful employees working in every area of Great Western.

This is an exciting time to be a part of the telecommunications industry. I know you will out-think the competition and continue to succeed in a very competitive arena.

I hope you will continue to take the moral high road and compete in a way that upholds our reputation for decency and honesty, not only within our industry but within the larger business community, as well. That's what will give Great Western the staying power to survive and succeed.

It has been an honor to serve as your president. I look forward to traveling with my wife, Phyllis, and perfecting my golf game. Those of you who have seen me play will understand that will be a full-time job.

My very best to each and every one of you.

Sincerely,

John Wellman

When the board meeting adjourned, everyone lined up to shake Max's hand and congratulate him. When Claudia reached him, they comfortably hugged in place of a handshake.

"Congratulations, Max. You've worked long and hard for this day. I'm not flying back with you, so I need to let you know that I'm resigning. I'll fill you in on the details later. I'll do whatever I can to make the transition successful. When you have some time, I'd be happy to share my thoughts on my replacement." She made sure that Sumner heard every word.

"I'm a little surprised. But you need to do what you need to do," Max smiled. Then he moved on to the next-well wisher.

Claudia was surprised that Max's reaction — or lack of reaction—stung a bit. He didn't ask why she was leaving or plead with her to reconsider. GWC wasn't going to miss a beat without her. Despite ten years of long hours catering to the demands of others, no one would be sorry to see her go.

Chapter 14

S umner Jackson made certain he was the first passenger to climb aboard the Gulfstream for the return trip to Omaha. He placed his briefcase on the seat directly behind and across the aisle from the front seat where he knew Max would ride. He'd flown often enough to know that no one sat in the seat next to Max unless they were personally invited to do so. By the time they landed in Omaha, Sumner was determined to be the next vice president of corporate communications.

Max looked forward to enjoying the pre-flight ritual he had established months earlier. When at home, he enjoyed this end-of-day passage in his study. But for some reason, he found it even more satisfying on the jet. Perhaps it was the small act of public rebellion he enjoyed. Once all the passengers were seated, he would slide shut and lock the specially designed door that separated the two front seats from the rest of the plane. Then he would light an expensive Cuban cigar and savor it for all of five minutes. For a man who threatened termination of any employee found smoking on company grounds, the hypocrisy somehow escaped him.

After all, he was Max Riley. The rules didn't apply to him. Three exaggerated puffs on the cigar and it was fired up. Next, he removed the paper lid from the Waterford tumbler. One of the responsibilities of the on-duty pilot was to measure three shots of Absinthe into the tumbler before anyone boarded the plane.

Leah had introduced Max to this forbidden liquor. He wasn't sure if the stories about it being a hallucinogen were true or if people just felt what they wanted to feel. But he didn't care. It gave him an immediate euphoric buzz and made him feel invincible. Van Gogh and Hemmingway swore by the stuff. Both claimed it unleashed the creative genius within. Hemmingway had long been Max's literary hero—such a man's man. If Absinthe was Hemmingway's drink, then it was good enough for him.

When Leah first introduced Max to Absinthe they savored it like they did their lovemaking. The ritual was slow and deliberate. Leah had ordered the entire "kit" from England. Before making love she would ceremonially prepare their drinks. After pouring a shot of Absinthe into a tall Absinthe glass, Leah would lay the specially slotted spoon across the top of the glass and place a sugar cube on it. Next, she very slowly poured ice water over the sugar, drop by drop, by drop. The sugared water dripped into the Absinthe, turning it a milky green. They sipped it slowly and passed the concoction back and forth between their thirsty mouths. It heightened the thrill of the lovemaking that would follow.

But the slow Absinthe ritual had gone the way of their long nights of repeated lovemaking. Max wanted his alcohol buzz and sexual release to be fast and powerful. If his partner didn't get off, well, that was her problem.

These days, Max instructed the pilot to have his

tumbler of Absinthe and sugar water mixed and waiting for him. After drinking all but an inch of the Absinthe, Max would drop his lit cigar into the liquid. He liked to watch it sizzle and smoke.

Sometimes, after indulging in this ritual, Max would slide open the door that separated him from the rest of the passengers and socialize. Other times he would keep the door closed to be alone with his thoughts or sleep.

As Quentin Saunders drove him to Centennial Airport, Max thought about the cigar and Absinthe that were waiting for him—and Leah.

Chapter 15

B rad Wilson sat in the cockpit and took pleasure in knowing that his passengers would have to suffer the flight back to Omaha without a refreshed supply of alcohol and snacks. Besides preparing Max's Absinthe, it was the pilot's responsibility to see that the coolers on board were stocked with the favorite brands of food and drink of the ranking officers and their spouses: Guinness for the vice president of marketing; Fat Tire for the board member on today's flight; pinot grigio for his wife, Diet Cherry Coke for Liz Rocker, the born-again vice president of human resources. Today, they'd all have to settle for whatever was left on board. And forget about preparing the Absinthe cocktail. After all, what was Max going to do? Fire him? Again?

James Beck, on the other hand, refused to believe he was really terminated. He was certain Max would come to his senses and when he did, he didn't want to piss him off all over again by not properly performing the demeaning bartending duties he so loathed.

James arrived at the jet two hours before the scheduled takeoff. When he discovered that Brad had not filled the coolers, he jumped back in his car in search of a good liquor store. He returned with a less than satisfactory assortment of snacks but it would have to do. He threw them in the cooler and returned to the front of the cabin to prepare Max's cocktail. He carefully removed the paper lid and gave the murky green liquid a quick swirl. Three shots mixed with sugar and ice water. He was surprised to see the concoction was already in place. At least Brad fulfilled that part of his responsibilities, James thought.

Within an hour of being tossed out of the condominium, Brad was on the phone to pilots at other Omaha corporations. He lined up three interviews for the following week and was feeling good about his future. He had painstakingly put together the security plan that James claimed credit for. That plan got James an on-the-spot bonus. The fact that he failed to implement the plan gave Max the excuse he needed to fire them both. Brad was a likeable guy and known in pilot circles for his superior skills in the cockpit. By the end of the week, he'd walk away from Great Western and James Beck with a pension, two years severance pay, and a better position with another company. Brad hadn't felt this good in years.

James was waiting when the SUV carrying Max Riley pulled up to the Gulfstream. He opened the passenger door before Quentin could turn off the car engine.

"Max, could I have a minute before you board?"

"Sure."

"Max, if you haven't already, I'm begging you to reconsider what happened back at the condominium. I recognize it was said in the heat of the moment."

Max shook his head. "Sorry, James."

"My first loyalty is to you and the company," James pleaded. "You know I would never betray you. I will never repeat what I saw. If you like, I'll sign a non-disclosure agreement, a loyalty oath. Anything you like. But please, let me keep my job."

"James, this was a business decision as much as anything else," Max lied. "I announced to the board of directors today that we are selling three of our jets and right-sizing the pilots accordingly. This will mean a significant savings for the company. You and Brad should actually benefit from being the first to go. We're going to eliminate eight additional pilot positions. By that time, you and Brad will have found new positions. Those we let go later will find a much tighter job market."

James was speechless. Max inwardly congratulated himself. He hadn't lost his touch. He could still make bullshit look like Shinola.

When Max climbed onto the jet, sixteen of the

eighteen occupants erupted in spontaneous applause. Ann Beck and Cindy Wilson, wives of the newly-unemployed pilots, sat silently. Max was relieved to see Ann and Cindy on board. He wouldn't have to worry about James or Brad doing something foolish with their wives on the plane.

Max waved in acknowledgment of the warm reception. "With apologies to Lou Gehrig, 'Today, I consider myself the luckiest man on the face of the earth'...Next to the day I married Trish and the births of my three children, this is the most remarkable day of my life. Thank you all.

"Now, if you'll bear with me, I know we're all anxious to get home to our families but I'm waiting for some papers to be delivered before we can take off. So, kick back and enjoy some refreshments and we'll be in the air as soon as possible."

Max slid the divider door closed and locked it. As he closed the door to the cockpit he told James, "I need some privacy. I'll let you know when I'm ready to take off.

Quentin eased the car as close to the jet as possible. If he angled it just right, the passengers might not see the reports being delivered. Out of the car slid a shapely woman wearing designer jeans and a cream-colored silk blouse. The open-toed stilettos showed off freshly pedicured red toenails against Leah Beaulay's perfect olive skin. Under her arm she carried an accordion file tied with a string that made a perfect figure eight from paper button to paper button. In the folder lay twenty-five sheets of blank white paper.

Chapter 16

Leah laid the folder on the empty seat and straddled Max.

"Unbutton your blouse," Max breathed.

He grabbed her round firm breasts with both hands and began massaging them hard enough that Leah worried they might bruise.

"Can you feel what's happening under that sweet ass of yours?" Max asked.

"I want you in me," Leah sighed.

"There's no time. Get on your knees and take care of me."

Leah dutifully unzipped Max's pants and unleashed his throbbing package. She watched it pulsate as she held it in her hands like a fragile, precious gift.

Max bit off the tip of his illegal Cuban cigar. He struck a wooden match and lit it, puffing three times before it ignited.

"You'd better start puffing, too. Your president needs a quick blow job," Max smiled.

Leah devoured him. Max held the cigar in his left hand and held Leah's head firmly in place with his right. It took less than a minute for Max to climax. Leah took a wet washcloth from the small plastic baggie inside her purse. She warmed it for twelve seconds in the microwave. Max looked out the window as Leah wiped the outside of her mouth with the damp cloth and then wiped any remnants of semen off his genitals. As she buttoned her blouse, she said, "I remember a time when pleasing me was as important to you as pleasing yourself. Now everything you do is fast...detached. We don't even share a glass of wine or Absinthe anymore.

"When are we going to finish our conversation about my move?" Leah continued.

"I've got a planeload of people waiting to take off. This isn't a good time."

"Let me get this straight," Leah continued. "There's time for me to give you a blow job but no time to discuss my future. People do desperate things when they're made to feel as powerless as you make me feel. I've about reached my breaking point."

"Please be patient. It will be months before I can pull the strings I need to get you to Denver. I know you love me enough to wait."

"You know I love *you* enough? What about you? Do you love me? Before you know it, months will be years," Leah countered. "You think you can use me forever, but you're wrong. There's a limit to how long I'll wait. After all, I'm not Trish."

Max flashed at Leah. It was one thing for him to disparage his wife, but he would not tolerate some-one else criticizing any member of his family.

"That's right. You're not Trish. She is the mother of my children and has more class in her little finger than you'll ever have. I never want to hear you speak her name. This conversation is over."

Chapter 17

Leah backed down the stairs of the plane and into the waiting car. Max knocked on the door of the cockpit and James opened it. The pilots knew the routine without instruction. James stood, pulled up the steps, and closed and locked the door. Max sat down and opened the refrigerator. His Absinthe was waiting.

Sumner watched Quentin drive away. He recognized the passenger sitting in the back seat. Fifteen minutes alone with Leah Beaulay was bound to put Max in a receptive mood, Sumner thought. He tapped on the sliding door that separated Max from the rest of the passengers. Without getting up from his seat, Max slid the door open about ten inches.

"Can I talk to you, Max?"

"I've got this report to work through," Max lied. "So if you want to state your case for replacing Claudia, it will need to be quick."

Sumner slid the door open and walked into Max's cabin. He was not about to let the most important conversation of his career be overheard by anyone.

"Okay, Max. I appreciate your straightforward style and will get right to the point. I do want Claudia's job. I will represent you far better than she ever could. She should never have been given the job in the first place. She wasn't strong enough for the position. Plus, we all know corporate headquarters is moving to Denver. She would never have agreed to a transfer. You need your officers and key communicators sitting right next door to you. I'll move wherever and whenever I'm needed."

"Well, Sumner, you may be right. But I'm not sure a sniveling, backstabbing, kiss-ass is the right person for the job, either." Max arched his eyebrows at Sumner and in a split second, broke out laughing. Though Sumner's was more of a courtesy laugh.

"That's the first time I've ever seen you laugh at anything, Sumner. That's good to see. The decision is not mine alone to make. But rest assured, you're on my short list. Now enjoy a glass of Shiraz and let me get at these reports."

Classic Max Riley. He successfully put Sumner in his place, made him feel special, and remembered his favorite wine, all in under sixty seconds.

Max slid the door shut. He removed the lid from the tumbler, added a handful of ice from the ice bucket, and gave the Absinthe concoction three clockwise swirls and three counter-clockwise turns with his right index finger. He quickly knocked back all but an inch of the Absinthe, then extinguished his cigar in the remaining liquid as he watched it sizzle.

He lifted the armrest of his seat and pulled out a bottle of Old Spice aftershave. He splashed it on his face and neck and dug into his pants to run his hand over his genitals. Old Spice was the only fragrance Trish liked and it did an excellent job of concealing the smell of another woman. Within moments, Max fell into a deep sleep.

Chapter 18

James opened the door to the aircraft and dropped the stairs. He exited without looking at or talking to Max. He had eavesdropped on Max's encounter with Leah and Sumner and both conversations repulsed him.

Max was always the last to leave the airplane. He enjoyed saying goodbye to everyone as they left. It made him feel loved. Liz Rocker, anxious to get home, was the first to exit. She slid open the privacy door, squeezed Max's shoulder from behind, and told him to have a nice weekend. When there was no response, Liz looked down. Max's face was a milky grey and there was a slight trace of vomit on his mouth and chin.

Liz dropped her briefcase and placed her thumb and forefinger against his carotids. "James, call 911," Liz yelled down the stairs. "It's Max."

Chapter 19

Detective Jake Sullivan and Nan Levine were in an unmarked car three miles from TAC Air when they heard the dispatcher send out a cruiser. Jake turned the car onto the tarmac just as the young uniformed cop was ascending the stairs of the jet. Jake flashed his badge and the cop stepped aside. Max was alone on the plane. James and Brad were talking to the ambulance attendant as he filled out paperwork and tried to convince the pilots that ambulances don't transport dead bodies to hospitals.

"How many passengers were on today's flight and where are they now?" Jake asked James.

"Well let's see...there were nine. Liz Rocker is on her way to Max's house to be with the family and the rest went home."

Jake looked through James and over to Brad. Jake could smell a pompous ass and he wasn't going to be condescended to by the likes of James Beck. "Nobody thought it might be a good idea to stick around until the police got here?"

"I'm not sure anybody saw a reason to baby-sit a corpse," Brad answered. "Max was no stranger to hard living. It finally caught up with him. I'm no doctor, but it looks like a massive heart attack to me. Are you thinking something different?"

Jake shrugged. "Maybe."

Nan inserted her five-foot, hundred-pound body between Jake and the pilots. She flashed her FBI identification at them and informed them that they were no longer in charge of the aircraft. Without looking either one in the eye, she smugly announced, "I doubt either one of you would know the difference between a heart attack and indigestion, let alone foul play."

"Listen here, little lady," Brad glared. "I have had a very, very bad week. To tell you the truth, Max's death wasn't even the worst of it. If you want to turn a heart attack into something more, be my guest. But watch your tone. I seriously doubt you know what the fuck you're talking about."

Nan flashed a look at Jake for support, but he just smiled and continued to dial Charlie Platt's number into his cell phone.

"Platt speaking," Charlie barked into the phone.

"Charlie, You'd better get over to TAC Air, right away. We may or may not have a homicide here, but you ought to take a look. I'll wait for you," Jake said.

Nan bristled. "If you haven't noticed, Jake, I'm standing right here. That phone call wasn't yours to make. I'm calling my boss. If this turns out to be a homicide that took place in the air, it will be our case."

"I see," Jake nodded. "Is that your law degree or your FBI training talking? I know your boss better than you do. He won't want to get his hands dirty until he absolutely has to. Standard procedure is that the OPD Homicide Department will do all the dirty work, and then the FBI will swoop in at the last minute to claim all the credit once the cameras arrive. Trust me, Nan, your boss doesn't want you to jump into this mess just yet. Besides, the pilot's probably right. Most likely a heart attack. So don't get all excited and embarrass yourself."

Chapter 20

Charlie Platt looked more like a caricature of a homicide detective than an actual detective. Despite the fact that he hadn't touched alcohol in over two years, his round red face looked as though it might explode at any moment. He was a heart attack waiting to happen. His beady blue eyes nearly closed when he laughed and his sandy, unkempt eyebrows came to a point above the exact center of each little eye. He wore a familiar too-tight tweed jacket (purchased ten years and twenty pounds ago) and khaki pants on his five-foot-ten, 215-pound frame. His tie, a birthday gift from one of the kids, lay loose against the unbuttoned collar of his white oxford shirt. His head appeared to sit directly on his shoulders. No neck. Buttoning the collar was not an option.

"Jakey, how the hell are you?" Charlie gave Jake a bracing handshake as he blocked him with his left shoulder.

"Platt! I heard you quit drinking. Obviously you haven't quit eating. Have you ever missed a meal?"

"Not a one. When I gave up the smokes and the booze, I had to take up something. Marie does only one thing better than cook and I'm taking full advantage of both her talents."

Charlie dug into his pocket and pulled out a toothpick and a quarter. He stuck the toothpick between his right front tooth and his chipped eyetooth. The tooth almost looked as though it had been filed away to make room for the ever-present toothpick. He walked the quarter from finger to finger on his right hand, occasionally catching it in his palm, but never dropping it.

"There, now the picture is complete. That's the Charlie Platt I know and love," Jake smiled.

Chapter 21

Did Riley have any health problems that you know of?" Charlie asked James.

"Not to my knowledge. He was real driven. You know the type, uber-ambitious, Type A. He smoked cigars and drank every day. If this is a heart attack, he brought it on himself."

"Yeah, that's probably it," Charlie agreed. "But if he wasn't being treated for any sort of chronic illness, he's going to have to be autopsied. I'll have the coroner come get him. Then I want you to pull the plane into the hangar. We're going to treat this as a suspicious death until the coroner tells me otherwise."

Charlie pulled a pair of latex gloves from his coat pocket before boarding the plane. He looked at the cigar snuffed out in green liquid. It looked like alcohol and smelled like black licorice. As he leaned over the body, he caught the smell of Old Spice. It reminded him of his old man. He noticed the white washcloth in the small wastebasket next to Max. He carefully lifted it to reveal the only other piece of trash, a cigar tip with bite marks on one end. The aftershave bottle sat on the pullout table. To Charlie, these bits and pieces looked like the remnants of a life of privilege and excess. Maybe it was coronary arrest. But Charlie knew from twenty years on the job that these seemingly innocent bits and pieces could tell a story of their own. Besides, it just didn't feel right. And he'd learned never to ignore that gnawing feeling in his gut.

Before Charlie telephoned the coroner, he took one last look at the lifeless body slumped in the seat. "Max, my name is Charlie Platt. Help me do my job," he whispered to the corpse. "Talk to me Max. Guide me. Work with me. Then you can rest."

Chapter 22

Marie Platt massaged Charlie's calves as he snored on the family room sofa. Vana White was turning letters on *Wheel of Fortune* when Charlie's phone rang. Startled, he answered on the first ring.

"Platt!" he barked into the phone.

A young female voice on the other end asked, "Is this Detective Platt?"

"Yes ma'am," Platt shot back. He could tell by the faint echo in her voice that she was talking to him from a sterile room walled in white tiles and furnished in stainless steel.

"Please hold a second. Cooper Dansk would like to speak to you."

She held the phone next to Cooper's ear, taking care not to touch his skin or scrubs. His gloved hands were covered with blood. His scalpel continued to probe the tissue in and around Max Riley's heart.

"You asked me to call the minute I knew anything. I've got a long way to go, but I can tell you, Max Riley's heart was in perfect condition. I don't want to say more until we get all the lab reports back, but I think our boy was poisoned. His skin is raw and irritated wherever the poison touched his mouth, his throat, his face, hands-all over."

"What kind of poison?"

"I won't know for sure until we run some tests on the tissue samples, but I've got a hunch. And you can rule out accidental poisoning. I'd say somebody went to a lot of trouble to get this much poison into him. It looks like he drank it. There was some vomiting but the poison also entered through pores on his neck, face, chest, hands, and—are you ready? His genitals —especially through his genitals.

"I can't imagine who would want him dead or why," Cooper volunteered. "I've known Max Riley for years. His seats are next to ours at Creighton basketball games. The whole city knew him and everybody liked him."

"Not everybody," answered Charlie. "Not everybody."

Chapter 23

Charlie didn't bother to stop by his desk or check in with the secretary. Instead, he headed straight for the crime lab. He spotted his favorite criminologist hunched over a light table.

Beth Johns was the senior criminologist in the Omaha lab. Prior to taking this job, she worked in the delicatessen at Baker's Supermarket. She loved her job and was grateful to have logged so many years in the position before the CSI craze took off. Last month she received over 200 unsolicited resumes from twenty-somethings with criminology degrees, many with master's degrees. Beth got her start in criminology when a degree in the field was rare.

She had been drawn to medicine since she was a little girl but couldn't pass chemistry. Too bad. She would have made a great nurse, or perhaps a doctor, but she couldn't get past the chemistry she would rarely use. Beth did everything with intensity. Her fine motor skills rivaled the most accomplished surgeon. There was not a sight, sound, or smell she could not identify. And nothing made her queasy.

There was nothing glamorous about criminology. It paid poorly and the hours could be long. Beth was dedicated to finding answers and giving prosecutors the tools they needed to bring justice for victims. She gave every case her full attention and was often frustrated that there was usually so little the crime lab could bring to a case.

Television had ruined the "gee whiz" element of physical evidence. At least once a day, she had to explain to someone the difference between what television crime labs do and what real world labs were capable of. Beth was all about justice for the victim. But it was becoming increasingly difficult to convince a jury to convict on circumstantial evidence alone. When there wasn't an abundance of forensic evidence, it was difficult to get a conviction. Television had unrealistically raised the bar for what the jury expected.

Beth was five feet two, inches and weighed 103 pounds. Her long hair tucked into her turquoise paper cap made it billow like a cartoon chef's hat. Her hands were small and delicate, which served her well when handling evidence. Next to Charlie, she looked like a first-grader.

"How's my favorite gumshoe?" she asked Charlie without looking up from the light table.

"Not too bad. How are things in the land of blood and guts?"

"We are buried—no pun intended. It's the only job I know where things are the busiest when things are dead," Beth smiled. "Damn, I'm clever."

"Has anybody started working on the Max Riley evidence, yet?" Charlie asked. "You'd be doing me a big favor if you took care of this one personally, Beth. And it needs to move ahead of anything else you're working on. This was no heart attack."

Chapter 24

Cooper Dansk spread the Max Riley autopsy notes out on the left side of his desk. On the right side, he laid out the lab notes and preliminary toxicology report. After thirty minutes of reading and writing, Cooper picked up the phone. He hoped he could pull off his cool demeanor, but his heart was racing.

"Platt speaking."

"Charlie? Cooper. No surprise, you've got yourself a homicide."

"Tell me everything you know, Coop."

"This is a first for me. The complete toxicology results might not be back for months but I've studied my duplicate samples and the preliminary reports. Max Riley was poisoned with nicotine. Whoever did this really went overboard. It looks like Max drank a deadly cocktail of Absinthe and nicotine."

"What the hell? I've never heard of Absinthe or liquid nicotine."

"I hadn't either. Absinthe is a nasty tasting green liqueur flavored with wormwood and anise, tastes like black licorice. It was outlawed in the U.S. for a few years, thought to be a hallucinogen. That turned out to be false so it was legalized a few years back. You're supposed to sip it like a liqueur but some people think if you knock it back, you'll get a faster buzz. My guess is that the killer soaked cigarettes in a small amount of liquid, strained it, and added it to the Absinthe."

"That can kill you?" Charlie asked.

"Oh, most definitely. It will take an hour or two, and it makes you pretty sick to your stomach. But it will do the job. That probably explains the vomit in Riley's mouth. But I doubt the nicotine in the Absinthe is what killed him.

"My theory is that Riley drank the Absinthe before he splashed the aftershave on his hands, neck, face, and genitals. The Old Spice was also spiked with nicotine. He probably expired ten minutes after applying it. Nicotine administered through the pores works that fast. If he had applied the aftershave first, I doubt he would have had time to down his drink and vomit.

"Of course, this all has to be considered speculative until the final toxicology reports come back. I've taken lots of duplicate tissue samples for analysis. There's no way we're coming up short on this one. I'm releasing the body to the family for burial."

"Any idea when Riley might have died?" Charlie asked. "Denver police aren't interested in investigating this. But if Riley died in the air over Colorado, they should take it."

"I can't help you there. But since Riley was alive when the plane took off, I think the Denver police could have a point. Since we do know he was dead when the plane landed, given the interstate airways laws, shouldn't this be an FBI case?"

Charlie chuckled. "Have you ever known the FBI to ask for work? No. I'll work the case, and if there's a lot of media attention—and there will be—they'll step into the spotlight and take all the credit once the case is solved. But that's okay. I just want to dig into this thing and catch the bad guy. I'm not looking for attention."

Chapter 25

The Catholic tradition of burial within three days after a death would have to be broken. Charlie wasn't ready to release Max's body until Cooper was absolutely sure he had everything on ice that might be called upon at trial.

Great Western wanted to fly in the board of directors and assemble the officers for the funeral. At the risk of appearing insensitive, they would call an emergency board meeting while they were at it. Until the board could hire a new CEO, John Wellman agreed to remain at the helm. Max's brother, Father Frank, was vacationing in Italy and his other brother, U.S. Senator Tom Riley, was in Japan. Charlie could never understand what the big rush was when it came to funerals, anyway. This one would have to wait a week.

Three surveillance vans were dispensed. One was positioned in front of Heafey, Heafey, and Hoffmann Funeral Home, another with a front door view of Christ the King Catholic Church, and a third at the gravesite. Charlie knew the killer might want to attend the funeral. He had taken too much care with the details not to follow the job to the grave.

In a televised press conference, Charlie told the media that Max's death did not appear to be suspicious but that it would be at least five weeks before the complete toxicology report came back. That would buy him some time to observe possible suspects unaware. At Charlie's request, Cooper would see that the final report was slow to materialize.

Chapter 26

Claudia hated wakes and visitations. Watching families accept condolences was like standing in a receiving line at a wedding — only this line was heavy with grief. She felt painfully uncomfortable for herself and the family. It seemed an odd custom to Claudia — almost as odd as parading the corpse from the funeral home to the church and then from the church to the cemetery. If this had been just another wake, she would have signed the guest book and slipped out the back. But there were five good reasons for Claudia to wait in line alongside city leaders, GWC employees, and a host of nameless faces. Those reasons were Trish, Korey, Katy and Tim Riley, and Ruth O'Kiefe. Claudia loved the Riley family and despite her best efforts, she loved Max Riley, a charming, good man, who was deeply flawed. There was no sin Claudia found more abominable than adultery. But she also understood the human condition.

Claudia's wait in line lasted over an hour. When she reached Trish, her eyes welled up. "He was so proud of you all," Claudia said as she embraced the young widow. Trish forced a smile and gave a knowing look.

"I mean it, Trish. Max loved you. He may have lost his way for a time, but never doubt that you and the kids meant everything to him. I'll see you tomorrow."

Claudia pulled Ruth aside and gave her a hug. "How are *you* doing?"

"I'm hanging in there. But I'll be better—we'll all be better—after we get the next few days behind us."

"Now that I'm on my way out of GWC, we should plan on walking every day. I need it for mental health as much as anything else. We both do," Claudia said. "And the doggies will be thrilled." Ruth agreed and promised to resume their routine.

"Listen, I know everybody says 'if there's anything', but I really mean it. I will be ticked if I'm not at the very top of your 'go-to' list. Jake wants to help, too. Can he sit at the house tomorrow during the funeral to make sure nobody wanders in?"

"That would be great."

It took Claudia another twenty minutes to walk to the door of the funeral home. She knew almost everyone in line and greeted them by name with genuine warmth. When she finally reached the door, she spotted Charlie and Marie Platt.

"Hi, Charlie, Claudia Sullivan, Jake's wife."

"Sure. I know you. I watched you work the line. Anybody here you don't know?"

"A few," Claudia smiled.

"I'd like to talk to you privately. Mind if I give you a call?" Charlie asked.

"Sure. I want to talk to you, too. I've resigned from Great Western and I'm taking the private investigator's exam in a couple of days."

"Yeah, Jake told me. You're gonna do fine. Maybe we can help each other."

Chapter 27

C laudia arrived at Christ the King Catholic Church thirty minutes before the funeral was scheduled to begin. Even then, the church was nearly filled to its capacity of 1,172 mourners. She found a spot on the right, near the front of the church and squeezed herself in at the end of the pew. Watching mourners take their seats reminded her of the parable of the fishes and the loaves of bread. As more people filed into the church, the pews' capacity seemed to miraculously expand.

The last time Claudia attended Christ the King was at her own father's funeral, two years ago. She had declined invitations to three weddings there for fear she would be overwhelmed with sadness. Churches, in general, made Claudia weepy. She hated to cry and abhorred crying in public. But church was the one meditative place where she could not busy her mind and crowd out her emotions. Today would be a challenge, but she was determined to stay strong. Too many people were watching. It would be unprofessional.

There were over 300 large bouquets around the altar and along the sides of the church. Another 200 had been left behind at the funeral home. The sweet smell of stargazer lilies overpowered the other flowers and their fragrance hung heavy in the air.

Twenty members of The Omaha Symphony Orchestra were assembled in the choir loft playing some of God's most inspired music: Mozart, Mahler, Pachobel.

As the orchestra played, Claudia listened and observed the crowd. The service wouldn't begin for fifteen minutes but many of the mourners were already crying. Funerals transport people to their deepest personal loss, she thought. We cry not for the dead of that day, but for those closest to us, already departed. At funerals we are reminded, even when we are capable of staying composed, that those raw feelings lay painfully close to the surface. In a moment of calm, feelings can float up to your throat and choke you.

Claudia willed herself not to cry. Seeing other adults blotting their eyes made that a challenge. The sight of two little girls standing on either side of their mother, sobbing into softball-sized wads of tissue, almost did her in. But she stood firm.

When the orchestra played Mozart and Pachobel,

Claudia dug her fingernails into the palms of her hands. When they played Mahler, she dug deeper and bit the inside of her cheek. Anywhere, anytime, the sheer beauty of Mahler could bring her to tears. But she persevered.

At 11:00 am, the music stopped, the bells tolled, and the soloist signaled those gathered to stand. Two altar boys, hands folded under their chins, walked on either side of Father Loseke as he led the procession to the front of the church. He swung the incense burner, anointing the way for the coffin that followed. Trish, on Tim's arm, followed directly behind the coffin. Next came Korey and Katy on either side of Grandma Ruth, hands held tight. Max's brothers, nieces, nephews, and cousins followed somberly behind. As they filed in, filling the reserved pews, the soloist sang a cappella, "On Eagle's Wings", a haunting version of Psalm 91 and a Catholic funeral favorite:

"You who dwell in the shelter of the Lord, Who abide in this shadow for life,

Say to the Lord 'My refuge, my rock in whom I trust!"

The soloist turned to the congregation and spread her arms to indicate they should join her in the refrain. Claudia swallowed hard but could not sing. This was the music that ultimately got to her at funerals. "On Eagle's Wings" took her back to every Catholic funeral she had attended in the past ten years, especially her father's.

Refrain:
"And I will raise you up on eagle's wings,
Bear you on the breath of dawn,
Make you to shine like the sun,
And hold you in the palm of my hand."

By the end of the hymn, the large extended Riley family was seated. The inside of Claudia's cheek was bleeding. And she was weeping.

Father Loseke opened the service with the standard prayers. Next came three eulogies that chronicled Max the boy, Max the young man, Max the adult, husband, father, and friend.

Max's brother, Father Frank, spoke first. He recalled their storybook family life and carefree boyhoods in a series of small Iowa towns. On one of their walks, Ruth had shared with Claudia that Max lost all respect for his father once he discovered what a philanderer he was. Claudia wondered if Father Frank knew about his father's infidelities. He spoke of their mother as if she was a saint and their father a devoted husband and involved dad. Had he rationalized away his father's infidelities? Was he even aware of them? Or was that one of many secrets little Max shouldered on his own?

Ben Weaver was next to take the pulpit. As he spoke, he frequently raked his fingers through his hair to keep it out of his eyes. This aging hippie lightened the mood with tales of youthful pranks and long summer days. Ben was a childhood friend of Max and later a fraternity brother at the University of Iowa. He recalled the day he and Max were at the student union and first met the perky coed, Trish Wervey.

"Trish's personality just lit up the place. It was as if Max was sucked into her energy field by some super human power. He was helpless. And that was just fine with him."

Ben looked over the podium and directly into Trish's watery blue eyes. "Trish, you were the love of Max's life. I mean that. He loved you every single day of his life. Even on the days he didn't know it."

Ben's words confirmed what Claudia had suggested to Trish at the wake. Max had never stopped loving his wife.

Finally, John Wellman got up to speak.

"Max Riley was the most charismatic person I have ever known. The outpouring of affection I see here today is evidence of that. But, like the rest of us, Max was human, and so he was flawed. I worked alongside Max all his days at Great Western Communications. I could spend my time here today reminding you what a great corporate leader he was or how his business genius will be missed, but that seems pretty hollow to me.

"So instead, I'll tell you what a treasured friend Max was, how he loved his family, and how important his faith was to him."

In one way or another, John Wellman's words connected to every person in that church. Max was all John said he was. Claudia saw it, too. Max was a good man who had done some terrible things. He was flawed. Fatally flawed.

Claudia spotted the surveillance van on her way into the church. Rumors that Max had been murdered had started to circulate around the company. Claudia had been doing damage control long enough to know one thing about rumors - they were usually true. She began to scan the church looking for the person who might have killed Max. She knew the odds were he or she was sitting in church today. So many suspects to consider. Claudia had read enough true crime novels to recognize that love was more of a motivator to kill than was hate. But perhaps love and hate were one and the same thing.

Claudia eyed union president Frank Johnson. Max had very public words with him. He had humiliated Frank in a room filled with union members. No one crossed Frank and got away with it. Then there was that sniveling Sumner Jackson. Could losing the promotion he felt so entitled to have caused him to snap? Leah's husband was there. So were some of Leah's former lovers—the ones she screwed on her climb up the corporate ladder en route to Max. Much as it pained Claudia, she knew Trish and the kids also had to be considered. Maybe even John and Phyllis Wellman.

But Claudia's eyes kept drifting back to Leah's husband, Peter Anderson. He had to know Leah and Max were having an affair. Like every other man she beguiled, he would do anything—endure anything—to keep her. Peter stood out in any crowd. His round, brown eyes were curtained by heavy eyelashes that seemed too heavy for his eyelids to lift. Flawless tanned skin dramatically contrasted his over-whitened teeth. He stood six feet, four inches tall and had the body of a man who spent hours in the gym —probably working out his frustrations. There were plenty of women who came onto him. But he remained faithful to Leah. He wasn't even tempted.

Strangely, Peter appeared genuinely saddened by Max's death, even wiping away the occasional tear. What was really behind his tears, Claudia wondered. Could he be mourning the loss of his marriage? The pain Max had caused him? The sadness he felt for Max's family? Claudia scanned each row, pew by pew, face by face. Nowhere could she find the face she most hoped to examine. Leah Beaulay was not in attendance.

Chapter 28

Claudia was climbing into bed when the phone rang. It was Charlie Platt.

"Hope it's okay to be calling so late," Charlie began.

"No, you're good. I'm still up and of course, Jake isn't home from work yet."

"Has Jake told you anything about Max Riley's death?" Charlie asked.

"Do you know my husband at all? Of course he hasn't told me anything. He never does. Everything's a secret with him. It drives me crazy but he claims it's because he could be asked to take a polygraph. Anyway, I know it's bullshit, but I gave up trying to squeeze information out of him years ago."

"Hmm. Well, Jake tells me that, in addition to all the GWC employees, you know everyone in the city of Omaha. Is that true?"

"Not exactly. But pretty close."

"He says it keeps him honest. With all the people you know, he'd never get away with anything," Charlie laughed.

"Good. Let's keep him thinking that way. Did he tell you I passed my P.I. test?"

"No. But congratulations, I think. You'll be a natural, if that's what you really want to do. But I hope you're not planning on getting rich in this business."

"Yeah, Jake isn't thrilled to see me walk away from a steady paycheck. But I am so burned out. I do need to hit the ground running and line up a client or two. If the rumors are true, Max's death is going to require a lot more investigation than you might think. You'll be surprised at all the players who had reasons to want Max dead."

"That's kind of why I'm calling," Charlie said.

"I don't suppose you're calling to hire me as a consultant on this case."

"I'd love nothing more, Claudia, but we have no budget. I'm calling to see if you'd be interested in hanging out with me on this one. It might give you some good experience and exposure. But I can't pay you."

"Are you kidding? I'd love to, Charlie. I know I can

learn a lot from you and I promise I won't get in your
way. I've got ten years worth of dirt on potential
suspects within the company that may surprise you.
I'm all yours."

Chapter 29

Claudia pulled her car around to the Tudor-style
carriage house tucked behind the Riley's stately
sandstone mansion. Claudia found Ruth's little
house far more appealing than the Riley mansion.
Ruth's was a 1,500 square foot, ivy-covered cottage.
The living room, with its fireplace and perfectly
scaled velvet sofas and chairs, reminded Claudia of an
old Manhattan brownstone. The furniture made her
want to kick off her shoes and snuggle in with a good
book. It just felt right.

At Max's insistence, Ruth moved into the carriage
house several years after her husband's death. Max
and Ruth had a warm relationship. They genuinely
liked one another. She agreed to move onto their
property, not because she needed them, but because
they needed her. Max and Trish depended on Ruth
far more than she depended on them. "We could
never enjoy our lifestyle without Ruth," Max once
commented. "She is always there when we need her. I
couldn't ask for a better mother-in-law."

Ruth lived in her separate quarters, independently
and out of the way. But she was always available to

help with the children, provide taxi service, and sleep in 'The Big House' whenever Trish and Max were out of town. After one of their marriage counseling sessions, Trish made a list of reasons to stay married to Max and a list of reasons she should end the marriage. Near the top of her "to stay" list was how good Max was to her mother.

Claudia and Ruth looked forward to getting back into their routine of daily walks with their dogs. Both agreed it was better than therapy. The dogs had been pound mates at the Nebraska Humane Society. Ruth and her grandkids were the first to adopt. She thought she was looking for a little lap dog but when a five-month-old black and white Australian shepherd in the last kennel locked eyes with Ruth, she knew this was the one. The Humane Society was the fourth home in as many months for the young dog with too much energy for the apartment owners who finally took her to the pound. Ruth's grandkids loved grandma's new dog and quickly changed her name from Abby to Sparky. It fit.

When Ruth got home with Abby/Sparky, she immediately called Claudia. "There's a dog at the Humane Society with your name on it."

"You know I travel too much to have a dog right now," Claudia protested. "What does she look like?"

"Just go. You'll know him when you see him."

"Him?"

Claudia and Jake liked big dogs. "If you're going to get a dog, get a *dog*," Jake would say. There were twenty-three dogs in clean, well-lit kennels at the

Humane Society that day. Claudia was taken by the variety of purebreds looking for homes. She identified three German Shorthairs, a Weimaraner, Beagle, Chocolate Lab, and two Black Labs. She wondered what their stories were but knew she couldn't bear to hear them. The tall, eighty pound red dog with wiry hair and bushy eyebrows cocked his head and perked up his ears. "You must be the one," Claudia said out loud. And he was.

Shamus was a four-year-old Airedale/Irish Wolfhound mix. An unscrupulous breeder in Topeka took the entire litter of accidental mutts to the pound there. At the Topeka pound, he had three days to find a home or it was curtains. Lucky for Shamus, a sad little woman named Clancy rescued him and took him to the one-room house she shared with nineteen other animals. A year later, social services persuaded Clancy to check herself into a mental hospital. She reluctantly agreed to let her neighbor take Shamus with him to Omaha to visit his parents. He explained that the Nebraska Humane Society was a model, no-kill facility where Shamus would be well-tended until he found a forever family. And so he was.

Chapter 30

Ruth opened the front door to her carriage house as Claudia opened her car door. Shamus flew over her to get to his old pal,

Sparky. They ran around the houses stopping just short of the street. Max had paid to have Invisible Fencing installed at his house and Claudia's. "If you two are going to be dog sitting for each other, it's the least I can do," Max said. Neither dog responded to the word "come" unless they felt like it. But when Ruth and Claudia held up their leashes, "the kids" came running. They loved walking their humans.

"A homicide detective was here to see Trish this morning. He's coming back after the children get home," Ruth said. "It's hard to grasp that Max was murdered."

"Yes. You probably met Charlie Platt. I'm going to be working with him on the case. Pro bono, sadly. But it might turn into something. I'll make sure I come back with him tonight. Most of what I know is rumor but I'll tell you anything you want to know. The chief of police is holding a televised press conference tomorrow morning to announce the autopsy findings. I assume Charlie has or will brief Trish before that happens."

Ruth wanted to know everything. After answering her questions, Claudia cautioned, "You know, Trish will be a person of interest. So will the kids. Maybe even you. The police don't think that any of you actually killed Max, but nine times out of ten the killer was sitting across the breakfast table from the victim the morning before the murder. They have to be investigated. Jake would advise you to have your lawyer present, even if you don't think you need one."

Ruth understood. "Good advice. I'll talk to Trish

about it. Now, let's move onto a happier topic. I hope you and Jake aren't letting your new career get in the way of making a baby."

"Quite the contrary. Now that I'm not on the road, we actually might be together when I'm ovulating."

"If memory serves, you're thirty-two years old. It's time to get busy if you want to have more than one child."

"Oh, we do. Or, at least I do. I think Jake is having a hard time with the whole idea of fatherhood. But he'll get used to it."

"Nobody knows better than I do that you have to hedge your bets when it comes to having children," Ruth said. "You know, we lost a child when I was about your age."

Claudia's mouth dropped. "How did I not know that? What happened?"

"She was our first born. I had just come home from the hospital with a new baby and Annie, my seven-year-old, looked like a different child than the one I had left just three days earlier. Her coloring was bad and she was extremely tired. I wasn't one to run to the doctor with every little thing, but my maternal instinct told me that this time something was terribly wrong.

"Long story short, Annie had leukemia and went into a coma that night. One week later, she was gone."

Claudia was dumbfounded. "I am so sorry. Why didn't you ever tell me this?"

Ruth shrugged. "How do you bring something like

that up? It makes people so uncomfortable. But, I guarantee you, it's something you never get over. Having your child wrenched from your care changes you forever. I've learned that it doesn't matter if your child is six days or sixty years old, when they pre-decease you, the pain is the same. Even when you force yourself to control your grief, it lives just under your skin. Annie died forty-eight years ago and it feels like it was yesterday. I would have done anything to save her. Anything.

"So at the risk of sounding cold," Ruth continued, "You really need to hedge your bets. I could never replace Annie, but if she had been my only child, I would have had no reason to live. Motherhood does that to you. I had three more babies after Annie died, five children in all. Even now, I wish I'd had more. I'll always feel that I'm one short."

Chapter 31

Claudia pulled into Trish Riley's driveway again at exactly 3:15 pm. Charlie was already setting up his tape recorder at the kitchen table. Claudia was there to observe. Charlie had a reputation as one of the finest homicide detectives in the country. His interview skills were legend but his purpose today was not to interrogate.

As Jake had advised, Trish's lawyer, Joe Duprey was present. Everything about Joe was likeable. He was a comfortable old shoe of a man with kind looks and a deep, soothing voice. He stood five foot seven inches tall and was built low to the ground, a la *Seinfeld's* George Costanza. His clear blue puppy dog eyes were hooded by heavy, creased eyelids. His droll, self-deprecating sense of humor made him a favorite with clients and judges. He was simply the kind of guy you wanted to do business with.

While a law student at Creighton, Joe joked, "I'm the very definition of an average white boy. I wish I was more interesting." His friends decided that called for a good nickname so they began calling him 'Jose' and it took.

"Jose! What a nice surprise," Claudia said as she walked behind Joe and gave his shoulders a two second massage. The two had dated briefly when Joe was between marriages. They had felt an immediate warmth for each other but there was no romantic spark, no sexual chemistry. They remained close and Claudia breathed a sigh of relief, knowing her friends were in such good hands.

Charlie was behaving more like an advisor than a homicide detective. "You are in for some very difficult months," Charlie grimaced. "My old man was a real son-of-a-bitch. After cheating on my mom for eighteen years, he up and leaves us one day for some ugly woman ten years his senior with kids of her own. It was devastating. I was sixteen and I didn't want to talk about it. In those days, we didn't talk about our parents' marriage. Your kids won't be so lucky. The details of Max's personal life are going to come out. You might want to consider breaking the news to them yourself."

"They know about Max and Leah Beaulay, if that's what you mean," Trish said. "The girls elected to bury their heads in the sand but Tim confronted his dad. Protecting his mom, I guess. We let the kids think that Leah was his only affair—a onetime mistake on Max's part. Do you think they need to know more then that?"

"It's certainly up to you," Charlie sighed. "But before this is over, the details of all of Max's affairs will become very public. I just want to give you a heads up on this so you can decide how you want to handle it."

Claudia was surprised at the lack of depth in Charlie's questions. The whole thing felt more like a getting to know you session. Claudia was always interested in the back stories. She not only wanted to know who did what, but why and what motivated them. Jake had warned her that clients wouldn't be willing to pay for that level of detail and perhaps she was better suited to be a therapist. Claudia knew that she'd go crazy if she was a talk therapist. "Are you kidding? I don't have the patience to listen to indecisive people fret about their lives. I'd want to tell them what to do and suggest that the walking worried get over themselves."

Charlie asked Ruth and Trish who they thought might have something to gain from Max's death. Neither could, or would, suggest a suspect. Forty minutes later, Charlie was closing up his notes and explaining that he would need to talk to them again in the next few days. "I'll want one of my investigators to talk to you and each of your children separately next week. I wanted to give you some time to discuss Max's personal life before we interview the kids."

As Trish walked Charlie to the door she said, "Thanks so much for being sensitive to our situation. I guess there's no choice but to give the kids the gory details of Max's affairs. We're already seeing a family therapist. I think I'll ask him to help. This might sound strange, but Max was a wonderful father and—for the most part—a good husband. Please find out who did this to him. Whoever killed Max took him from us just as we were getting our marriage—and our family—back on track. I still love my husband and I want his killer brought to justice."

Chapter 32

Claudia followed Charlie to his car. "Could you meet me at the police station tomorrow at 8:00 am?" Charlie asked. "We're setting up a war room, listing all the possible suspects, eliminating some, making a timeline, assigning interviews—really getting organized."

"I'll be there," Claudia said. "I was surprised at the way things went this evening. This was nothing like what I see on television. I hunger for details. I expected the questions to be more pointed. Maybe you're planning on doing that later?"

"Maybe. Tomorrow we'll get a better idea of who we need to take a harder look at. We want to interview anyone and everyone who had means, motive, and opportunity. We'll start with motive. I was led to believe that everybody loved the guy, but I'm finding out there were plenty of people who had beefs with Riley. I'm hoping you can add to the list with what you know about his activities at Great Western."

"The list is going to be very long on motive, but short on means and opportunity," Claudia said.

"Yeah," agreed Charlie. "I don't think there were all that many people who had access to the airplane."

"Tell me what you're thinking, Charlie. I'll bet you've already got some thoughts on who the killer is."

"I don't want to be accused of being a 'linear thinker' again. The public defender once called me that and it still pisses me off. There was a case we investigated the hell out of but he still accused me of pre-judging his client and then setting out to prove him guilty without seriously considering other suspects. So, if Max gave anybody reason to do him harm, we're going to investigate them."

Claudia wasn't going to let him sidestep her question. "So are you saying you don't have any prime suspects?"

"We've got to work the case and follow up every lame lead that comes our way. But we'll make an arrest and get a conviction on this one. It's less of a 'who done it' than it is a 'why done it'. That's what we'll be investigating."

Chapter 33

C harlie met Claudia in the lobby of the Omaha Police Headquarters. The building was relatively new but already dingy and showing signs of wear. Jake claimed it was because the construction contract had been awarded to an unqualified minority-owned company. Claudia thought that was just Jake being Jake, but she had to admit the construction was shoddy and the fluorescent lighting made the station all the more depressing. After signing in and getting a long term visitor's pass, they wound their way to the elevators and up to the fourth floor.

Claudia expected the offices to be a somewhat drearier rendition of the GWC branches she had visited over the last ten years. She expected a generic maze of corporate cubicles that housed employees like so many prairie dogs. But when the elevator doors opened onto the fourth floor, she was taken aback by the bleak office space. Dark grey steel desks were butted up against each other in one giant room. No artwork or potted plants here. Each desk was shared by the employee's counterpart on the night shift. No privacy. Claudia wondered what these conditions did to the quality of their work, never mind the quality of their lives.

The interview rooms were even worse. Every room was identical: eight-by-twelve feet, white-walls, a grey steel table, and two grey chairs. "Just when I didn't think the place could get any more depressing, it does," Claudia smiled.

"That's by design," Charlie answered. "I don't want anything to distract the suspects and I don't want them getting too comfortable."

The walls of the conference room were lined with glossy white eraser boards. On one long wall was the beginning of a crude timeline of the day of the murder. With Claudia's help, the opposite wall would soon fill with the names and possible motives of people of interest. Detectives Dan King and Jim Smith were working on the timeline when Charlie and Claudia walked in. "Damn," Claudia thought as she eyed the young detectives, "this *is* a cute profession."

Charlie laid stacks of charts on the table. There were GWC employee organization charts, lists of personal acquaintances and their relationship to Max, family members, a chart of the neighborhood, a list of Centennial airport personnel, lists of Max's therapists, physicians, and confidants. To make it to the wall, a name had to have a motive, no matter how slight. By lunchtime, there were eighty-three names on the wall.

The secretary brought three sacks of food from Taco Bell in for lunch. Charlie picked up the tab and the four dug in. After lunch, they went about the task of highlighting the names on the wall that were possible suspects in yellow and those who were not suspects but could provide meaningful information in pink. Claudia thought the highlighted list of suspects was longer than it needed to be. But she remembered Charlie's caution about not wanting to be labeled a linear thinker, and she understood.

The suspect list included everyone who boarded or had access to the plane in Denver, Max's immediate family, employees with known grudges, former mistresses, Leah Beaulay's husband, and Leah's former lovers.

The names listed in pink included Max and Trish's marriage counselor, John Wellman, Ruth O'Kiefe, Father Loseke, Max's secretary, and Claudia.

Claudia did a double-take when she looked at her watch. How did it get to be 6:15 pm? She was pumped and pleased with the contribution she had made. So this is what it feels like to be excited about your work, she thought. It had been a long time since she had experienced that feeling.

Charlie walked Claudia to her car. The station parking lot was dimly lit and surprisingly unsafe.

"Well, how'd you like your first day working homicide?" Charlie asked. "You are going to be a tremendous asset to this investigation."

"I loved it. This is my kind of work. I enjoy digging into things and learning everything I can about a subject. I can be a little obsessive, but I think that might serve me well here. You know, as busy as I was at Great Western, I was oddly bored most of the time. Not today."

"Well, I can promise you that when you're working

a homicide, you'll never be bored. We'll start the interviews tomorrow. We thought everybody at Great Western loved Max, but you've opened our eyes. Seems there is no shortage of people who hated his guts. We've got a lot of suspects to eliminate."

"I just wish we had a better sense of when the poison was put into the aftershave and Absinthe. It's going to be difficult to clear suspects without knowing exactly when they need an alibi," Claudia added.

"The interviews will really help the pieces fall into place. If we do our jobs right, we'll be able to hand the county attorney a case he can not only prosecute, but win."

"So tell me confidentially, Charlie, of that long list of suspects, do you have a top three?" Claudia asked.

Charlie shook his head and smiled. "No, I can't say I have a top three. We have to do our jobs and run down every possible lead. But I know who killed Max Riley. And I suspect you do too. Of all those names on the wall, I can think of only one person who had the means, motive, and opportunity. Confidentially? I don't have a top three. I only have a top one."

Chapter 34

The red light was flashing on Claudia's answering machine when she walked into her house. Two messages.

"Hi, sweetie. It's your loving husband. I won't be

home for dinner. Don't wait up for me." Beep.

"Claudia, it's Joe Duprey. How would you like to investigate the Max Riley case *and* get paid for it? Call me."

It was 7:00 pm so Claudia called Joe at home and tried to control the excitement in her voice. "Hey, Joe, I just got your message. What gives?" Claudia was trying to sound cool but she was sure her pounding heart could be heard in her voice.

"After you left the Riley's, Trish and Ruth and I had a long talk about how to best prepare the children. Your name kept coming up. They love you, Claudia. And they believe in you. Trish and Ruth think that your 'soft skills' (their term, not mine) are so good, you'd be more successful at getting at the truth than Platt. You could help soften the information to the kids as it presents itself. Ruth wants to be supportive of your career and they both think you've got innate investigative skills. They have authorized the law firm to hire you to investigate this on the family's behalf."

"Wow. I'm flattered. Should I do this?"

"Absolutely. You'll be working as a private investigator for me. You'll be able to investigate without some of the restrictions put on police. Every month you'll turn in a time sheet, we'll bill the Riley's, and you'll get paid. You've fallen into one hell of a first assignment. Come down to my office at ten tomorrow morning and you can sign a quick contract. And one last thing. Congratulations. "

Chapter 35

Charlie Platt was genuinely happy for Claudia. After ten years in corporate America, Claudia was taken aback by his show of support. In all her years at Great Western, she never felt a peer was happy for her success. He assured her she was still welcome to shadow his team on interviews and sit in on meetings. Charlie sincerely wanted Claudia to succeed.

Since Max's death, Leah had not returned to Connecticut. She worked out of her old Omaha office and was negotiating for her old job back. Wayne Winston was working hard to make that happen. Leah's husband, Peter Anderson, was glad to have his wife back, in every sense of the word.

John Wellman agreed to stay on at Great Western until the new CEO was settled in. The board quickly offered the CEO spot to renowned SOB, Sam Batio. Publicly bullying employees at AT&T was Sam's management style. He was universally hated for his arrogance, personal greed, and humiliating tactics. At five feet-four inches tall, his receding hairline made him look older than his forty-seven years. The joke was, if you looked up Napoleon complex in the dictionary, you'd find a picture of Sam Batio. But he had earned a reputation as a dealmaker and the board liked that. He had consistently over-shot his annual revenue targets while at AT&T. At least that's what his numbers said. His abrasive personality was an assault on the sensibilities of every Omaha employee.

Sam Batio was everything that John Wellman was not. As much as John had initially dreaded this forced retirement, now that he had publicly stepped aside, he looked forward to handing over the reins and getting on with his life.

Claudia called John at home to ask if it was okay to drop by with Charlie after dinner. Phyllis Wellman served decaf coffee and ice water straight from the tap before excusing herself for her evening stroll. Charlie presented a list of all the Great Western employees he hoped to interview.

John's name was on the list along with twenty others. "Some we'll want to interview in the office and some we'd like to accompany us back to the station," Charlie explained. John promised his full cooperation and said he would arrange for Claudia and the OPD to have easy access to the Great Western facilities and employees.

After Charlie left, Claudia asked John if she could interview him, personally. "Am I a suspect?" John laughed.

"Not to my way of thinking. But if I didn't know you, and if the OPD is keeping an open mind, you should be. You certainly had the opportunity and some would say a motive."

"What would be my motive?"

"Well, with Max out of the picture maybe you'd still be CEO. Or maybe you found out he was still seeing Leah and you felt betrayed. You had easy access to the jet and everything on it."

"If I need an alibi, I've got one. I wasn't alone for two minutes the entire time I was in Denver."

"You're not a suspect. But Charlie and I will want to know everything you know about Max's relationships with the people on that list."

"I'm happy to help. But you can eliminate most of the names on that list. I can tell you one thing for certain. I know enough about human nature to know that Max was murdered by a woman. A man would never have taken the time to carry out such an intricate plan. And a man would have acted with more violence."

Chapter 36

Jake had worked late every night for the past three months. Working on interstate drug trafficking had recently paired him with Nan Levine, a young FBI agent who was as far away from her own profile as one could imagine. At five feet, Nan was delicate and feminine. Her long, strawberry blond hair fell in corkscrew curls over her frequently exposed shoulders. Her clear blue eyes and alabaster skin made her look Scandinavian or Irish. In fact, she was neither. Her parents were Jewish immigrants from Russia who fled the country in 1960, to escape continued religious persecution.

When Claudia discovered that Nan was nothing like the stereotype she had imagined, she felt guilty (a daily emotion she was trying to tame). Equality, fairness, and truth were the passions that drove Claudia. When she caught herself pre-judging Nan she wanted to make amends. Despite skepticism from a couple of police women, Claudia was determined to make Nan feel welcomed.

A recent graduate of University of Virginia Law School, Nan was heavily recruited by the FBI and the CIA. She selected the FBI because they were willing to give her the assurance that her first assignment would probably be New York or Los Angeles. After spending the last seven years of her life in small-town Virginia, she was anxious to move to a more cosmopolitan setting - one that would better appreciate her intelligence, good looks, and prestigious education.

When, instead, her first assignment landed her in Omaha, Nan was not amused. A move from Podunk, Virginia to Podunk, Nebraska, was not what she had signed on for. The FBI, much like the military, was famous for promising recruits the moon until they had them in their grasp. Bait and switch was standard practice.

Nan was the only agent from her graduating class at Quantico heading to Omaha. Her FBI classmates threw a going away party for her on the beach. The wives and girlfriends were happy to see her go and looked forward to celebrating her departure. "It's kind of like seeing the stake go through the heart of a vampire," one skeptical wife drawled. "I came here tonight so I can talk to the little vampire and make sure she's actually leaving. Hell, I might volunteer to drive her to the airport and put her on the plane."

Laklin Jennings, a second year law student from Grand Island, Nebraska, didn't know Nan but attended the party with her FBI boyfriend. "You're in for a nice surprise. People don't often move to Omaha willingly, but once there, they never want to leave," Laklin gushed.

"I doubt that," Nan replied as she turned her back on her. Why bother making conversation with someone who could not advance her career or life in any way?

"No, really," Laklin continued. "Nebraskans are famously friendly and Omaha is getting tons of big name concerts. The social and cultural scene is surprisingly good. Plus, you'll have the opportunity to shop at the largest, finest furniture store in the entire country and buy a whole apartment full of furniture at amazing prices. Warren Buffett owns it!"

Nan's laugh dripped with condescension, causing the surrounding conversations to quiet. "A small town filled with small-minded people with small aspirations. Gee, I can't wait. Furniture shopping. Wow."

Laklin felt like a child who had been called down by a teacher in front of the entire class. One of the wives grabbed her by the arm.

"Help me get these kabobs on the fire," she said. "Don't let Nan get to you. You're not alone. That's the thanks you get—the thanks many of us have gotten— for trying to invite Nan Levine into our lives and keep her out of our husbands' beds." She purposely said it just loud enough for Nan to overhear.

Chapter 37

Nan was assigned to work with the Omaha Police Department's Drug Trafficking Task Force. This was way beneath her. She viewed FBI agents and even DEA agents as the cream of law enforcement. Now she found herself, along with three male agents, working with a bunch of cops she assumed were mostly renegades who made their own rules during undercover drug busts. Most of the cops were married. But that didn't stop them from flirting and trying to impress their new co-worker. The two female officers on the task force disliked Nan as much as she did them.

Nan was teamed with Jake upon her arrival in Omaha. Two weeks later, Claudia fielded an anonymous telephone call: "Watch out. Nan is gonna be all over Jake. She's real stuck on herself and, when it comes to investigative work, she's as worthless as tits on a boar. He's already doing his work and hers, and—I swear to God—she acts more like his girlfriend than his partner!"

Claudia knew the caller meant well and thanked her for the warning. She hung up and knew immediately how to head this off. She would invite Nan into her home and her circle of friends. Claudia was determined to be supportive. At Great Western, she was often frustrated by the lack of support women gave one another. She set out to prove to Nan that Omaha was a well-guarded urban gem and that the women here could be as savvy as their New York sisters.

When Jake spoke of Nan, it was obvious to Claudia that he was developing an innocent crush on her. The value of winning Nan over to her side early in their partnership was not lost on Claudia.

Claudia invited four of her favorite couples and two unattached women to their home for dinner. When she telephoned Nan, her unfriendly tone caught Claudia off guard.

"Hi, this is Claudia Sullivan, Jake's wife."

After an awkward pause, Nan answered, "Yes?"

"Jake and I are having a little dinner party on Saturday. We'd love it if you could join us. You're welcome to bring a date, but there will be a mix of singles and couples so, either way, you'll fit right in. It will give you a chance to get to know some people outside the cop shop."

"Sure. Okay. I guess I can stop by. What time?"

Claudia hung up the phone and took a moment to digest the conversation. Had she misinterpreted Nan? Had Nan been rude? Caught off guard? Shy?

Claudia, an astute observer of human behavior, believed that shy attractive people were often misread as being aloof. She knew that Jake wouldn't befriend someone who thought she was better than he was. Nan's ego may be sizeable but Jake's was huge and Claudia knew it.

Jake suggested to Nan that she come early. Claudia wanted to get to know her before the others arrived.

At 7:00 pm, Nan arrived with two bottles of expensive wine. Claudia was deep into food preparation and had already opened a bottle of Rosemont Shiraz, one of her favorites.

Claudia greeted Nan with a warm hug. Nan's body stiffened. "I don't cook, but I like good wine," Nan said as she handed Claudia the bottles.

"You'll fit right in," Claudia smiled. "Not many of the women you'll meet here tonight are into cooking. They work long hours—lawyers, executives, business owners—and don't have time to cook. I, on the other hand, find it very cathartic. It's a great creative outlet for me. Plus, the projects I work on drag on forever and I get a great deal of satisfaction from starting a meal and seeing a finished product an hour later. The best part is, it gives me an excuse to put on great music and drink good wine. The cook always drinks, you know."

"I'll drink to that," Nan smiled.

Chapter 38

Jake's hair was wet from the shower. He was still getting dressed as he walked into the kitchen. "Zip it up, big guy, we've got company," Claudia warned.

"Nan! I didn't hear you come in. I hope you're not helping Claude with the cooking. I'd hate to kill our friends," Jake chided.

"Jake knows I don't cook. I have many talents, but cooking is not one of them," Nan laughed, never taking her eyes off of Jake.

Claudia's friends welcomed Nan into the group and made her the center of attention. The diversity of the gathering was pure Claudia. Jake envied her natural ability to attract and nurture meaningful friendships. The professional make-up of the group surprised Nan. She had prepared herself to spend the evening with a group of suburban office drones and housewives. Claudia pointedly introduced each guest to Nan in a way that let Nan know that their backgrounds far surpassed hers. There was Lisa Vialobos, a highly regarded Douglas County prosecutor born in Venezuela, graduated first in her law class at University of Nebraska. Lisa's handsome husband with the deep FM voice, Dr. Stone (short for Rhinestone) Spence, a liver specialist on the renowned Nebraska Medical Center organ transplant team. Pam Rovier, a divorce attorney came without her husband. Phil Rovier, a vice president for Borsheim's Jewelry, was on a camping trip with their son. Jack and Patty Bee, Claudia's oldest friends, kept the party jumping. Patty, a bubbly Type A, was owner and president of the family business, George Labs. The Labs conducted controlled medical studies for clients around the world. Patty was also a favorite actress for the Omaha Community Playhouse. Her husband Jack, was the antithesis of Patty. He had quit his job as a draftsman at age thirty-eight to be a stay-at-home dad. The kids were now out of the house but

Jack was busier than ever. He spent his days turning small tasks into lifelong projects, taking karate classes, practicing tae kwon do, frequenting health food stores, and volunteering on the spot to help strangers and friends, alike. Patty and Jack were an oddly matched couple who gave new meaning to the notion that opposites attract. But their core values matched and Claudia thought that was why the Bee's had the strongest marriage of any of her friends.

Claudia introduced Ruth O'Kiefe as, "The most evolved spirit I know. She's an accomplished downhill skier and can out-hike anyone in this room. She has more life and travel experience than anyone I know. She is my hero."

Including The Sullivan's, there were nine guests. Last, Claudia introduced Nan. "Nan is our guest of honor, I guess. She's FBI, and working with Jake on whatever it is my secretive husband works on these days. She's brand new to Omaha and I wanted her to meet some people outside of law enforcement."

"Good party," Patty proclaimed as she and Jack were leaving. "Excellent party," added Pam. "It didn't suck at all. You should throw dinner parties for us every week."

"Good food, good wine, and good company. It doesn't get any better than that," Stone smiled as he kissed Claudia on the cheek. Her heart skipped a beat whenever Stone touched her. That voice, those hands, the sex appeal of his superior mind were all very appealing to her.

Claudia found that she genuinely enjoyed Nan.

She could see why Jake liked her. She was glad they had gotten to know one another. If she had felt the least bit threatened, that feeling was gone.

Nan walked unsteadily to the door, it was clear she had been over-served by her hosts.

"Let me drive you home, Nan. Have one last glass with Claudia while I take a leak and then I'll drive you. We'll get your car to you tomorrow."

"Good idea," Claudia agreed as she poured the last of the pinot grigio. "The cook always drinks, and so does the dishwasher. That's me, too."

"I am so glad we finally got to meet," Claudia said as she walked arm in arm with Nan to the car. She helped her in and Jake did the honors with the seat belt.

Claudia kissed Jake. "I like her," she whispered into his ear. I want to fix her up with my brother. Find out if she's interested."

Jake arrived home some ninety minutes after he and Nan left for what should have been a forty minute round trip. Claudia was returning the last of the crystal to their quiet little resting place in the dining room hutch.

"I was getting worried. What took you so long?"

"Nan was a little more inebriated than we thought. I got her home just in time for her to start puking. Being the consummate host, I held her hair back while she let it fly. I'm practicing for fatherhood," Jake smiled.

"I love you, Jake. You are a decent man and a good friend." Claudia knew Jake had a weak stomach when it came to body fluids and was repulsed to see a woman vomit. Jake could never be attracted to Nan after tonight.

"Did you tell her I want to fix her up with my brother?"

"I did. She wanted me to tell you that she is capable of getting her own dates. And she said it with attitude, my dear. Clearly, Miss Nan thinks she can do better lining up her own romantic encounters."

"Wow. That kind of surprises me. No. Actually, that pisses me off. Who does she think she is? Don't my friends or my brother for that matter - meet her high standards? I'm offended. Tell her I was relieved that she doesn't need any help getting dates. Tell her I was worried she wasn't hot enough for my brother, anyway!

"Am I really such a bad judge of character? I bust my butt to welcome her into our home, and that's her response? Do you know, I've been warned that Nan is after you? Everybody thinks she is a cutthroat bitch who wouldn't mind screwing my husband. But, oh no, I insist on supporting her and trusting you!"

Jake grabbed Claudia from behind by her wrists and pulled her close to him. "Settle down, tiger. I think you're missing something. First of all, you have nothing to worry about when it comes to me and Nan, or any other woman for that matter. I stopped screwing around the day we got married. I will never cheat on you. Did it ever occur to you that Nan might be a lesbian?"

Claudia laughed. "Please. Man hungry is more like

it. Didn't you see her flirting with Stone? I guarantee you his wife did."

"No, I'm serious," Jake insisted, "I think she's a lesbian. Just some things she's said to me. And a couple of single guys on the task force have taken a run at her—good looking guys—and she's shot them down. I think that's why she doesn't want you fixing her up."

Claudia shook her head. "As your old friend, Ronnie Reagan would say, 'There I go again'. I'm not proud to tell you I was a little jealous of her. She seemed way too familiar with you, not to mention downright flirtatious. I actually felt like a third wheel and that she was your date."

Jake pressed his cheek into hers. "You've got to start trusting me. I know I was a shitty boyfriend, but I'm an excellent husband. Until tonight anyway, Nan saw me as the only friend she had in Omaha. I'm her buddy. And I'll bet you a head shot she's gay."

Chapter 39

Claudia was drinking bad coffee from a paper cup in the station conference room when Charlie walked in.

"We've got half a dozen interviews scheduled for today. They've all agreed to come down to the station," Charlie instructed. "I'll introduce you and tell them you're investigating this independently on behalf of the Riley family. At the end of the interview, I'll ask if you have any further questions." Claudia understood.

First up: Brad Wilson.

Within one week after Max relieved Brad of his pilot's job at GWC, he was flying the private jet of a local entrepreneur. He was happier than he'd been in years. He was no longer required to wear a suit to work, he was flying fewer hours, and making more money. Best of all, he was free of the day-to-day corporate bullshit of working for James Beck. His only concern was that the non-disclosure statement he signed stipulated that if he talked about Great Western, he would forfeit his $140,000 severance check. When Charlie explained that a criminal investigation trumped the non-disclosure, Brad smiled broadly and relaxed in his chair. "Fire away."

Brad gave a detailed account of the scene at the condominium. Despite being fired, he didn't appear to harbor ill feelings towards Max. When asked to elaborate, Brad shrugged. "Max was a charmer, but I knew him for what he was—a phony asshole. I didn't care if he lived or died."

"Can you tell me anything about the nature of Leah Beaulay's visit to the jet just before takeoff?"

Oh, this is sweet, Brad thought. "I could certainly give you an educated guess, but you ought to ask James Beck about that. He electronically eavesdrops on everything that goes on behind the cockpit. He doesn't know that the other pilots know about his seedy little audio switch, but we're all onto him."

Finally, it was Claudia's turn. "Do you know anyone who might have reason to want Max dead?"

"How long have you got? Of course, Leah Beaulay has to be at the top of anybody's list. Word on the street was that Riley had to get rid of her in order to become CEO. That couldn't have made her very happy. Then there are all the people who lost or were about to lose their jobs thanks to Max. Maybe the girlfriends who preceded Leah were pissed off at him. I heard John Wellman had a big blow out with Riley a few months back. And of course, my favorite suspect, James Beck. We were both fired that day and Beck was terrified of being pulled off the corporate teat. Once Max was dead all bets were off. Max's death meant Beck kept his job. I could have, too, for that matter. But my personal belief is that life is random and full of serendipitous opportunities. When I got fired, I was glad to see what the future held for me. Not many people at GWC share that philosophy. Certainly not Beck."

"Do you really think James is capable of murder?" Claudia asked.

Brad reluctantly shook his head. "Nah. But I sure hope you'll screw with him."

Chapter 40

As Brad exited the conference room he noticed the familiar black cashmere top coat perfectly folded and draped over the grey metal chair. As he walked to the elevator, he practically bumped into James Beck dipping a decaf tea bag into a foam cup. James saw Brad and quickly averted his eyes. Why be cordial to a former employee who had nothing to offer him? That was okay with Brad. "Good luck, asshole," Brad said under his breath.

Claudia introduced James to Charlie Platt and read Beck's short, glowing bio. "James has been a pilot at Great Western for twenty years and head pilot for ten. Prior to Great Western, James was a pilot in the Air Force, stationed at Offutt Air Force Base. He's married with two adult children. He is active in his church and community. His golf handicap is a four and he plays racquetball every Saturday morning. Executives at GWC like and respect him. He's a class act. That about cover it, James?"

"Very flattering, Claudia."

"Thank you."

Charlie explained they were interviewing everyone on the jet the day of Max's murder. He verified that Max had been poisoned but would not comment on other details. Charlie asked James to recount the scene at the condo. It matched Brad's story, but James stopped short at the point where Max fired them. He provided useless, vanilla information about each of the passengers.

"Anybody on that plane have a motive for murdering Max?" Charlie asked.

"Maybe Leah Beaulay," James said. "Max had recently ended a long affair with her and she was very unhappy about it."

"Can you give us the details of the time they spent together right before takeoff? Did you hear any of their conversation?"

"No."

"Come on, James, we know you eavesdrop on Max and anybody else within ear—or should I say microphone shot."

Claudia jumped in. She didn't want to scare James into shutting up. A little more flattery might open him up again.

"You're an excellent judge of character, James. In your heart of hearts, who do you think killed Max?" Claudia smiled.

"I'd really rather not say. I'd hate to bear false witness," James said. "But Leah Beaulay was very unhappy with Max. She even threatened him. I heard her suggest more than once that if he didn't hurry up and fix things, maybe she'd hire somebody to have him whacked. She was kidding but still. What was it Shakespeare said, 'many a truth is first said in jest'? Bottom line, she's a whore. I felt so sorry for Max's family. Trish is a great girl. She didn't deserve the treatment Max and Leah gave her. Leah definitely had a motive—and the means. Not many people knew about Max's Absinthe ritual. But Leah did. In fact, she was the one who introduced him to it."

"What about Brad Wilson?" Claudia asked. "Max fired him, couldn't that be a motive?"

"Brad didn't even care that he'd been fired. And if Max's Absinthe was poisoned—well, Brad isn't sophisticated enough to pull something like that off."

"What about you, James? Are you sophisticated enough? You had the means, you had the motive—after all, with Max dead, you keep your job. And you had free and open access to the jet while it was on the ground. That's opportunity. You're not a suspect. Not yet, anyway. I just wish someone could substantiate your claim that Leah threatened Max," Charlie said. The room fell silent for what seemed like an eternity.

James swallowed hard and studied his manicured hands, folded on the table. "The microphone in the cockpit was hooked up to a hidden tape recorder. I have Max and Leah's last encounter all on tape."

Chapter 41

Trish agreed to let Claudia interview each of her children privately. She warned them that the next few months would get ugly and that she could not protect them from the rumors—true and false—that would be made public. She assured them that Max's behavior was not their fault and that his love for them was constant. They flashed each other looks when Trish said that. They had all heard a heated argument between their parents when their mother was pleading to keep the family together. When she begged Max to think about what he was doing to the children he shouted, "I don't give a damn about the kids." He didn't mean it, of course. But they would never be convinced of that.

Trish promised to answer any questions they had, no matter how difficult or sordid. She also suggested that they not dig too deeply into the ugly details of their father's life.

Tim sat quietly while his sisters asked questions for nearly an hour. "What about you?" Trish finally asked Tim. "Do you have any questions?"

"I'm not at all curious about dad. But, please, don't tell me he loved us. When he wanted to leave you, he wanted to leave all of us. He had a choice. Would he rather be with us every day or with his whore? He wanted to live with his whore more than he wanted to live with us. I hate him. I always will."

Tim was hurt and angry, not because he hated his father, but because he loved him. Trish knew that the opposite of love was not hate, but indifference. She also knew that Tim was not ready to hear that. Not now. All she could do was love her youngest child and only son. Even though Max's infidelities began on the day of Tim's birth, she never held Tim responsible.

Trish had suspected the underlying cause of Max's first affairs long before their shrink suggested it. But the therapy sessions revealed the painful details of earlier indiscretions. She couldn't let herself go there. She would not allow herself to speculate on how different their marriage might have been if Tim had not been born.

The adventure that ended in Tim's birth began in South Dakota sixteen years ago. Every detail was fresh in Trish's mind as she sat down to share the story with Claudia.

For some unexplained reason, after the Riley girls were born, Max's sperm count went south. When Trish could not conceive with what she had always dreamed would be the third of their four children, she quickly put the wheels in motion to adopt.

At the time, Trish had been awarded a government grant to test precious Native American children living on the reservations for learning disabilities. She had always assumed she would quit working when her own children were born. But she loved the work and the Native American children too much to abandon them.

Conditions on the Rosebud Indian Reservation were shameful. The human debris left by alcoholism could be seen everywhere. Children with alcoholic parents wandered from house to house, seeking care and refuge from loving extended families and neighbors. Unwed pregnant girls generally kept their babies and raised them alone, digging an impossibly deep hole their children could not escape.

Trish loved these teenaged mothers, and knew

that this was where she wanted to adopt. There was never any question that she could make a significant contribution to one human being's life by adopting and loving an otherwise doomed child.

The first day Trish laid eyes on two-year-old Delores, she made an instant connection. Delores' mother had died of AIDS at the age of sixteen. One night, lonely for love, Farrah White Horse went to bed with a townie, as Rosebud girls referred to the white boys who lived outside the reservation. Gregg Potter was a handsome nineteen-year-old with a high school degree and junior college in his future. It was easy for him to charm Farrah into what he knew would only be a one night stand.

That was the last night Farrah, or anyone else, laid eyes on Gregg. Six months later, during a routine checkup, Farrah tested positive for HIV. She prayed obsessively that her baby would be born without the virus. Her prayers were answered, but Farrah was not so lucky. Two years after Delores' birth, Farrah died. The shame of her condition did not allow Farrah to seek the medical treatment that could have extended her life. Despite the fact that little Delores repeatedly tested negative for HIV, fear of the disease resulted in many in the community shunning her.

Trish approached the tribal council for permission to adopt. She knew that despite the love and privilege she could offer this innocent outcast, it would be a tough sell. The Indian community rarely let one of their own be adopted outside the tribe without a fight. But Delores' fate might be different. No one wanted her.

Trish sought legal advice and was discouraged from pursuing the adoption. But she was determined. She provided character witnesses, brought Max and the girls to visit Rosebud, presented financial statements and photos of their house and Delores' future bedroom.

The tribal hearings dragged on for three months. During that time, Delores was in foster care. Trish ached every day for her soon-to-be daughter. Knowing she was in foster care when she should have been home with The Riley's, kept her up nights.

Trish received a call one morning from the chief of the tribal council. "We meet tonight to rule on Delores' placement. You should be here."

That call was every bit as exciting to Trish as those first labor pains announcing the eminent births of Katy and Korey. "What time? We'll be there. Can we bring her home tonight?" When Trish stopped for a breath, the chief repeated, "We meet tonight." Then he hung up the phone.

Max was in Minneapolis attending a presentation at Great Western's advertising agency when he was called out to take Trish's urgent call. "Get on the plane and come home. Now. We're driving to Rosebud to pick up Delores."

Ruth threw a nightgown and toothbrush in a paper grocery sack and headed across the backyard to The Big House. She would care for Katy and Korey while Max and Trish made the six-hour trek to Rosebud.

The best car seat money could buy was installed in the back seat. A basket of small travel toys and a pillow sat next to it. Max could hear his heart pounding in his ears. Trish thought she might explode. "You know, Trish, I'll never forget the drives we made to the hospital when our girls were born. I can't believe it, but I feel exactly the same today."

He slid his hand over and onto hers. "I love you so much." He said, "Tonight, one unfortunate little girl will become the luckiest child in America, thanks to you."

When the Riley's arrived, the meeting was already underway. The council normally met with few onlookers in attendance. But tonight the shabby meeting room, which doubled as a bingo hall, was packed. Trish was a popular visitor on the reservation, especially among young women. She was flattered to see so many friends had come to support and celebrate the event.

Max quietly opened the door, hoping not to draw attention. The eight councilmen were seated at a long table at the front of the hall quietly debating who should be awarded the contract for the bingo hall's cigarette vending machines. Should they award the contract to a business owned by a fellow Native American from Yankton, or should the contract go to white men from Sioux City who were offering the reservation twice as much of their profits?

When Max and Trish entered the meeting hall, council members became noticeably uncomfortable. The room fell silent and the air grew thick. All eyes turned to Max and Trish. Lillian Truth Seeker,

Trish's friend and assistant, buried her hands in the skirt of her flowered blue cotton dress and began to cry. In that instant, Trish knew what every mother knows before any words are spoken. She knew that something terrible had happened to her child.

Council chief, Joseph Ravenhead quickly tabled the vending machine discussion and postponed that decision for another week. He asked the Rileys to take a seat but neither moved.

"We'll stand," Max answered.

Ravenhead looked around the room and called out, "Raymond White Horse, please come forward. Raymond White Horse. Raymond White Horse." No one in the room moved a muscle.

"We will proceed without him", Ravenhead continued. "Trish, on behalf of the entire Sioux Tribe, I extend our appreciation for all you have done for the people of Rosebud. You have shown a generosity of spirit that we rarely see here. But we must do what is best for Delores. And that is what we have done. As you know, it is always best to keep an Indian child with her people. In Delores' case, we have been able to place her not only with a member of the Sioux Tribe, but also with a blood relative. Raymond White Horse is Delores' maternal grandfather. She has been placed in his care. With the help of all who live on this reservation, he will raise her in the ways of our people."

Trish stood, immobilized. It was as though she was having an out of body experience. As she stood mute, some force overtook her body and spoke.

"Chief Ravenhead, you know what great respect we have for your culture. We will bring Delores to Rosebud regularly and do everything we can to maintain her proud heritage. But we can give her that and so much more. We love her beyond measure. She will enter a safe, loving family that can meet all her spiritual and material needs. I beg you. God has granted this child—our child—a second chance. He will not forgive you if you deny her the blessings He is bestowing on her."

"I'm sorry. We must do what we know to be right," Ravenhead answered.

"I don't have to tell anyone in this room, including you, what type of man White Horse is," Trish continued. "He is a hopeless alcoholic who never took proper care of his family. He neglected Farrah. He can't even take care of himself. Delores will not be safe with him. Where is he tonight? Where is my child? Delores will die in his care. Can you live with that?" Trish dropped to her knees. Max attempted to pull her up and put an end to the pathetic scene but she would not budge. She laced her fingers and pleaded, "Please, for the child's sake. I beg you. Delores belongs with us. Don't do this to her."

"Delores belongs with her people. This is where she will stay. It is done. The council is now adjourned."

As the men exited, the women began to chant. Trish did not recognize this as any of the native chants she had come to know. It was the sound of mother animals wailing in unison over the death of a child.

Chapter 42

As Max and Trish walked into the cold Dakota night, the women followed. The chanting continued as they walked to their cars and homes. These women wanted nothing more than to see Delores go home with the Rileys. Years of a powerless existence had muted the Sioux women's senses. But the events of this night, the terrible injustice, brought their long buried pain and screaming to the surface.

Max put his arm around Trish's shoulder and held her tight. He feared if he loosened his grip, she might collapse to the ground. "You were perfect in there tonight," Max whispered. "You said and did everything right. Now it's my turn. This isn't over. I can fix this."

Trish smiled at Max. He understood nothing of the realities of life on the reservation.

As Max opened Trish's car door, she saw a figure emerge from behind the meeting hall. He stood alone in the moonlight. It was Raymond White Horse.

Chapter 43

T hat's him," Trish whispered. "That's Delores' grandfather." Max started towards him but Trish caught his elbow. "Let him come to us."

White Horse gathered himself up and staggered with the same practiced determination he exhibited when attempting to walk a straight line for the Rosebud police. The results were the same. He weaved his way over to the Rileys. "Where's Delores?" Trish demanded.

"What is it you want?" Max snapped.

White Horse turned to answer Max. As far as he was concerned, Trish did not exist. "The girl is fine. I'm taking real good care of her," White Horse slurred.

"Where is she?"

"She's home in bed. Probably fast asleep by now."

Trish marveled at how so many children somehow made it to adulthood with little or no adult supervision. She forced herself to remember that as she pictured Delores sleeping alone in White Horse's shabby trailer. "Who's with her right now while you're out drinking?"

Trish already knew the answer. No one.

"She's fine. She's just fine. You worry too much," White Horse answered.

Trish knew this could not end well but Max saw it as just another business challenge to overcome. She had worked on the reservation long enough to know that Delores would never be theirs. Dragging the process out any longer would be damaging to everyone. But Max was used to winning. Corporate power brings with it the expectation that you will get what you want outside the business world, just as you do at the office.

"Let's hear what the man has to say. What can I do for you, Mr. White Horse?"

"My Farrah was very precious to me. And she made a beautiful child when she made... Dee Daw, uh, my grandchild. I think Farrah would want you to take her. But this is a big sacrifice for me. You need to make it right."

"How much?" Max asked, not hiding the disgust in his voice.

"Forget it," Trish interrupted. "I know the power of the tribal council. We can't buy Delores. He'll get the money and we'll end up in jail." Max knew she was right.

Still, he repeated, "How much?"

"$10,000."

"You fool. You could have asked for $100,000." Max turned to get into the car.

Then, in one seamless movement, he swung around and knocked Raymond White Horse out cold. By morning he would not remember the encounter or what had happened to his jaw.

Chapter 44

Trish knew it was over. But Max was just getting started. "Do you know where White Horse lives?" Max asked.

"What are you going to do, kidnap Delores?"

"No. But I'm going to take pictures of the dump she's in. We're going to get social services and the lawyers on this. You know it's best for Delores. This isn't over. Not by a long shot."

Max wasn't accustomed to failure. Especially when he knew he was right.

"Max," Trish put her hand on his leg, "You have to listen to me on this one. I have worked here for a long while and I know that a ruling by the tribal council carries more weight than the United States Supreme Court. This is my fault. I've known from the very beginning how they feel about letting their children be adopted outside the tribe. I fooled myself into believing they had come to see me as one of them. I was wrong. I'll talk to Lillian. She'll see that Delores is well cared for and loved. White Horse isn't capable of caring for her, and he doesn't really want to. He just wanted the money. But, despite the living conditions, there is a great love of children on Rosebud. The women here will take good care of her. I promise."

They sat in silence as Max turned the car onto Highway 18 for the long drive back to Omaha. The silence was broken by a small voice coming from the floor of the back seat.

"Mrs. Riley is right."

Chapter 45

Sweet Mary, mother of God!" Max exclaimed. As he instinctively turned around to see where the voice was coming from he simultaneously wheeled the car off the road and onto the flat, frozen cornfield where it finally came to a stop.

Kathleen Cerone grabbed hold of the back of the driver's seat and pulled herself up with a long rooting pig-like grunt. Trish recognized Kathleen immediately from her work on the reservation. She was the shy girl who cashiered at the Gas 'n Go just outside the Rosebud entrance. The moonlight danced on her straight, shiny black hair. Trish once told Kathleen that she looked exactly like what she had imagined Indian princesses looked like in the books she read as a child.

In all the months Trish had been gassing up her car for the long drives back to Omaha, the shy Kathleen had uttered nothing beyond "Thank you," or "Have a nice day". Trish tried to engage her in conversation, but without success.

Now, here she sat, boldly stowed away in the backseat of their car. Kathleen Cerone was twenty-two years old, single, and looking very pregnant.

"Are you alright?" Trish asked.

Kathleen nodded and sat silently, her big brown eyes, the color of well-oiled espresso beans, darted back and forth between Trish and Max.

"I need your help," Kathleen pleaded. "Please let me tell you my story all in one piece before I lose my courage."

Max and Trish leaned against their respective doors and nodded.

"My mother knows what I am doing and has given me her blessing. She will talk to my father and make it right with him. Their approval is important to me, but it doesn't really matter. I am moving off the reservation and I am twenty-two-years-old so no one can stop me.

"As you can see, I am going to have a baby. I was in love with the father. I am a good girl. I have only slept with the baby's father, no one else. He wants nothing to do with the baby. He even tried to talk me into having an abortion, but I said no. He joined the Army to get away from the reservation. Before he left, I got him to sign a paper saying I was free to do as I pleased with our baby. We even had his signature witnessed and notarized.

"I want my baby to have things I could never give it—things no child living on a reservation could ever have. I am going to Omaha to start a new life. Now that I am off the reservation, I am free to have my baby and choose its parents. I choose you."

Max shook his head emphatically from left to right, again and again. "We can't just trade one baby for another. I'm not ready to jump from the frying pan into the fire. How do we know you won't change your mind? No. I'm calling the shots from now on and I say no."

Trish's eyes were glued to Max as she addressed Kathleen. "We would be honored to adopt your child. I did not believe in predestination until this very moment. I think all the horrible events of the evening have been leading to this moment. This is your destiny, Kathleen. This is our destiny. We will work with our attorney from the very beginning this time. We will cover all your medical expenses and help you find a job after the baby is born."

Max knew he would have no say in this matter. He felt impotent in every sense of the word. He had lost his ability to father a child and with it, he had lost his place of power in the marriage.

The next few months went smoother than anyone could have hoped. Kathleen moved into the carriage house with Ruth. Korey and Katy warmed up to Kathleen and the new sister or brother she was carrying. Legal work was completed with relative ease. The process was simple, but expensive.

At the end of the month, Trish, with Max's blessings, sat down to write some checks. The first was for $100,000 which she deposited in a joint money market account she had opened for Lillian and Delores. She called Lillian and explained she was to spend it on herself and Delores any way she saw fit. Delores was now living with Lillian's family and

Raymond White Horse was relieved to be free to stay drunk without worrying about his granddaughter. Lillian protested, but Trish was insistent.

"We would have spent more on Delores in her lifetime if we had been allowed to adopt her. It is the least we can do. This way, I can feel that I have helped create a wonderful family and a better life for that precious child, even if I couldn't be her mother. Consider it a baby gift."

Next, Trish wrote out a check to their lawyer, Joe Duprey, for $5,000. She knew that his bill could have easily been three times that amount, but that wasn't Joe's style. "Hell, Kathleen did the important legal work when she had the father sign a waiver to his rights," Joe conceded.

Then she wrote a check for $50,000 to be deposited in an account she had opened for Kathleen. She'd keep it a secret until after the baby was born. Kathleen wanted to go to nursing school and Trish and Max wanted to make that happen.

Finally, Trish wrote a check in the amount of $10,000 to Kathleen's obstetrician. Without health insurance, the office needed a check up front or they wouldn't accept Kathleen as a new patient, never mind that the need for prenatal care was nearly behind her. When Trish presented the check to the office manager Trish said, "It's hard for me to believe that someone can cross our borders illegally and deliver a baby free of charge, but you won't help this Native American, a people we owe so much to, without a check up front."

The office manager had heard plenty of reasons why a patient couldn't, wouldn't, or shouldn't have to pay. But this was a first. As she took Trish's check she said, "I'm sorry. If it were up to me...I'm sorry."

On that first visit to the obstetrician, Kathleen made a confession. "I am ashamed to tell you that I have not stayed away from alcohol altogether during my pregnancy. When I found out I was pregnant, I was in great despair and I started drinking."

"How much and how often?" Dr. Albert Bass asked without a hint of judgment in his voice.

"A lot. And then sometimes not so much. On the weekends I would maybe drink a bottle of wine each night, or maybe a six-pack of Pabst Blue Ribbon. But then, during the week, I might not drink at all."

"When did you last have a drink?"

"The day the Rileys saved me. That was the last day I touched a drop of alcohol." Kathleen smiled at Trish and Trish squeezed her hand.

Dr. Bass explained to Kathleen that because no one knows how much alcohol is too much alcohol for a pregnant woman, the safest thing to do is not drink at all. "But, the truth of the matter is some studies show that the last trimester is the most critical. You should be fine. Just don't drink anymore until after the baby is born."

The two women breathed audible sighs of relief. Both had witnessed the devastating effects of alcohol on newborns at the Rosebud reservation. This was a piece of Indian "tradition" Kathleen had prayed she would not pass along to her child.

Dr. Bass instructed Kathleen to get dressed and meet him down the hall in his office. He gestured with his head for Trish to join him outside the examining room.

"There was no reason to beat up on Kathleen about her drinking. What's done is done. And I meant it when I said we're not sure when the damage from alcohol is done to the fetus. But I am concerned. You may very well be adopting a child with some level of brain damage. You may want to reconsider this adoption."

Trish smiled and took the doctor's hand. "You're too late. God has already placed this precious life in our hands."

On March 18th, Kathleen gave birth to a nine pound, four ounce baby boy, Timothy Edward Riley. His black hair stood on end like the down of a baby duckling. Trish and Max witnessed the birth of their new son. Max cut the cord and the baby was handed to Trish as Kathleen had prearranged. Then Max left the new mothers at the hospital and went home to tell his girls.

Max was overjoyed. But at the same time, he couldn't shake the sense of sadness he was feeling. He had often joked privately to Trish about his low sperm count. But despite his jokes and her repeated reassurances, she knew it bothered him. Max knew his thinking wasn't rational, but he couldn't help it. He felt like less of a man.

Trish did everything she could to lift Max's spirits and make him feel sexy. She made love to him every night and never failed to let him know that his performance in the bedroom just got better and better. They sought counseling, individually and as a couple.

Max tried anti-depressants for awhile but they weakened his sex drive so he stopped. Perhaps a couple of Scotchs would lift his spirits tonight.

Ruth, Max, and the girls celebrated Tim's birth around the kitchen table with sacks of malts, fries, and Tastee Treats (loose meat sandwiches) from the B&G Restaurant. All agreed it was the finest food within a five mile radius of the Riley house. Max told Ruth he needed to leave for a few hours and she agreed to stay with Katy and Korey.

He drove to M's Pub in the Old Market, a quaint, cobble-stoned area on the edge of downtown Omaha, and sat at the bar drinking Scotch on the rocks for the next hour. He struck up a conversation with a pretty twenty-eight-year-old blonde, a well-educated middle manager with ConAgra.

She was perfectly attired in a fitted black business suit that just grazed her knee. The jacket was buttoned and she wore a black silk camisole underneath. When she reached across Max to grab a napkin, she brushed against him and he could feel that she was not wearing a bra. Her breasts were rock hard and her nipples erect. Max was thinking, *what I wouldn't give to hit on that piece of ass*, when the blonde suggested, "I've got much better Scotch at my place. Want to follow me home?"

Max followed her to her trendy townhouse, a mile south of the Old Market. Once there, Max and the blonde wasted no time tearing each others clothes off. They did it hard and fast in the entryway. Then again on the floor at the top of the stairs. An hour later, they finally made it under the sheets of her bed.

That night, the night of Timothy Edward Riley's birth, would be the first of many one-night stands for Max Riley. He still had what it took. The blonde made that all too clear. But one night wouldn't be enough. Max would require constant reassurance.

Chapter 46

"Claudia, I am so sorry. Look at the time," Trish said. "I've been rambling on for over an hour with one irrelevant sob story after another."

"Not at all," Claudia reassured her. "This is exactly the sort of thing that interests me. We can learn so much about people by examining the events that trigger behavior. This has been very insightful and I appreciate your candor. The reasons behind Max's personality shift, for lack of a better term, might be very relevant. Can we back up to something?"

"Sure."

"Would you be willing to contact your therapist and give him or her permission to answer a few questions?"

"Sure. There's no point in keeping things quiet now. His name is Larry Walton and you'll like him. He's very intelligent and has a passion for the truth. I thought Max might take advice from a man more than he would a woman. No matter what was going on in our marriage, I found Larry to be very helpful. The kids and mom went to see him, too. We'll sign any permission forms he needs to free him to answer all your questions. Charlie's too."

"One other thing," Claudia hesitated. "Did you ever have Tim evaluated for fetal alcohol syndrome?"

"I know what you're thinking, and you're wrong. Tim would never hurt his dad. Besides, Tim was skiing the entire time the jet was on the ground in Denver."

"Was he ever tested?"

"Yes, Tim has some developmental delays, possibly due to Kathleen's drinking."

"Trish, I know I don't have to tell you that one of the most prominent symptoms of fetal alcohol syndrome is the inability to discern right from wrong—a consistent lack of conscience."

"I want you to interview my entire family, including Tim," Trish repeated. "I'm not worried. Tim knows right from wrong. Despite what he says, he adored Max. He did not kill his father."

Chapter 47

Claudia interviewed the girls separately. First Katy and then Korey. Their responses were nearly identical. They were aware that their parents were having problems and that they were seeing a marriage counselor. Korey suspected Max of adultery early on. Katy had not. Both agreed that at the time of Max's death, their parents were getting along much better and were openly affectionate, even playful.

Both remembered meeting Leah. She had been at the Riley house on several occasions for company parties. They recalled being introduced to her, but that was all. Per Charlie Platt's advice, Trish had answered her children's questions about their father's life. They didn't ask for many details. Despite Trish's admonitions, Korey and Katy insisted on referring to Leah as "dad's whore". Neither shed a tear during Claudia's interviews. They hated Leah. And they hated Max. "If you think *we* hate dad," Korey concluded, "wait until you talk to Tim."

Tim was going through an awkward stage, but one could easily imagine that dark good looks were just around the corner for him.

Before Claudia eased into her first question, Tim blurted out, "I didn't kill my dad, but I'm glad somebody did."

Claudia began with the timeline. Was Tim skiing the entire weekend? Was he ever alone? Did he return to the plane at any time? Did he know when his father died? Did he know how he died? Did he know his parents were having marital problems?"

"Yeah, they told us they were working things out."

"Did you know what their problems were about?"

"Not at the time. They just told us it was normal stuff."

"Did you think your dad might be having an affair?"

"No. Why would anyone do that to my mom? She is so beautiful and so nice. Everybody loves her. Only a monster would hurt her like that."

"When did you find out your dad and Leah were having an affair?"

"About a week ago. When my dad was alive, I thought he loved us. Sometimes he'd say mean things, but my mom said he didn't mean them. Now I know that he didn't love mom and he never loved me."

"That's not true," Claudia protested. "I've known your dad for many years and I saw how proud he was the day after you were born. He was wrong to be unfaithful to your mom, but he loved you all very much."

"If he loved me so much, why did he start cheating the day I was born?"

Claudia didn't have an answer for that. But she knew Tim didn't kill Max. He may have hated his dad enough to want him dead, but he didn't know how much he hated him until he was already gone.

Chapter 48

Larry Walton rose to greet Claudia as she entered his office. His coarse, unkempt grey hair and bewildered demeanor made him appear older than his fifty-five years. He had kind, steel blue eyes and a warm smile. He was a gangly six foot, seven inches tall wearing a wrinkled shirt and ill-fitting tweed jacket. Claudia thought he looked more like a disheveled professor than a respected therapist.

"Trish gave me permission to divulge anything from our therapy sessions that might be useful to you. Before I start working with a client, I assure them that our sessions are confidential. Even the kids, whom I sometimes saw separately, gave me permission to speak candidly with you. You know, despite Max's failings, he lived his life pretty much as an open book. Our sessions were confidential from my perspective, but Max and Trish were very open with each other."

Larry didn't have much to add to the information Claudia had compiled from her conversations with Trish and the children. Without shedding additional light on Max's affairs, Larry did share some insightful philosophies on infidelity in general. "The impetus behind Max's need for multiple sex partners is not unusual. Trish was a great wife, but then, I see great wives in here all the time. Max's affairs were not about Trish. There was nothing she could have done to prevent them. Intellectually, Max knew that a low sperm count had nothing to do with his masculinity. But emotionally, he needed to prove his virility by bedding a long list of women."

"Is there anyone on that long list we should be looking at for Max's murder?"

"No. Most of the affairs were brief and purely sexual in nature, at least for Max. A few of the women got their hearts broken, but that was long ago. They got over it. Max was lucky not to stumble into any "fatal attraction" relationships, but he really didn't. He never hid the fact that he was married and would never leave his family."

"Until Leah Beaulay?"

"Yes, until Leah Beaulay."

"Do you know what the real danger is in having affairs?" Larry asked.

"Well, you could bring home the AIDS virus and kill your innocent spouse."

"Yes, of course you're right. But beyond that, the danger in having affairs is that sometimes you fall in love."

"Is that what happened to Max?"

"Yes. He fell in love with Leah. He wanted a divorce, but Trish wouldn't hear of it. She asked me once what I thought she should do and I told her that I thought she should divorce him. I could have lost my license for that. I'm not supposed to tell people what to do. They're supposed to reach their own conclusions, but the Rileys didn't want me to operate like that. I told Trish that I thought Max wanted desperately to end the marriage but he didn't have the guts to pull the trigger. Trish would have to do that. She refused. She saw no need to rush things. She was hoping the affair would die of its own weight. But it never did.

"Want to guess who feels some responsibility for the unhappiness in the Riley marriage? Ruth O'Kiefe."

Claudia motioned Larry to tell her more.

"Ruth gave me permission to talk to you as well as

Trish and the kids or I wouldn't be telling you this. Often, dysfunctional relationships are a learned behavior. Ruth wanted Trish to leave Max, but she refused. By all accounts, Ruth had a good, long marriage. But her husband had a year-long affair when Trish was in high school. Ruth found out about it and so did Trish. She watched her mom live through it and put it behind her. Ruth blamed herself for modeling the long suffering wife behavior.

"Max was repeating family history, too. His dad was a real skirt-chaser. Max adored his mother and resented his father's cavalier attitude. Much as he hated his dad for mistreating his mother, he subconsciously learned it was his birthright to behave likewise. He thought his mother was a saint. He expected Trish to be one, too. Max became his father."

"And Trish became her mother," Claudia interrupted.

"Trish may have mentioned my fascination with how events can mold character. I have to admit to being obsessed with details. You can take the girl out of journalism school, but—Maybe I'm over-thinking this. It seems to so often come down to sex. The human sex drive must be terribly powerful."

"Oh, it is. I see people every day who, despite their moral convictions, can't fight the pull of one sexual demon or another. But it's never simple. Sex is rarely just about sex."

Claudia took a minute to digest all this. She needed to refocus on the final days of Max's life. "In the end, Leah was forced to take a downgrade and transfer to Connecticut. By all accounts, Trish and Max were getting along much better with Leah out of the picture. Would you agree?" Claudia asked.

"That was just an elaborate front Max put up until he was installed as CEO. The affair never ended, not even after Leah was transferred. Max promised her that when the time was right, he would move to Denver and see to it that she moved there, too. Trish wouldn't divorce him, but she couldn't prevent him from filing for divorce. I think he was getting closer to pulling the plug. But Leah didn't believe that and she was getting impatient. He was seeing a side of Leah he didn't like. Her demands were starting to annoy him. I know enough about scorned women to know what that sounds like," Larry said.

"What's that?"

"A motive for murder. And I'll tell you something else. There was a time when Max wanted me to see Leah alone on a separate matter. He was concerned about her state of mind after she ran over and killed a young boy."

"I heard about that," Claudia said. "The kid came out of nowhere on a skateboard on Center Street. I understand it wasn't Leah's fault. She wasn't ticketed. Still, I can't imagine getting over something like that. She must have been devastated."

"Quite the contrary. Leah refused to see me. She felt no guilt whatsoever. She never called the boy's parents, nothing. Max once told me that he never saw her shed a tear. You'd expect her to feel terrible, even though it wasn't her fault. But she felt nothing.

"I wish Leah would have agreed to see me. I think, psychologically speaking, Leah and Max were a lot alike. People who feel no guilt, no empathy, generally have an incident in their early lives that cause them to pull away. They decide they aren't going to feel pain and they can't feel empathy for others.

"Sociopaths can be obsessed with sex. They use it like a drug. Max didn't feel alive if he wasn't in a highly charged sexual relationship. Classic sociopaths have lost control of their lives. They believe life is dragging them somewhere they don't want to go. Max felt that way. I shouldn't try to diagnose Leah, since I've never met with her. But, from what Max told me, she certainly fits the definition of a sociopath. It would be interesting to know what made Leah feel so out of control."

Chapter 49

Claudia knew where she wanted to go next with her investigation. But would she be looking for Max's killer or simply satisfying her perverse curiosity? The police were making short work of their list and Claudia began to wonder if they were seriously looking at anyone other than Leah. She'd better touch base with Trish before making her next call.

"Look, Trish, I don't want to run up your bill chasing information not relevant to the case. But I think the back stories of the people involved in Max's life might give us some more answers. I'd like to interview Leah's current husband and her first husband and maybe find out what makes her tick. Did you know she has two kids by her first husband and that he has custody?"

"I didn't know that. In fact, I wonder if Max knew. I'll run it past mom but I'm sure she'll want you to keep going. Technically, she's paying for the investigation. She didn't want it to look like I was out to get Leah. I would love to know what makes that woman tick. What makes her think it's okay to destroy families. So have at it. I'm well aware that Max wasn't the first man who wanted to dump his wife for Leah. You know, a couple of the other betrayed wives have told me that their husbands never got over Leah. Do you think one of them thought that with Max out of the way they could have Leah back?"

"It's possible." Claudia said. "But wishing Max dead and actually killing him are two entirely different things."

Chapter 50

Rick Johansson and his wife packed up Lindsay and Ned for the long drive from Indianapolis to Omaha to visit Leah. It was their spring break and the kids were looking forward to spending time with their mother. That meant that Rick and his wife would also spend the week in Omaha. The children made Leah nervous and she could only be around them for so long before she became irritable. Rick wanted to make the time they spent with their mother as happy as possible, so he agreed to get a room at the Holiday Inn so the children could stay with him at night. The big indoor pool and pinball arcade were a hit with the kids.

"Mom would love to have you sleep at her house, but I would just miss you too darn much," Rick said.

His children meant everything to him and he wasn't about to let Leah's indifference hurt them more than it already had. So, for their sakes, he covered for her.

Rick's current wife, Ruby, had known Leah even longer than Rick had. In fact, she was maid of honor at Leah and Rick's wedding. Claudia met them for lunch at Spezia, a cozy restaurant near their hotel. Rick's only request was that they meet anywhere but a chain restaurant. Spezia met the requirement. The food was consistently excellent and their large booth offered plenty of privacy. Claudia explained what she was doing and asked them how they met Leah and what she was like as a young woman. Rick's wife took a deep breath and in a slow, soft-spoken manner, began her story.

Lawrence, Kansas

When Leah Beaulay left the Choctaw Indian Reservation for Haskell Indian Institute, she was given a hero's send-off. At the bus stop, her mother kissed her goodbye and said, "I know you will never live here again. But please remember where you came from and that we love you and are so proud of you."

Leah held her mother tight. She, too, knew she would never return to the reservation. She swore that she would never live in poverty again. She would earn her teaching certificate and work for some suburban school near Kansas City or St. Louis. Fulfilling that dream would make her the most financially successful member of her family, or her reservation, for that matter.

Leah easily settled into her room at Haskell. The grounds and dorm were beautiful. In comparison to the reservation, this was paradise. There were two twin beds in the twelve by fourteen foot room she shared with Ruby Littlefoot. Physically, the roommates were the Mutt and Jeff of Haskell, but Leah didn't take notice.

Ruby felt rich in any environment. She was quick to laugh and slow to anger. Her room at Haskell felt like a five-star hotel. She couldn't believe her good fortune. At five foot, two inches, Ruby was a full head shorter than Leah. Her face was perfectly round, her jet black hair shiny and straight. When she laughed, her dark brown eyes turned into slashes against her pretty mocha colored skin.

Three weeks into their freshman year, Ruby suggested to Leah that they venture off campus. "Let's take the bus around the KU campus and eat dinner on Massachusetts Avenue," Ruby suggested.

Leah found the idea both terrifying and exhilarating. She managed to show Ruby her excitement but not her fear. Ruby recruited Alice and Marilyn, two other freshmen, and headed to the edge of the Haskell campus. To Leah, it might just as well have been the edge of the universe.

There they were. Four Indian girls on a warm autumn day boarding the bus to tour the University of Kansas and the quaint town of Lawrence. The campus sits high on The Hill and is arguably the prettiest campus in Middle America. On this day, the sky was clear and the turning colors of the sugar maples and burning bushes made Leah feel like she had just driven onto the pages of a children's picture book.

At the top of the hill, the bus driver stopped in front of the Chi Omega fountain. Two girls with dark blonde hair boarded. They sat quietly in their sweater sets and khaki slacks. Identical new penny loafers, looking uncomfortably stiff and tight, peaked out from under their perfectly pressed ankle-length pants. The two got off the bus two blocks away from where they boarded and were replaced by two blonder, even prettier girls. One block later, the dance repeated itself.

Ruby, Leah, Alice, and Marilyn quietly took it all in. They may as well have been touring a foreign country. After circling the campus twice, they got off the bus. They looked at each other and broke into relieved laughter. "Have you ever seen so many blonde girls in one place?" Ruby asked.

"Gorgeous blonde girls," Leah added. "Don't they allow ugly girls to attend KU? I'd never want to go to school there. It would be impossible to compete for boys with those girls. I'd never get a date."

The foursome fell silent. All eyes were on Leah, who did not make the connection. She was oblivious of her astounding good looks.

It was 4:00 pm before the girls remembered they hadn't eaten lunch. They had been trying on clothes at Hawklette's for an hour—clothes they could not afford and had no intention of buying. Ruby didn't want to hang up the sizable pile of discarded clothes she had tried on her short, square frame. And she didn't want to face the snotty clerk who made no attempt to hide her mistrust of these Indian girls.

"We'll go next door and grab a table while you finish getting dressed," Ruby said to Leah through the closed dressing room curtain. "And take your time. We'll probably have to wait for a table."

The aromas that hung in the air at the Larrytown Burger Basket were a tangible reminder of why greasy food—even bad greasy food—is so irresistible. The smell of grilled onions, fried potatoes, burgers on the grill, and fried buffalo chicken wings could not completely conceal the musty odor that laid claim to

Larry's. As tantalizing as the aroma was, the food's flavor was pretty ordinary. Every entrée had the same fried food taste. But this was *the* spot for KU students who wanted to see and be seen while filling up on cheap burgers and 3.2 percent beer.

The girls were greeted at the door by a handsome college boy dressed in a Kansas basketball t-shirt and well-worn blue jeans. "Welcome to Larry's, ladies. How many are we today?"

Ruby blushed. No one had ever called her a lady. And the host's smile was so genuine and engaging, she felt sincerely welcome at this hub of KU's off-campus student life. He led them to their booth. No one stared or stopped talking. These three Indian girls from the poorest parts of America fit right into this friendly place. They were glowing. They had arrived.

A shapely blonde with big, perfectly round blue eyes placed four glasses of water in front of the girls. "What can I get you?"

"It's our first time here. What do you recommend?"

"Well, I hear all the burgers and the chicken strips are good. I always get the tossed salad. That's good."

"Great," Marilyn laughed. "Now I'll feel guilty when I order the blue cheese burger with fried onions."

Two frat boys wearing t-shirts identifying their affiliation popped up from the adjoining booth. "The blue cheese burger is an excellent choice. May we recommend a round of beers to go with that?"

This reception was not at all what the girls expected. They had been cautioned that KU's rival,

Kansas State, referred to the pretty campus on the hill as Snob Hill. Perhaps that was to counter KU's nickname for K-State: Silo Tech. But the girls were finding this hangout to be remarkably friendly. The place was lousy with gorgeous coeds, yet these boys were paying attention to three Indian girls from Haskell. What a feeling.

It was fifteen minutes before Leah walked in. The fraternity boys looked Leah's way and their conversations stopped. Mouths dropped open like human dominos falling one by one. And not just the boys. Every girl in the place stared at Leah as she entered the Larrytown Burger Basket. Suddenly, the room grew quiet.

Ruby stood up and gave Leah a wave. The boys scurried to their seats like frightened mice. Leah was wearing the tight-fitting pink angora sweater she had just purchased. All eyes were on Leah as she squeezed into the booth. Pretty blondes continued to crane their heads to get a look.

Leah was oblivious to the attention she drew. Ruby shook her head. "Leah, you are a rare bird. You are always the most gorgeous girl in the room and you don't even know it. That makes you all the more beautiful. Now that I've enlightened you, please don't get all conceited on us."

Leah cocked her perfectly oval, olive-skinned faced questioningly towards Ruby. Her lips were parted just enough to reveal her naturally straight, paper-white teeth. She had curled her hair that morning and it billowed over her shoulders with a shine that rivaled the old Breck Girls on the back of a *Seventeen Magazine*. Her nose had a slight bump near the top and was long and regal, a feature that only added to Leah's exotic good looks. Her complexion was flawless. Every nail on her hand was perfectly shaped and polished. Her legs and arms were long and thin and her breasts were in perfect proportion to her long, lean body. Her big almond eyes were set off by impossibly long eyelashes and full, naturally-arched eyebrows.

"We were talking about you behind your back last week," Ruby smiled. "We think you are a cross between Raquel Welch and Sophia Loren—only way prettier. We are proud that you are one of us, an Indian girl. You may look more Greek or Italian, but you are a beautiful Indian girl and it's about time you saw what everyone else in this room sees."

Leah was sincerely bewildered by Ruby's declaration. The Beaulays were part Choctaw and part French. Most of her ancestors remained in Louisiana and Mississippi where they lived in the poverty of small southern towns or on the reservation — the worst of both worlds. Leah Beaulay had never slept in a nicer place than her room at Haskell. The KU campus tour was the prettiest landscape she had ever seen. And now, Ruby told her she was beautiful. Leah knew at that very moment that she was living the best day of her life.

Chapter 51

Rick Johansson looked up from the grill to see why the room had suddenly gone silent. There wasn't an inch of unoccupied real estate on the giant fry top. It was hissing and smoking but, through the haze, Rick caught a glimpse of Leah. He was thunderstruck. It wasn't just her room-quieting good looks. It was more like an electric current connecting them. He put down his spatula and picked up an order pad.

Rick's fraternity brothers described him as, "The nicest guy you'll ever meet—even if he is a rich kid." He was the son of two prominent Kansas City surgeons, and a fourth year pre-med student who fried burgers on the weekends just because he enjoyed it. He liked interacting with his co-workers where all were equals. He was cute and likeable and had that certain spark that made girls develop an instant crush on him. At the end of his burger flipping shift he felt a sense of accomplishment, a feeling his studies rarely gave him. His parents never pressured him into medicine. But everyone took it for granted that Rick would continue the family tradition. Medicine was not his passion and he certainly wasn't enjoying the class work. But then, he hadn't found any other course of study that excited him, either. Like so many of his friends, it was hard to follow your bliss when you couldn't identify it.

Rick walked over to Leah's booth like a puppy

heading towards the smell of peanut butter. His movements were also reminiscent of a pup.

"Hi. I'm Rick. Can I take your order?" he asked Leah, blind to the other girls in the booth.

Ruby, Alice, and Marilyn ordered a variety of pub grub. Leah ordered a tossed salad and double chocolate malt.

"Hmm, an intriguing combination," Rick mused.

Rick personally fried up most of the orders. When he delivered them to the table, he handed the bill to Leah and asked her to read it to herself.

The bill was marked 'PAID'. A note read: Please consider this our first date. My name is Rick Johansson, and I've never done anything like this before. I'm a senior from Kansas City. I'd like a chance to get to know you. May I have your phone number and permission to call you? (Ask any of the waitresses and they'll tell you I'm a decent guy.)

Leah wrote down her number and address. If this guy didn't want to date a girl from Haskell, better to know her address up front. She walked with confidence to the fry window, handed her number to Rick and said, "By the way, my name is Leah Beaulay."

"Excellent," Rick smiled. "Beautiful and excellent."

Chapter 52

Rick was in love. Leah was happy when she was with Rick, but she didn't miss him when they were apart. She wasn't about to fall in love with a fry cook. When she learned he was pre-med, she grew fonder of him. When Rick took her home to meet his parents and turned the car into one of the old-money mansions that line Ward Parkway, her eyes popped. Maybe she *was* in love.

The day after Rick Johansson graduated, he married Leah Beaulay in Danforth Chapel on The University of Kansas campus. Rick's parents flew Leah's entire family in and paid for the wedding and reception. They had never seen their son so happy and they loved their new daughter-in-law. Nineteen-year-old Leah was happy to be Mrs. Rick Johansson. She was thrilled to be the future Mrs. "Dr." Rick Johansson.

Rick's parents put a generous monthly stipend into Rick and Leah's joint checking account. They wanted Rick to focus his energy on medical school and not burn the candle at both ends. But Rick wanted to work. He liked going to a job away from the KU Med Center and he wanted to feel that *he* was supporting his new bride.

Leah got a job as a clerk at Southwestern Bell Telephone. They rented an apartment in an old house near the Med Center. What Leah remembered most about those early days was that she was tired all the time. When she began to fall asleep at her desk at 3:00 pm, Rick insisted she get a physical

Every morning at exactly 6:30 am, Leah took her birth control pill. She got pregnant anyway. Twenty-year-old Leah was sick to her stomach and in her heart. Rick was over the moon.

Lindsay arrived eight months later. Ned, another surprise, arrived sixteen months after Lindsay. After each birth, Leah returned to her job at the phone company. She felt like she was suffocating and she missed getting dressed up and talking to adults. Three days after each birth, Leah zipped up her size four jeans and left the hospital. As her looks matured, she became even more striking.

Rick's devotion to Leah and the kids came naturally. He was born to be a husband and father and he relished both jobs. A part-time job selling vacuum cleaners at Sears quickly led to a promotion to assistant manager of the department. He liked his job.

What he did not like was medical school. His grades were good but he was struggling with the ambivalence he continued to feel towards his chosen profession. The motivations of his fellow students sickened him. Those who weren't in it for the money were there to feed their enormous egos. Only a few wanted to make a difference or enjoyed the science of medicine. Rick, however, was a natural at the relationship side of doctoring. He looked forward to getting to know his patients and their families. But after three years of med school, he was beginning to see that his Norman Rockwell concept of the doctor/patient relationship no longer existed.

Rick tried to discuss his misgivings with Leah but he didn't find a sympathetic ear. She routinely cut him off with, "Grow up on an Indian reservation and you'll understand why I can't feel sorry for somebody whose biggest problem is a lack of job satisfaction." He hated it when Leah played the "poor little Indian girl" card. He never gave her a real reason to play it, but when played, Rick knew that the conversation was over.

Chapter 53

Rick joined four other third year students for lunch in the hospital cafeteria. He had two helpings of ground beef goulash on his tray and two cartons of chocolate milk. Rick loved cafeteria food. It reminded him of his happy childhood and the taste and smell made him feel loved. When he sat down, the others were in mid-rant about his favorite class, *Healing the Spirit*, taught by sociologist Sue Landers, PhD.

"I can't believe I'm forced to pay tuition to listen to some sociology major tell me how to play nice with patients. That woman has nothing to teach me," Paul barked. "I am in medical school, not touchy-feely school. As a doctor, I'll be saving lives. Let the hospital social worker deal with the families. I don't have time for hand-holding. It's not even cost-effective."

Rick didn't usually let himself get sucked into these thinly veiled doctor-as-God conversations. But he couldn't resist. "I believe strongly in the mind-body connection. If you want to heal the patient, you have to treat the whole person, the whole family. I think this is the most important class we'll take."

"Then be a shrink, or maybe a chaplain. I don't care how much of that voodoo, holistic crap you've bought into. I signed up to practice Western medicine."

Two residents at the next table stood up to bus their trays. Ian was a skinny, dark-haired man who looked about fourteen. His glasses and protruding Adams apple set off a terrible haircut that camouflaged a yarmulke. The other resident, Randy, stood six foot five and had the rugged good looks of a pro-soccer player. Good looks, brains, medical resident—Randy got laid a lot.

"Rick, I once felt like you do about being a compassionate physician—healing from the heart, serving the entire family—for about two years," Randy said. "Let me save you a few years. Unlearn everything Sue Landers teaches you. Being a doctor is like being a landlord. You keep a certain distance from your patients. If you show compassion or try to be their friend, I promise you, it will come back and bite you in the butt. The patient is your enemy. They are clients, and enemies. If you let them, they'll suck the life right out of you. They'll expect you to work for free, and then they'll sue your ass. If you don't keep a healthy distance from them, you'll go crazy, and broke. The good country doctor is dead and buried. What insurance companies didn't do to him, malpractice attorneys did. The patient is the enemy. Remember that."

Rick went to his job at Sears that night with a heaviness he hadn't felt in a long while. It was easy to forget about medical school the minute he hit the revolving doors at Sears. But not tonight. He demonstrated a couple of vacuums and sold one to a pretty young woman as she balanced a toddler on her hip. "Who would have guessed that buying a vacuum could actually be fun. You're good at what you do," she smiled.

Oh shit, thought Rick. *I just had an epiphany at Sears and Roebuck. I don't want to practice medicine. I'd rather sell vacuums.*

Chapter 54

L eah's affair with Randy began three days after Rick announced he was leaving medical school. After sneaking around with Leah for three months, Randy announced his engagement to his college sweetheart. When Leah was offered an entry level management job at Northwestern Bell in Omaha, she filed for divorce. Despite Rick's devastation, the divorce was amicable. Rick got custody of Lindsay and Ned. Leah didn't want them. Rick gave Leah a generous settlement and agreed to alimony. She had convinced him that the career bait and switch he pulled, robbed her of completing her education and a more financially secure life. Rick didn't want to upset Leah. He still harbored hopes that one day she would come back to him.

Before Leah moved to Omaha, she made a few changes. She had plastic surgery to remove the bump on her nose. At the same time, she treated herself to breast implants. Rick did not think either procedure was necessary.

"Leah's good looks were unconventional. Now she looks like just another gorgeous white woman. But she's happy, I guess," Rick told his parents. After the divorce, Leah Johansson changed her name back to Beaulay. It was a prominent name in the Indian community and Leah planned to take advantage of every EEOC consideration she could muster.

The Spezia waiter interrupted with their order. Rick shook his head in an attempt to jolt himself back into the present. Ruby Littlefoot Johansson stroked her husband's arm. "I know what you want to ask, Claudia. You want to ask Rick if he is still in love with Leah but you don't want to say anything in front of me. The answer is yes. He still loves her, and so do I. Leah is my best friend. She is kind and good and very messed up. But if you knew her better, you'd love her, too."

Rick kissed Ruby. "This is the love of my life. We have never had a cross word. She accepts me for who I am and Lindsay and Ned couldn't ask for a better mother."

"Thank you for being so candid. I think I understand why Leah is so drawn to successful men. Poverty must be terrifying. But it's no excuse. Ruby, your life experiences are very close to Leah's. But you haven't wavered from your values. Why is that? I've seen people who have suffered terrible child abuse who go on to be successful adults and loving parents. But I also see abused kids who use their childhoods as an excuse for a life of crime. At some point, you have to say, okay, I've had some bad breaks, but I'm taking control of my life now. I doubt Leah was any poorer than you were, Ruby. Yet look at what a bright, selfless soul you are."

Ruby smiled. "I think once Leah realized she could buy her way into the white man's world with her great looks, it really sent her down the wrong path. My great beauty never got in the way," Ruby laughed.

Claudia was beginning to grasp what Larry Walton meant when he suggested that Leah was a sociopath. It was the fear of returning to a life of poverty that drove her.

"Tell me this. If Max Riley had promised to marry Leah, but changed his mind, do you think that might have made her angry enough to kill him?"

Ruby and Rick looked at each other and answered in unison. "No. Never."

Chapter 55

Charlie agreed to let Claudia sit in on his last interview of the day, Leah Beaulay. She filled him in on the relevant parts of her lunch with Rick and Ruby Johansson.

"They have every reason to despise Leah but they don't," Claudia said. "I never realized how driven she is by her fear of returning to poverty. Wealth is everything to her. If she killed Max, it might have been about money. And another thing, Leah doesn't seem to have a conscious. She never takes responsibility or apologizes for her actions. And she may not be as dumb as I thought."

Claudia was impressed with Leah's articulate answers to Charlie's questions. She was also impressed with her candor. When asked about her relationships with various men, Leah offered as much detail as Charlie requested. Despite her amoral behavior, Leah mentioned her devotion to the Evangelical movement whenever possible. Claudia had been biting her tongue for twenty minutes when she finally blurted out, "Isn't adultery against your religion?"

"Yes, it is. But did you know that only men can commit adultery? Those laws were written for men, not women. Read your bible."

Claudia was stung by the comment. Charlie shot her a cautionary glare.

Charlie went easy on Leah. Claudia wondered if he might be falling for her, too. He asked for a sample of her DNA and she agreed without hesitating. "You're going to find my DNA on Max. I told you what happened before the plane took off. But I didn't kill him. I don't even know exactly how he died."

"And if you did kill him, so what?" Charlie shrugged. "If adultery doesn't apply to women, I suppose Thou Shalt Not Kill doesn't either."

As the interview ended, Leah looked to Claudia for support. "Next time, I'll bring a lawyer, huh? How could anyone think I had anything to do with this?"

"Don't look at me. Your friends all tell me what a nice person you are, but I don't think nice women fuck husbands that don't belong to them. Period. I think you may be selfish enough and nasty enough to murder, but I doubt you're clever enough."

Charlie called Claudia later that night. "Leah told me she doesn't want you in the room if I interview her again. Want to know why?"

"Because I've got a big mouth?"

"No. Because you have a dirty mouth. She reminded me again that she is very religious. Your language offends her."

Claudia wanted to explode. "In-fucking-credible. Please tell Leah that I am very sorry that my language offends her. Also tell her it amuses me that fucking someone else's husband is okay, but using the word is not."

Chapter 56

Claudia looked forward to her one-on-one interview with James Beck. Charlie had all the information he needed from him, but Claudia wanted to watch him squirm. He was nice enough to her when she worked at GWC because he knew she was tight with Wellman. Claudia had heard he had issues with women in the workplace. Madonnas or whores. There was no in-between for James. Mothers, nuns, teachers, daughters, wives, all were put on a pedestal.

Then there were the girls James saw fit for the drive-in but not the prom: waitresses, any woman with less education or a lower IQ than James, store clerks, non-white women—these were the whores. He had no respect for them. He didn't hate them or love them. He merely categorized them. It was easy to make snap judgments when he was growing up in rural Missouri. Women in a position to praise and elevate James were clearly Madonnas. The rest were whores. The Catholic school he attended, his parents, and his six brothers nurtured those beliefs.

But corporate life was different. This was unfamiliar territory to James. Women in power positions were attractive, well-dressed, and for the most part, conservative. They treated James with respect but did nothing to elevate him the way his mother and wife did. He didn't know what to make of them and he certainly didn't know how to treat them.

Much as Claudia wanted to take him down a peg, she knew that to squeeze information out of James she'd have to kiss up to him, a skill she had perfected at Great Western.

"You have more exposure to the executives than anyone else in the company. Any thoughts on who might have wanted to see Max dead?"

"I've certainly thought about it. But most of the vice presidents got where they are because of John Wellman and Max Riley. Why would they want to kill the guy responsible for their success?"

"What about Sumner Jackson?" Claudia asked. "He was the last person to talk to Max. I know he was ticked off when I got the VP job he wanted."

"No. With you and Wellman gone, Sumner will get your job. He was tighter with Max than you might think. Max loved a good yes man and Sumner is certainly that."

"Got any idea who might have done this?"

"Leah Beaulay has to be the prime suspect, doesn't she? They were having an affair. She threatened him. She was used to getting what she wanted. Maybe she couldn't handle getting dumped. She was the last person alone with Riley. It all adds up."

"You don't like her, do you?"

"Not even a little. I didn't like Max either. Neither one had a moral bone in their bodies."

"So you'd put your money on Leah?"

"No. Leah isn't smart enough to pull something like this off. But she could have talked somebody else into doing it. There are some men at the company who would do anything she asked. "

"You know what frustrates me, Jim?" James shot Claudia a piercing look in response to being called Jim. She did it on purpose and he knew it.

"What frustrates me is that we have several people who had the means to kill Max, and quite a few more with motive. But with no airport security policy in place, everyone had opportunity. Do you feel at all responsible for that? Does this make you want to press full speed ahead with Brad's security plan?"

James shrugged. "Maybe. We'll see what the new guy wants to do."

Chapter 57

Claudia had grown accustomed to attending social functions without Jake. But tonight's dinner at the Wellman's was to be just the four of them and she was irritated when he called at the last minute to say he couldn't make it.

Jake never said no when asked to work overtime. His own father worked like a dog but still the family could barely make ends meet. Jake and Claudia lived below their means and saved regularly. Yet there would never be enough money in their nest egg for Jake to feel secure.

He respected Claudia's earning power and worried that would change once she became pregnant. He once called a friend of theirs who was staying home to raise three kids, "a drain on society." Claudia knew that her six-figure salary at GWC was one of the things that attracted him to her. Her new career was going to test the marriage. Being an executive in a big corporation put Jake in social circles most cops never saw. His fellow police officers were impressed with Jake's social status, and he liked that.

Jake genuinely liked the Wellmans. While he felt flattered and important to be a part of Claudia's social circle, he would have enjoyed the friendship of John and Phyllis Wellman under any circumstances. Claudia liked the way John's personality rubbed off on Jake when they were around each other. She knew one way to have a happy marriage was to surround yourself with other couples who are happily married. That defined the Wellman's. Jake would never cancel on them without an urgent, unavoidable reason. They all understood that.

Phyllis answered the door and gave Claudia a long, warm hug. "I'm sorry Jake couldn't make it. But John and I selfishly love having you all to ourselves, too. We're trying out some new wines tonight. I put clean sheets on the bed in the guest room. Maybe you'll sleep over?"

"I hope I don't drink that much. But we'll see."

The Wellman's house was a sprawling multi-level built in the late '60's. The house sat angled on the corner making the backyard secluded and inviting. A waterfall led down the hill to a large koi pond. The walled patio was surrounded by a dense English garden. Something was always in bloom. John had done most of the landscaping himself. More than once, Claudia caught him working in the yard in a pair of old wing tips and cut off pin striped suit pants. Yard work was his therapy. This sanctuary was where the Wellmans entertained and spent every waking moment that the harsh Nebraska climate allowed.

The inside of the house was well built and neat as a pin. Claudia wondered how different the energy of the house must have been when the Wellman boys were growing up. The silence in the house hurt Claudia's ears. Jake loved the ticking of the grandfather clock but she found it depressing. The carpets were "little old lady mauve" as Claudia referred to the color. Dated, but in perfect condition.

"I used to really care about every detail of a house," Phyllis sighed. "When John was uprooting us every three years, I looked at every house we bought as my new assignment. He never held me back. I could do whatever I wanted in exchange for pulling up stakes and not complaining. But we've been in this house for 10 years. It's the first time we've lived anywhere long enough that I've had to tear out and update my own renovations. Frankly, I just don't have the interest anymore. So, I've got a proposition for you. When you're done with this investigation, if you have some down time, what would you think about me hiring you to be my interior decorator? No, that's not right. How about you agree to be my interior designer?"

"Are you kidding? I'd love to. I'd have gone into

interior design in a minute if I thought anyone would hire me." Claudia gushed.

"Great. Maybe you'll reconsider this private eye business—too dangerous. I'll give you a budget and you can do whatever you see fit. I just want someone to breathe some life into this house. I want it to look young - fresh."

Some eastern cultures believe that inanimate objects can actually take on energy. Phyllis bought into that philosophy. When her boys left home, that energy seemed to leave with them and their belongings. It felt dead to her. She hoped Claudia could remedy that.

John was sautéing Morel mushrooms in an iron skillet when the women walked into the kitchen.

"What is that smell?" Claudia asked as she gave John a squeeze. "Oh, dear Lord, you've been mushroom hunting. I have just died and gone to heaven."

Phyllis opened an ice cold bottle of Ironstone Chardonnay and carried it to the patio with three enormous, hand-blown wine glasses from the Adam Whitney Art Gallery. They had been a retirement gift from Claudia and Jake, true works of art. John followed behind with the Morels. George Benson and Teddie Pendergast serenaded them through the screen door. "What a lovely life I have," Claudia heard herself say.

The evening flew by. The three discussed an upcoming trip to Tuscany the Wellman's were planning, movies they had seen and needed to see, the ridiculously high Douglas County property taxes, and promising politicians. By 9:00 pm, they were feeling no pain.

"Okay, let's talk about the elephant standing in the middle of the room," Phyllis suggested.

They discussed it from every angle. "Considering how much it hurt when they initially pushed me out of the company, now I can't wait to be gone. The whole place is distracted with the murder investigation. You just never expect something like this to happen," John said.

Claudia updated them on the details of the investigation. Neither had ever heard of Absinthe. Phyllis googled it and printed up some information. "I'm ordering some first thing tomorrow. And who would ever have thought that nicotine could poison a person?"

John sat quietly and digested this new information.

"You know, John, you were right about James Beck," Claudia said. "If he had put any sort of security plan in place, this might not have happened. Anybody at any time could have slipped onto the plane and poisoned the Absinthe. You ought to re-fire that arrogant ass while you still have the chance."

"You don't believe James had anything to do with this do you?" John asked as he opened another bottle of wine. Without waiting for an answer John restated his own theory. "It wasn't James, or Sumner, or Frank Johnson, or Leah's husband. There were plenty of men who might have wanted Max dead, but none of them killed him. They would have shot him or used some other quick, macho method. Whoever killed Max put a lot of thought into it. I think there must be some significance in the Absinthe/nicotine method that you're missing. There's some message there we're not seeing. Whoever did this is highly intelligent and thoughtful. There's got to be some symbolism intended here. This took a lot of planning. I don't know who killed Max, but I'll say it again. It was a woman. Men are all about violence and power, let's get the job done, boom. Women are more thoughtful. I hate to admit it, but women are a lot more intelligent than men, more complicated, more evolved. A woman killed Max Riley. I'd bet my life on it."

Chapter 58

11:30 AM

Claudia called home and listened to the sound of her own voice on the answering machine. She felt like a newlywed whenever she heard herself say, "You've reached the Sullivan's." She loved those little personal reminders that she was Jake's wife. She hung up and tried his cell phone. Jake didn't answer his cell either so she left a message.

"Hey, I don't know if you remember me. My name is Claudia Sullivan—your wife? I thought if you were done working you could come retrieve me. But, I guess you're missing in action. I've had a little too much wine, so I'm spending the night at the Wellman's. I'll see you tomorrow. I love you."

Claudia took two Advil with a big glass of water as a precautionary measure. She slid her naked body between the crisp white sheets of the queen-sized bed in the Wellman guestroom. Clean sheets were one of life's under-appreciated little pleasures, Claudia thought. The pillowcases were ironed, something she hadn't experienced since leaving home for college. She could hear John and Phyllis Wellman talking and laughing gently. She dozed off to the unmistakable sound of their lovemaking. How sweet, Claudia thought. I miss Jake.

7:30 AM

Claudia was jolted awake by the sound of Sly Stone singing "Hot Fun in the Summertime". It was her cell phone. She answered with a chipper, wide awake voice.

"Claudia Sullivan."

"Jeez, I'm sorry, it's Platt, did I wake you?"

"No, no, not at all, what's up?"

Why do people always feel the need to deny to early morning callers that they have interrupted their sleep?

"We are arresting Leah Beaulay this morning."

Without thinking, Claudia responded, "What for?"

"You were sleeping, weren't you? We're arresting her for the murder of Max Riley. The chief is holding a news conference at 10:00 am. Thought you'd want to know."

"Thanks. Have you told Trish, or would you like me to?"

"I'll call her, but it might be helpful if you were with her when my call comes in. We're confident that we have enough evidence to convict. Otherwise we wouldn't be making the arrest. Like I said from the beginning: means, motive, opportunity. Leah had it all."

"I can't argue with that. But you know Charlie, I've conducted quite a few interviews in the last few weeks. Some of those interviews were with people who had every reason to dislike Leah. But to a person, none of them thought Leah capable of murder."

"That will be for a jury to decide now. We heard a lot of people describe Leah as the nicest person you'd ever want to meet. That doesn't mean squat to me. Nice people murder their lovers all the time."

Chapter 59

Claudia threw on her clothes and quietly pulled away from The Wellman's. If she hurried, she could grab a quick shower before heading over to Trish's. As she rounded the corner, she saw Jake's car pull into their driveway.

"You just getting home?" she asked as he held her car door open.

"Yeah. I am beat. Looks like I'm working every

night this week. I just came home to grab a couple of hours sleep."

They kissed as Jake unlocked the door.

"I missed you last night. Think you could keep your eyes open long enough for a quickie?"

"Why not," Jake smiled.

Claudia stripped off her clothes and jumped into bed while Jake brushed his teeth and splashed water on his face. He took off his shoes, socks, and jeans and left them in a heap on the floor before joining his wife.

"Aren't you going to take off the rest of your clothes?" she asked.

"Don't spoil my surprise. I thought I'd take care of you for a change. You lay still. I'll take care of everything."

Jake positioned himself on top of Claudia. He kissed her neck and arms. "Don't move," he commanded. His movements were slow and slightly painful. Claudia wondered if this might be all she'd need to climax. Jake threw her legs over his shoulders and wedged his head between her legs. She was going crazy.

"I want you in me," Claudia begged.

"Not today. Today I'm taking care of *you*."

Jake expertly worked his magic on Claudia. She couldn't hold back, and she didn't want to. Her climax was long and loud and as intense as any she had ever experienced. Immediately, Claudia felt guilty.

"I feel bad that you didn't get off."

"Next time," Jake said.

"You've never done that to me before. I mean

you've never just taken care of me. It was fun."

"It's supposed to be. I'll have to do it more often."

Chapter 60

Ruth and Trish were sitting on the front porch drinking coffee when Claudia arrived. Charlie had already called. Claudia's detour home had thrown her off schedule.

"Grab a cup and come join us," Trish said.

Claudia rummaged through the coffee cups until she found just the right one. Half of the cupboards in the recently remodeled kitchen featured glass doors that showed off dozens of matched cups and dishes. But behind the maple door next to the sink was where the really good stuff was kept: the mismatched mugs with the coffee stains in the bottoms; the green bean can covered with construction paper that held pens and pencils; a list taped to the inside with important phone numbers. Claudia was flattered to find her name on the list. The white clay mug was oversized and the handle just felt right in Claudia's hand. The chip on the rim fit perfectly against her lower lip. "Mom" was scratched into one side. "Love, Tim" was scratched into the other.

"I see you found your favorite cup," Ruth smiled.

"Right. I had to do some digging. I was afraid for a minute someone had broken it. By the way, Trish, if it ever does get broken, don't throw it away. I'll fix it. I don't quite know why, but I love this thing."

"It makes Tim feel good to see you use it. Funny how it's the little things that make a difference in life."

There was an awkward silence. Ruth broke it. "What do you think about Leah's arrest?"

"I think Charlie Platt is the best homicide detective in the country. He and his team have worked night and day on this case. He wouldn't be making the arrest unless he was sure he could get a conviction. I asked him how sure he was that he had the right person. I expected him to say ninety-nine percent. He said he was 110 percent positive that Leah killed Max. She had means, motive, and opportunity. And she was the last person alone with Max. Charlie knows what he's doing."

"What do you think?" Trish asked. "Do you think Leah killed Max?"

"No. I'm sorry. I just don't. She certainly had opportunity. But then, everyone had opportunity. The jet was never secure. She doesn't have the brains for it. The way Max was murdered took a much more complicated mind than Leah possesses. She just couldn't have executed such a complex plan.

"And motive? I don't think she had one. The prosecution doesn't have to show motive, but they certainly will throw their theory up. They'll say that she was a woman scorned. But, I think the defense will try to show that Max was intending to move her to Denver once he got settled there. And she never asked him to leave you, Trish.

"They say that love, not hate, is what motivates people to kill. I've interviewed a lot of people who know Leah well and I feel confident in saying that Leah didn't love Max. I don't think she's ever really loved anyone."

"Charlie told me that Leah threatened Max. He says they have it on tape," Trish countered.

"I've heard the tape. It's a pretty vague threat. She certainly doesn't threaten to kill him. I'll put this all in my report to you. I conducted lots of detailed interviews that Charlie's team couldn't. I assume Leah's arrest means I need to shut down my investigation."

"I'm not sure we're ready for you to shut down just yet," Ruth said. "This family has no love for Leah Beaulay. But we do want justice for Max. If you think there are more stones to overturn, then do it. I will be at the trial every day. Trish and the kids don't need to be humiliated by the evidence the prosecution presents. I want to represent the family. I can handle it, and I want to. Claudia, you know how much I respect your hard work and the insight you bring to this investigation. But I think we also need to consider the possibility, maybe the probability, that the police have arrested the *right* person."

Chapter 61

The explosion ripped through the morning air, jolting all three women to their feet. Trish's coffee splashed onto her white cotton sweater as her cup shattered on the cement. "What the—was that a cherry bomb?"

Claudia stared at them with a glare befitting the sternest Mother Superior. "Stay here. Do not leave this porch."

As she walked through the house, she knew what she would find. She just wasn't sure where. Her heart filled her throat, making it impossible to swallow. She could hear herself repeating out loud: "Please, God, no. Please, God, no. Please, God, no..."

Chapter 62

Tim Riley's bedroom was on the main floor, next to Max's study. Claudia walked quickly to his room. The door was open but Tim was not there. As she turned, she bumped into Ruth and Trish. Neither mother had heeded Claudia's admonition to stay on the porch. The door to the study was closed. Claudia opened it. Tim lay soundlessly on his back in the middle of the floor. The shotgun was clutched in both hands. A halo of blood spread under his head.

Trish ran silently to her son and knelt beside

him. In a state of shock, she went on auto pilot. She wrapped her arms around him and put her head to his chest. "Call 911 and get some towels."

Claudia called 911 and requested an ambulance. She also asked the operator to find Charlie Platt and tell him to get to the Riley house, immediately. Claudia carefully removed the shotgun before Trish began stuffing the white towels under Tim's head. Ruth held Tim's bare feet in her hands and alternately stroked them and kissed them. Claudia and Ruth both knew Tim was dead, but they didn't want to deny Trish the last opportunity she would ever have to take care of her little boy.

The ambulance arrived in seven minutes, thirty-two seconds. For some reason, Claudia felt the need to mentally note the time of the gunshot, discovery of Tim, arrival of the paramedics. The sirens started up as Trish and Tim left for Children's Hospital. Eight minutes later, Charlie pulled into the driveway.

Ruth and Claudia walked Charlie and the uniformed cop through the sequence of events. "I know this isn't your responsibility, but I appreciate you coming, Charlie. The family has enormous respect for you and I thought having you here might make things a little easier," Claudia said.

"You did the right thing. Mrs. O'Kiefe, would you mind if Claudia took me through a few rooms."

"Go ahead. I'll be in the kitchen."

Ruth wanted a cigarette. In her seventy years, she had never smoked a single cigarette. She hated everything about the filthy habit, but today it appealed to her. Instead, she inhaled and exhaled deeply as she methodically washed dishes at the kitchen sink.

The unlocked gun case in the basement was open and one of the shotguns was missing. The rug over the floor safe was thrown back and the safe was open. The box of shells was open and several were missing.

"Have you found a note?" Charlie asked.

"No, but we haven't really looked."

"I'll bet we don't find one. Sometimes suicides— usually girls and women, or men on a mission—even mail letters before they kill themselves. But boys are notorious for not leaving any explanation. That can actually be a blessing. I've seen families who, absent a note, talk themselves into believing that the victim didn't really mean to kill himself."

"I'd be surprised if Trish responded that way. This is a family of strong women. They don't like things sugarcoated. In their minds, finding and understanding the truth is extremely important. They won't want you to whitewash this. They've even asked me to continue to investigate Max's death. It's not that they think you have the wrong woman. It's just that if there is more to be uncovered, they want it uncovered."

Claudia and Charlie were in Tim's bedroom looking through the papers on his desk when Ruth walked in.

"Mrs. O'Kiefe, I can't begin to tell you how sorry I am for your loss. I lost a son several years ago. He was ill for about six months before he died. It was as painful for his grandmother—my wife's mother—as it was for my wife and me. She told me that her agony was doubled because she watched her grandson *and* her daughter suffer and there wasn't a damn thing she could do about it. If I could soak up some of the pain this family has endured, I'd do it in a minute. This is just so..."

Charlie's voice cracked and the words caught in his throat. Ruth took him in her arms like a wounded child. Then Claudia saw something she never expected. Ruth O'Kiefe broke down and sobbed. And Charlie Platt cried right along with her.

Chapter 63

Claudia arrived home at 1:30 pm. She heard snoring in the bedroom. A note on the kitchen table read: *Make sure I'm up by 5:00. Love, Jake.*

Claudia wanted to wake him and share the horrors of her morning, but she knew how badly he needed sleep. Whatever case he and Nan were working on gave him little time for rest. Jake was like a man on meth. He moved fast and appeared to have limitless energy. But when he finally got the opportunity to sleep, he crashed into a deep immediate slumber.

At 4:55 pm, Claudia stood at the bedroom door and called Jake's name. She knew not to wake him within arms length or she could end up with a black eye. When Jake awoke from a sound sleep, he woke up swinging, another lingering side effect from his years in the Marine Corps.

Claudia sat by his side. "Want a backrub?"

"Sure. What time is it? I've got to be at work by six."

"You've got time. Jake, Tim Riley killed himself this morning."

"Yeah, I heard you were there when it happened."

"You knew and you didn't bother to call or wait up for me?"

"You're a big girl. I didn't think you'd want me getting in your way."

Claudia's heart sank. She loathed Jake using her independence as an excuse to ignore her. "I'm also your wife. You're supposed to care about me. Be there for me."

"I'm sorry. I didn't think of it that way. How are you? How's Trish handling this?"

Claudia was hurt and pissed. How could he be so insensitive? Everything seemed more important to him than her emotional needs these days. She asked for very little yet received even less. His job, his friends, his daily workouts, Claudia was always at the bottom of his list.

When Claudia didn't respond, Jake got defensive.

"I said I was sorry. If you want to be a private investigator, you'd better develop thicker skin. You're the one who thought being an overpaid vice president with a big office wasn't meaningful enough. You did this to yourself."

"Jake, I'm not talking about the job. Someone I love has died and I'm hurting. It's that simple. Do you care so little about me that you can't imagine I might be in pain and could use a little support? You know it's difficult for me to ask for help, let alone tenderness.

We're married, for God's sake. Aren't married people supposed to be there for each other?"

Jake did not answer. He was asleep.

As Claudia stared at Jake, doubts muscled their way into her consciousness. Doubts a woman desperate to start a family dare not allow herself to acknowledge. Claudia recognized years before she married Jake that she was addicted to him. She wasn't sure if her addiction was coupled with love or in place of it. At this moment, that debate didn't matter. She was suddenly slapped in the face with an insight so simple and clear that it startled her. Claudia did not *like* her husband. And she hadn't liked him for several years.

Chapter 64

For the second time in less than a year Claudia found herself lining up for a funeral at Christ the King Catholic Church. It was the saddest gathering she had ever attended. Tim's funeral drew even more mourners than Max's. By the time the service began, teens and adults would be standing shoulder to shoulder on the plaza in front of the church, unable to secure a seat.

As Claudia inched her way up in line towards the guest book, she watched the slide show of Tim's life, expertly produced by Great Western's public relations department. It reminded Claudia that there was still some small semblance of family within the company. She would miss that.

The slideshow chronicled Tim's life from the day of his birth until just one week before his death. Claudia searched his face for some sign of despair that may have led him to take his own life. If it was there, she couldn't find it. Max was in many of the pictures. She could see that his smile, in the final few years of his life, had changed from genuine happiness and fatherly pride to one he had practiced for the camera. Anyone viewing the slides would surely conclude that Tim loved his life and adored his family. What could have gone so terribly wrong? As always, Claudia wanted answers. But for once, she would have to accept that there wouldn't be any.

The bells tolled and Claudia watched over her shoulder as one of the pall bearers removed Tim's red and white soccer jersey from the top of his casket. He folded it awkwardly and handed it to Trish. There were three teenaged boys on either side of the casket. Their eyes were red and swollen as they accompanied their friend and teammate's body to the front of the church.

Trish followed directly behind, holding the hand of Tim's biological mother, Kathleen Cerone. Tears streamed down both mothers' cheeks. Behind them followed Korey, Katy, and Ruth. Their behavior was quite a contrast to Max's funeral where great strength and poise were called upon. Today, the girls had to steady their grandmother as they made their way to their seats. They could not control their grief. And they didn't care.

Father Loseke spoke first. His vestments were so

grand, they looked almost cartoonish. Claudia thought he looked very pope-like. She held her breath, hoping he would not say anything that would add to Trish's burden.

Tears filled Father Loseke's eyes as he began to speak. "People sometimes joke about what we refer to as 'Catholic Guilt'. But there is no room in this church today for guilt. I know some of you are wondering if Tim's death is due to something you said or didn't say. Was it something you did or didn't do? Were you a good enough friend? Had you been unkind? None of those things led to Tim's death. Tim made a terrible choice. I can not condone or explain what he did. But I know the choice was his and his alone. No one in this room caused it and no one could have stopped him. I can assure you that God loves Tim and forgives Tim. And we should, too."

As the old priest took his seat, Claudia breathed a sigh of relief. She wondered if Father Loseke believed his own words. She knew that, like most religions, Catholicism teaches that suicide insures a straight shot to hell. A friend—a child psychiatrist—once told her that, as physicians, they don't argue with The Church's stand on suicide. "Sometimes that fear of going to hell is the only thing that stands between a patient and the barrel of a gun."

Next, Larry Walton stood. As he approached the altar he genuflected like a good, albeit aging, altar boy. Claudia was beginning to wonder if everyone in Omaha was Catholic.

"My name is Dr. Larry Walton. I counseled Tim

Riley and his family. I want to thank Father Loseke for his straight talk and I'd like to add to that. I know what killed Tim Riley. Tim had a fatal form of a disease called depression. Many who have it find medication that can cure them, much like chemotherapy can cure cancer. Again, like cancer, some die from it without ever knowing they have the disease. Depression is not a mental illness. It is an illness where the body cannot produce certain chemicals it must have to survive. Just like insulin can save the life of many diabetics, and statin drugs can save people from heart disease, there are medications that can help people produce the brain chemicals their bodies cannot.

"Tim didn't think he was depressed. At one point he was placed on some mild antidepressants, but he quit taking them. He thought they masked his true personality. He was wrong but we couldn't convince him of that. He tried so hard to show us all how happy he was. But he couldn't fool his brain. If he had let someone know, perhaps we could have helped him. Suicide is never the result of something someone did. It is always this terrible disease that takes the life.

"Tim shared much with me. His friends and family meant the world to him. He would not want to hurt those he loved so much. But it was out of his control.

"I beg those of you hearing this today, if you are miserable for any reason, don't let yourself do anything final. Don't do anything irreversible. Talk to someone. If you can't talk to your parents, seek out a teacher you trust or the parent of a friend. Call my office. I will always make time for you. There is no mistake that can't be corrected. There is nothing that can't be fixed. Except suicide. Just stay alive and I promise things can get better. Just stay alive."

The Riley family sat silent as the limousine drove to the cemetery. Kathleen Cerone broke the silence.

"This is all my fault. It was the drinking I did when I was pregnant."

Ruth quickly interrupted. "That is not so. If anyone is at fault, it's me. I should have seen that Tim was suffering. Grandmothers are supposed to see what others can't. I don't care what the priest said. I'll never get over the guilt. I'm to blame for this."

Trish shook her head. "Stop it. Both of you. It is a mother's responsibility to see to it that her children live to adulthood. I alone failed Tim. I'll take that to my grave."

Chapter 65

FOUR DAYS LATER

Shamus nearly knocked Claudia down as he bounded out of the car. Sparky was running circles around her as if herding her towards Ruth's front door.

"Do you think Trish might walk with us today? It would be good for her," Claudia asked.

"No. She's already gone on a run. No stretching, just took off going a hundred miles an hour—like she was trying to run herself to death. I am worried sick about her. She's not eating, she doesn't like to go out in public, not even to the grocery store. She says she can't shake the feeling of being a failure and she's embarrassed to go out as if her life is okay. She thinks, if she can't even keep her children alive, what's the point?"

As the dogs pulled their humans down the block, they were waved down by the neighbor across the street. Claudia remembered seeing this woman at Tim's funeral. Despite an obvious facelift, she looked every day of her fifty-five years. A van came over the crest of the hill causing her to jump back onto the curb.

"We need to get the city to put a speed bump in here. The cars just fly over the hill." She extended her hand to Claudia, "Hi, I'm Diane Dingman. We've lived across the street forever." After a quick minute of small talk, Diane got to the point.

"Ruth, I told Trish if there was anything I could do—well, I know that sounds hollow, but I mean it. I'm right here and I want to help. I just don't know what to do. So please, please, just ask. How is everyone doing?"

"We're hanging in there. Some days just barely. But we're hanging in there," Ruth said.

"I know your faith will see you through this, just like it did when Max died. It's just so unfair to have all this heaped on your family. You have suffered so much tragedy. Just remember, God never gives us more than we can handle."

As they walked out of earshot, Ruth said, "Ooh, so close. She almost said just the right thing, and then she had to say something stupid. If one more person suggests that God never gives us more than we can handle, I'm going to suggest they pay a visit to the Nebraska Psychiatric Hospital. That place is loaded with people who were given more than they could handle."

"I know what you mean. I'll just ask you right now to forgive me for all the stupid things I've said or will say. We all mean to say the right thing, we're so afraid of screwing up that we just clam up."

"Oh, I know that. When my daughter died, I think I heard every well-meaning, stupid attempt at condolence you could imagine: I know just how you feel because my dog died last month, my eighty-year-old grandfather has cancer, everything happens for a reason, you're lucky you have other children, you can still have more kids. I could go on and on. But I knew people meant well and I never really took offense.

"The only comment I couldn't bear without speaking up was: 'You're lucky Annie was so young when she died. Just think how awful it would have been if she was older?' That one made me crazy. I felt they were diminishing the importance of her life. And you'd be amazed at how many people said it. My husband and I got some counseling and the therapist even said it.

"I really took that therapist to task, kind of read her the riot act. It was important that she of all people understand how a grieving parent takes that remark. But apparently I didn't make an impact. A couple of sessions later, she repeated the same damn thing. I couldn't believe it. That was the last time we saw her. She just didn't get it. Some well-meaning people have said the same thing to Trish. Makes you wonder how old they think kids need to be before it's okay to be devastated by their deaths."

For the next mile, Claudia let Ruth continue to unload. Tim's death was crushing to the entire family. Korey, Katy, and Trish were just going through the motions. This was different from the grief they felt when Max died. This was so much worse. Trish feared she would never be happy again.

"I thought Larry Walton's eulogy at Tim's funeral was right on. I think Tim was depressed, even if no one knew it," Claudia said. "This may sound weird, but had Tim been ill, had a bug of any sort before he died?"

"Yes. The night before he died he said he felt nauseous and ached all over. He said he felt weird...off. Why do you ask?"

"Unfortunately, over the years I have known five other people who committed suicide. Every one of them had flu-like symptoms in the days before their deaths. I have nothing to back this up, but I wonder if a virus can throw off the brain's chemical balance. Or, maybe those chemicals are being depleted in an effort to fight off the virus. I think that could explain why some seemingly happy, healthy people suddenly take their own lives. Again, I have nothing to back this up. It's just something I've been thinking about. Have you ever wondered if Max's death was harder on Tim than we realized? Maybe it zapped him of the chemical reserves he needed to function?"

Ruth bristled at this and Claudia regretted bringing up Max. She had overstepped her bounds and apologized, acknowledging it was a stupid thing to say.

"You know Tim—and the girls for that matter—hated Max," Ruth said. "After a short grieving period, they were all happier—much happier—than when he was alive. When Max was alive, they had no control over their own lives, their own happiness. Max's death breathed new life into this family."

"Yes, I noticed that, too. You're right. I'm sorry. I just hate that we have to accept Tim's death without ever getting any answers. That's a tough one for me. I'm angry but I don't know who I'm angry with or why."

"When Annie died, I thought that the death of a child was the most painful experience on earth. But this is worse. The death of a child by his own hand is so wrenching, I can't even find the words to explain it.

"Trish told me she read something that for whatever reason, gave her some comfort. She said that we shouldn't feel guilty or responsible for the terrible tragedies in our lives because the world is a very random place—out of our control. She read that, scientifically speaking, the universe is becoming more and more random, not less. Einstein studied this extensively and it bothered him tremendously. He thought that as humans evolved and learned more, we should be able to have more control over what happens to us, but we have less."

"That is kind of comforting," Claudia agreed. "We just have to do the best we can, and then let it go."

They walked the last half mile back to the Riley house in a comfortable silence only true friends can share. As Claudia loaded Shamus into the car she heard a bizarre sound coming from inside the house. Perhaps an animal had gotten in. She ran to the kitchen. Trish was sitting on the floor, rocking and wailing as she held Tim's backpack tightly against her breast. Shamus pushed past Claudia and sat down next to Trish. He threw his head back and howled along with her, hoping to save her from this vicious, unseen intruder: despair.

Chapter 66

Davis Bunker looked like a bulldog. Not a bad look for a defense attorney. He stood five-feet, six-inches and was built like a block of ice. His eyes bugged out of his square face and his teeth were pointed like a prize winning pit bull. His dark hair was usually in need of a trim, not to mention a style. He walked with purpose, eyes darting from left to right. All that was missing was the spiked dog collar.

Davis was butt ugly. But that didn't seem to slow him down when it came to the ladies. His wife, a petite blonde from a wealthy old Omaha family, knew he had other women, but felt she was lucky to have him. Her self-worth and confidence registered at zero. Davis fed her insecurities. He knew a thing or two about unfaithful spouses and the women who pursued them. He was smart, focused, and the best defense lawyer in town. If you wanted to win, you wanted Davis Bunker to represent you. He relished digging his teeth into seemingly unwinnable cases and unraveling the prosecution.

Nobody enjoyed performing for the cameras more than Davis. So when his paralegal, Mary Nathan, raced into his office to tell him Peter Anderson was on the phone, she expected a bigger response. Davis had never heard of Peter. "Peter is Leah Beaulay's husband. She's been arrested."

Davis picked up the phone as if Peter was his long lost brother. He told Peter he had been following the case and would be pleased to represent Leah. He hung up the phone and smiled broadly at Mary. *This is going to be fun.*

Chapter 67

Leah's bail was set at one million dollars. Gene Knoll, lead prosecutor for Douglas County, made a strong case for denying bail altogether. But in the end, the judge did not think Leah was a flight risk. Within hours, Peter Anderson produced the $100,000 required to bail his wife out of jail. Peter and Leah drove from the jail directly to Davis Bunker's law office.

Leah had had plenty of time to think as she waited for her bail hearing. She knew that without Peter's money, she could never afford the kind of expensive defense Davis could provide. She also knew she couldn't lie to him about Max. She confessed to Peter everything that took place in Denver the day Max died. She knew it would come out in court.

When Davis asked her to explain what happened in Denver, she was truthful. When he asked her to detail any other affairs she might have had over the last ten years, she was stunned. She claimed infidelity rumors had plagued her for years and that Max was her only transgression.

"People at the company are jealous of me. They refused to believe that my promotions were the result of hard work and brains, so they started rumors that I was sleeping my way up the corporate ladder. It's just not true. I'm a born-again Christian. I'm obviously not perfect, but I believe in the Ten Commandments. I am not a slut."

Deny, deny, deny. It was a strategy Davis himself had used successfully, but not this time. It just wouldn't work. There was too much evidence. Besides, he knew that to get Leah off he might want to raise the possibility of other lovers having motive to kill Max.

"I want you to listen very carefully." Davis spoke in a low, deliberate tone as he locked eyes with Leah. "Contrary to popular belief, defense attorneys do not lie for their clients. I win acquittals by building cases with the information my clients give me. What you have just given me, my dear, is bullshit. Is that the kind of defense you want me to present? Bullshit in, bullshit out. That's how it works. If the jury thinks you're lying about other affairs—and they will—then they'll think you're also lying about killing Max. The prosecution has witnesses up the wazoo who will testify about your other extramarital activities. I'm going to leave you two alone for awhile. Leah, it's time for you to have a 'come to Jesus' talk with your husband. Then we'll begin again."

Davis stood outside the door long enough to hear Peter tell Leah that there was nothing she could say or do that would make him stop loving her. "Before we can repair this marriage, we have to get you out of this mess. I've signed on for the long haul, but you've got to be honest with me. I need to hear the truth, and I need to hear it from you."

Leah swallowed hard. "I'm really going to put that to the test. I have a lot to tell you. And the first thing I want to say is that I love you and I am so very, very sorry."

Chapter 68

Fifteen minutes passed before Davis bounded back into his office. "Are we good here?" Davis asked. Peter looked at him like a deer looking into the headlights of a Mack truck. "Because it's all going to come out," Davis said to Peter. "Leah needs you if we're going to win this. But if you can't get past this and support her, and that would certainly be understandable, can you at least play the forgiving husband until after the trial?"

Peter nodded his head in the affirmative, unable to speak.

Leah re-told the story of the last ten years of her life. This time she was candid. As Davis prodded her for details, she filled him in on her every indiscretion. He asked the management level of each of her partners. Her first affair was with a second level manager, then a third level, a director, then Max.

"Each new affair was with a higher level of management? So you *were* screwing your way up the ladder," Davis said.

Leah protested, claiming that the ascending ranks of her lovers were purely coincidental. Davis frowned and went into his "courtroom" voice. "So we've established that you were on the path of screwing your way up the corporate ladder. We won't even go into the affairs you've had with men outside the company. You've lied to cover up your affairs. That makes you an adulterer and a liar. Why should the jury believe that you didn't kill Max to get ahead, cover your tracks, get your old job back—any number of motives?"

Peter stood up and started towards Davis. The size difference alone should have frightened him, but he didn't flinch.

"Settle down, Pete. This is child's play. Wait until the media gets a hold of this. Hell, wait until the prosecution opens. If we decide to portray Leah as a big-hearted girl who just can't say no, it's going to get ugly. Actually, no matter what our approach, it's going to get ugly."

The months preceding the trial required the full attention of Davis and his staff. Finding and interviewing potential character witnesses, countering the prosecution's forensic psychologist with one of their own choosing, investigating others who may have had motive to kill, examining the prosecution's case, studying the physical evidence, the workload was daunting. Davis' billable hours would be astronomical. But he was worth every penny of it, and Leah and Peter knew it.

Chapter 69

The media speculated that jury selection might take days. Because of the extensive national coverage the case had attracted, many thought an impartial jury would be impossible to seat and that the trial would have to be moved out of Omaha. But Claudia knew better. Many of the potential jurors had never read about the murder or seen anything about it on television. As astounding as that was to Claudia, she had only to remind herself that the majority of Americans couldn't even name the current vice-president of The United States. Why would they know who Leah Beaulay is? Those who had followed the case but wanted to sit on the jury, claimed they had not reached any conclusions as to Leah's guilt or innocence and could remain impartial.

Claudia wondered why Davis had not opted for a judge instead of a jury. Several years ago she had listened to Davis pontificating to Creighton law students over beers at The Jay. "If your client is innocent or proof of guilt isn't there, a judge is your best choice. If your client is guilty and you want to get him off, ask for a jury. Somebody on the jury is apt to believe that the defendant wouldn't lie. With a judge, you only get one chance to get your client off. But with a jury, you get twelve chances."

As Claudia listened to the selection process, she thought she might do well working for the defense as a jury selection consultant. She was not impressed with the unasked questions that could make or break Leah's chance for acquittal. How did potential jurors feel about infidelity? Mothers who gave up custody of their children? Did they have friends who worked for Great Western?

It took only three hours to seat the jury. Chosen were six men and six women, four were Latino, three were African American, and five were white. Their occupations and educations didn't tell Claudia much. She wondered if the ethnic makeup meant Davis was going to lean heavily on Leah's Native American background.

What Davis didn't seem to take into account was how the jury—especially the women—felt about infidelity. If Davis thought his wife was typical of most cheated upon women or that Pete's steadfastness was typical of most cuckolded husbands, he was sadly mistaken. Claudia knew better. She sensed that several of the jurors would happily send Leah to prison for life for her outrageous adultery, alone. If Davis didn't have some very impressive lawyering up his sleeve, Leah was screwed.

Chapter 70

The attorneys for the prosecution took their seats. There was eager Gregg Boots, twenty-six and fresh out of Creighton Law School. Beside him sat seasoned prosecutor Lanie Reynolds. Lanie graduated from Nebraska Law School twenty-five years ago. During her tenure with the Douglas County Attorney's office she married, raised three children, and divorced. This was the only post-law school job she had ever had or ever wanted. But putting bad guys away had taken its toll. She thought if they won this case she might retire and go out on a high note.

Gene Knoll was serving his second term as Douglas County Attorney. Admired and liked by his peers, he won cases based on facts, hard work, and competence. His relationship with defense attorneys was cooperative and professional. No fireworks with Gene. Just a very skilled, likeable public servant that juries wanted to root for. He had faith in his staff, but this was the highest profile trial of his career and he wasn't going to miss a minute in the courtroom. All three of the prosecuting attorneys had one thing in common: they looked tired.

About two-thirds of the seats in the courtroom were occupied. The first two rows were filled with reporters. Claudia was struck by how most professions in America were populated with people who were sick of their jobs. Claudia was excited to be in the courtroom but most of the reporters appeared bored. Some were yawning. Perhaps people should be required to shift careers every seven years, she thought. Claudia could see where burnouts were a detriment to any profession.

The list of possible witnesses was long. Those on the list were not allowed to sit in on the testimony of others so many of the faces one might expect to see in the courtroom were not present.

Davis entered the room with a quick, confident gait. Leah Beaulay was at his side and his paralegal, Mary, followed close behind. Mary was dressed in a red suit with a short skirt and three inch heels. She was perfectly turned out and looking much flashier then she had at the office. Perhaps by dressing Mary up and toning Leah down, the suspect would look less threatening. *Mission not accomplished.*

Leah wore a dark grey shirtdress that fell just below her knees, a watch, silver stud earrings, and her plain, platinum wedding band. Makeup was limited to a little lipstick and mascara. Her hair was pulled back and clamped up on her head in a casual, schoolgirl way. She had to buy new shoes for the trial. They were the only pair of flats she would ever purchase.

Still, her natural beauty lit up the courtroom. Even the drab clothing and fluorescent lighting could not dull Leah's glow.

Chapter 71

Opening and closing arguments were the most interesting days of any criminal trial. The attorneys got to throw anything they wanted up against the wall. Witnesses rarely provided any revelations and the CSI evidence could be tedious. The real theatrics came on the first and last days.

First up, Douglas County Prosecutor Gene Knoll. "Over the next few days, you will hear a story of greed, lust, betrayal, and extreme egocentricity. Witnesses will recount the life of Max Riley. They are going to paint a picture of a good, charming man with the world at his feet. You'll learn what a good friend, husband, and father he was until he had the tragic misfortune of meeting the defendant, Leah Beaulay.

"You will see a pattern of cruel disregard for any wife or family that got in the way of Ms. Beaulay's ambitions. We will show how she manipulated her way into the beds of any married man who could advance her career. And she did it again and again and again without ever showing signs of remorse. Leah Beaulay never feels guilt for the pain she causes others. She adulterated her way all the way up to the executive suite at Great Western Communications, where she hit the jackpot: Max Riley. Never mind that Max had a wife and children who loved and needed him.

"We will demonstrate how over the length of the affair—two years—Ms. Beaulay got much of what she had plotted for: a promotion, money, expensive gifts, attention. But she did not get what she ultimately wanted. Max Riley would not divorce his wife for his mistress. For two years, Ms. Beaulay showed that she could be patient. Max had made promises that were worth the wait. But Leah's patience snapped the day Max Riley ended their affair.

"Witnesses will testify that when Max was given an ultimatum: transfer Leah, or lose the presidency of Great Western Communications, he was relieved to have a way out of the tangled web Leah had spun them into.

"But Leah was not about to let Max dump her. They argued on numerous occasions. We have witnesses who will recount how Leah threatened Max. In fact, you'll hear Leah's threats with your own ears. Then we'll show you how she went about making good on that threat. She was a woman scorned. It's the oldest motive in the world.

"You'll hear testimony from the Douglas County Crime Lab as to the twisted, very personal plot the defendant carried out. She introduced Max, her lover, to a forbidden form of alcohol, Absinthe. She encouraged Max's love of illegal Cuban cigars. Then, when Max ended their affair, she took this ritual she had created, the ritual that she and she alone fully understood, and twisted it into a ritual of death. How fitting, she must have thought.

"The prosecution is not required to show motive, but we will. We'll also prove that Leah Beaulay was the only person who had the means to murder Max Riley and she certainly had the opportunity. She was the last person alone with Max the day he died. We have witnesses and DNA evidence. On the day of Max's death, Leah again threatened him. Was she giving him one last chance before she carried out her very personal, premeditated plan? That's something you'll have to decide.

"You'll hear from seasoned homicide detectives in the Omaha Police Department. I am so proud of the work this team has done on the case. They have worked night and day conducting over eighty interviews with persons of interest and potential witnesses. They have interviewed anyone and everyone who may have had a motive to kill Max Riley. You'll hear from some of those potential suspects on the witness stand. Max Riley had his enemies. All successful executives do. The defense will try to deflect your attention to those people. But every one of them can account for their whereabouts in the days leading to Max's death. Not one of them had the means or the opportunity to kill Mr. Riley. But Leah Beaulay did. And we're going to prove it to you."

Chapter 72

D avis Bunker stood silently at the defense table for a full two minutes. His head was bowed and his hands were clasped behind him. Was he studying the words on the paper before him? Was he praying? Meditating? Gathering his thoughts? He'd let the jury decide for themselves. He had one final thought before crossing in front of the prosecutors' desk to address the jury: It's show time.

"We human beings are complicated animals. The prosecution has painted my client as an adulteress. And while she regrets that fact, she does not deny it. Leah Beaulay is deeply sorry for her behavior. She has admitted it and is extremely remorseful. We all know people who have had affairs. I wish we didn't, but we do. It's a very complicated flaw in the human condition. But this young woman is not on trial for adultery. She is on trial for a murder she did not commit, could not commit.

"The prosecution has promised to present a picture of an ambitious woman who would do anything to get ahead. But that is simply not Leah Beaulay. She is a wife, a mother, a friend, a Native American who grew up in poverty so extreme, I won't even ask you to imagine it. She was an excellent employee who earned her promotions in spite of, not because of, her affairs.

"A woman scorned as the prosecution would have you believe? Hardly. Max had not ended their affair and had plans to transfer Leah to Denver once he established himself there. But Leah didn't want any part of that. She was ashamed of her behavior and looked forward to forgiveness from God and a chance to start over half way across the country where Max Riley could not control her. She had no motive to kill Max Riley. None.

"As for means, anyone who knew anything about nicotine poisoning could have killed Max. Leah Beaulay, by the way, had never heard of nicotine poisoning. She hasn't taken a science class since high school. She's never seen any of the CSI television shows. She doesn't read mysteries or thrillers. In short, she's not a student of complicated ways to kill. Anyone who had access to cigarettes or cigars technically had the means to commit this murder. You can't rule anyone out when it comes to means.

"Opportunity? Lots of people had the opportunity to poison Max. But not Leah. She can account for her whereabouts from the time her plane landed in Denver, until the time she left to return to her home in Connecticut. We'll show an appalling lack of security measures taken by the Great Western Flight Department. Anyone could have driven up to the airplane and planted the poison concoction. Anyone with a motive. And there was no shortage of people who would be happy to see Max Riley dead. We'll introduce you to some of those people.

"You'll be asked to consider physical evidence from the police crime lab. That evidence will show you how Max died, but it won't shed any light on who concocted the deadly mixture. There is not one shred of physical evidence that ties my client to the murder. Not one. And there's a reason for that. Leah Beaulay did not kill Max Riley."

Chapter 73

L anie Reynolds called Charlie Platt to the stand. Charlie had taken great care to appear professional. He wore a camel jacket and dark brown pants. His loafers were polished to perfection and the diagonal striped tie pulled the look together. But try as he may, Charlie still looked like the old school cop he was. His head appeared to be stuffed into his new white shirt and his blotchy red complexion made him look like a dressed up tomato. He did not look comfortable in this courtroom costume.

"Will you please state and spell your name for the record?" Lanie began.

"Charlie Platt, P-l-a-t-t."

"Detective Platt, will you state your occupation and give us a little history of your employment record?"

"Certainly. I have been a police officer for nearly twenty-one years. I started out in a cruiser and later worked in Robbery and Sex for three years where I was promoted to sergeant. I spent the next two years in the Gang Unit. For the past eleven years, I have been a homicide detective. I have been a lieutenant for five of those years."

"What specific training have you had?"

"I have a degree in criminal justice from the University of Nebraska at Omaha. I have accumulated twelve hours towards a master's degree in crime scene investigation from Nebraska Wesleyan University. I have attended FBI training seminars in Quantico, Virginia. I've completed classes in interrogation techniques and have kept current regarding changes in state and federal laws through seminars given by the Reid Institute."

This educational resume seemed to surprise and impress several of the jurors.

"Lt. Platt, during your eleven years in the Homicide Department, how many cases have you personally led?"

"Thirty three."

"Would it be fair to say that this case is the biggest case you've ever investigated?"

"I look at every case we investigate as the biggest, most important case to date. It certainly is to the victims' families."

"Who was first to arrive at the airplane after Max Riley's body was discovered?"

"The pilot had called 911 and an ambulance was dispatched with two paramedics. About that same time, Police Officer Jake Sullivan arrived with some FBI agent he happened to be working with."

Ruth and Claudia were perhaps the only two in the courtroom who understood that Charlie's offhanded neglect of crediting Nan Levine was an intentional slight. It made them smile.

"Was it Officer Sullivan who notified you?"

"Yes. He made sure nothing was disturbed until I got there."

"Where were the pilots and passengers?"

"The passengers had all left the airport. But both pilots were there."

"What did you do next?"

"I put on a pair of latex gloves and boarded the plane. I looked at the body and observed a small amount of vomit at the corner of the victim's mouth. I took a pencil and poked through the items in the waste receptacle. I smelled the glass containing a greenish liquid and a cigar butt, opened the armrest and looked at its contents. I then called the coroner's office and the crime lab."

"What led you to believe Mr. Riley's death was a homicide?"

"Everything and nothing. I always assume the worse. We had a pretty pristine crime scene at that point and I wanted to preserve it. I didn't want to compromise any possible evidence."

"When was it determined that Max Riley did not die of natural causes?"

"Officially, after the coroner's report and the toxicology results were issued."

"And what did those reports conclude?"

"That Max Riley died of a lethal dose of concentrated nicotine that entered his body through the pores of his skin and through his mouth."

"During your investigation, how many interviews did you conduct?"

"Eighty-three."

"Tell the jury, in a murder investigation, what is an average number of interviews?"

"There is no average number. We take every lead seriously, no matter how insignificant it may seem. In this instance, we had eighty-three leads and we interviewed every one of them."

"Who interviewed the defendant?"

"Myself and homicide detectives Dan King and Jim Smith."

"How many times did you interview Ms. Beaulay?"

"Four times."

"Was it anything she said during those interviews that led to her arrest?"

"Well, she didn't confess. But she admitted she was the last person alone with Riley the day of his death. She revealed means, motive, and opportunity."

Through a hail of objections from the defense table, Charlie read from his interview notes. Leah's eyes never left her perfectly manicured hands folded neatly on the table in front of her.

Chapter 74

Davis Bunker wanted the jury to like him. He needed that. His opening line of questions to Lt. Platt was intended to short circuit any ideas the jury may have that he was beating up on a hard working police officer. His cross-examination would be surprisingly warm and would establish

Davis as somebody who liked to put bad guys away as much as the prosecution did.

"Lt. Platt, how long have we known each other?"

"Maybe fifteen years."

"Tell the jury how we met."

"We worked a few drug cases together when I was working the gang unit and you were an FBI agent."

"Over the past fifteen years, we've attended cookouts together, our wives have met, we've enjoyed some of the same parties, in short, we're friends. Would you agree with that?"

As a rule, Charlie hated all defense attorneys, often referring to them as "paid liars". But it was hard not to like Davis. He had earned his way into the Good Old Boys Club.

Charlie looked down and smiled. "Yes, I guess you could say we're friends."

"We're two old friends with jobs to do. So let's get started."

Davis turned away from Charlie and fixed his gaze on the wall above the jury.

"You testified that when you arrived at the airport, all of the passengers had left the scene. Did that seem odd to you?"

"No."

"They all walked past a dead body, got into their cars, and drove home. Did it occur to any of them that the police might have a few questions?"

"I guess not."

"Why do you think that was?"

"At the time, I think they all assumed Mr. Riley

had died of a heart attack or some such thing."

"So it appeared to people who knew Max Riley well, that no crime had been committed, is that right?"

"At the time, yes."

"So there is a possibility that no crime was committed at all?"

"No there is no possibility of that. The passengers may have thought so, but we now have evidence to the contrary."

"Did you ever consider the possibility that the murderer, if there even was a murderer, was on the plane that day?"

"We interviewed everyone who was on or near the aircraft that day. We considered everyone a suspect until we were satisfied otherwise."

"Including the pilots, how many people were on the plane that day?"

"Twenty-one including Max."

"So, twenty potential suspects. How did they exit the airplane?"

"Only one way to exit. Through the front door."

"And where was Max's body?"

"Sitting in the front seat, directly behind the pilots."

"So you're telling me that twenty potential suspects walked through the crime scene, unattended, before you secured it."

"Yes, I guess I am."

Davis returned to his notes, giving the jury a minute to let that last piece of information sink in.

"You testified that you and your unit interviewed eighty-three people, is that correct?"

"Yes."

"But let's be clear, you weren't looking at all eighty-three as possible suspects, were you?"

"No, we interviewed some of them to gather important information in the case."

"Some of them? Most were not serious suspects, would you agree?"

"That's correct."

"When did you first interview Leah Beaulay. Was it early in your investigation?"

"Yes, she was interviewed in the first days."

"Was she considered a suspect from the very beginning?"

"Yes."

"Was she considered the prime suspect from the very beginning?"

"I don't want to say that. We seriously considered everyone we interviewed. We didn't enter into this investigation with any pre-conceived notions."

"Let me ask that another way. Before you began questioning potential suspects, was there anyone...anyone at all...you suspected more than Leah Beaulay."

"Me, personally? No."

"You testified that you interviewed Ms. Beaulay four times. Before she answered your questions, did you read her Miranda Rights?"

"No, not before she was interviewed. There was no..."

Davis cut him off. "You've answered the question, Lt. Platt. Did you videotape any of your interviews?"

"No."

"Did you audiotape any of your interviews?"

"Yes, some."

"Did you audiotape any of your interviews with my client?"

"No."

"Why did you elect not to tape your interviews with Ms. Beaulay?"

"We're not required to. There were always at least two of us in the room with her. We all took notes and had a secretary sit in to transcribe, much like a court reporter."

"Why not audiotape all your interviews? Wouldn't that have been more accurate."

"Not necessarily. Sometimes words don't match body language and you actually get a false impression of what the suspect is communicating."

The minute the words left his mouth, Charlie regretted them. So did the prosecuting attorneys. They could predict at precisely what point in the trial that piece of testimony was going to come back to bite them.

Lanie Reynolds stood quickly to redirect Charlie.

"You testified that the defendant was not read her Miranda Rights. For the record, I will read the Miranda statement now."

Lanie couldn't believe there was anyone in the room who didn't know and understand the Miranda statement. Most could probably have joined in and recited it with her.

"Lt. Platt, why didn't you read the defendant her rights? You testified that she was a potential suspect early in the investigation."

"Ms. Beaulay was never required to answer our questions. She was never detained against her will. When we asked her to come down to the station, she did so willingly. The Supreme Court says a suspect is to be read his or her Miranda Rights whenever they are asked to do something not of their own free will. We read her rights when we arrested her. That's the law."

Chapter 75

The prosecution called Beth Johns. She took the jury through the physical evidence piece by piece. With each submission of evidence, the case became more alive, not just a two-dimensional newspaper story. With a gloved hand, Gene Knoll carefully displayed the glass that held the deadly drink. Next, he showed the jurors the bottle of Old Spice aftershave that was spiked with the lethal dose of nicotine. Beth explained that the lab results from Atlanta revealed that the nicotine was most likely derived from cigars that had been soaking in a small amount of liquid.

Beth had successfully lifted prints off of both items. The aftershave had a clear print that belonged to Max Riley. The drinking glass had two sets of fingerprints. One set belonged to Max, the other to James Beck.

Knoll introduced the washcloth retrieved from the waste receptacle next to Max's seat. Beth testified that the cloth contained trace amounts of Max's semen and two long hairs belonging to Leah Beaulay.

Finally, Knoll entered into evidence a large photo of Max Riley slumped in his seat and a close-up of the vomit on his lips and chin. The jurors frowned and some squirmed as they viewed the body of the dead man. Beth testified that she had taken the photos and that the vomit was later tested. In it was found nicotine and Absinthe. She then described for the jurors what Absinthe was and how tobacco was leeched from cigars and added to Max's drink. She explained the highly toxic nature of nicotine and how unusual it was to find it in such a high concentration.

Under cross examination, Davis asked Beth if the nicotine poisoning might have been accidental. "That would be pretty far-fetched," Beth answered.

"Why is that?"

"To obtain such a high concentration, a person would have to think ahead. The cigars, and there were probably at least three, would need to be soaked for several days or maybe weeks, to draw out a lethal dose of nicotine."

"So you're saying, someone with access to those cigars had to take considerable care and forethought to concoct the Absinthe/nicotine cocktail.

"That's right."

"Was there any evidence that someone had tried to wipe fingerprints off the glass or after shave?"

"No. The prints we lifted were very clean."

"And the only prints you lifted were from the victim and the pilot, James Beck, is that correct?"

"That's correct."

Chapter 76

Quentin Saunders was called to the stand. His turquoise and white print shirt was tucked neatly into his perfectly pressed khaki trousers. Paired with his white teeth and full dreadlocks, he looked like he had just flown in from Jamaica. It was always a surprise when he spoke with a Midwestern, All-American accent, which is to say no accent at all.

Lanie was drawn to Quentin's sexual energy and deep, melodious voice. When she addressed him, she held her gaze just above his right shoulder. She couldn't allow herself to make eye contact, but the jurors didn't need to see that.

"Please explain for the jurors what your responsibilities are at Great Western Communications."

"My job title is executive assistant. I do whatever I can to help the executives I'm assigned to. The better I do my job, the more productive they are."

"What kinds of tasks did you typically perform for Max Riley?"

"Whatever he needed. I was very familiar with his routine. I usually picked him up from the airport, took him where he needed to go, helped with his luggage."

"Did you wait for him while he was at the office, attending meetings, whatever?"

"Sometimes he would ask me to wait. But if he was going to be gone awhile, as he usually was, I'd run errands for him."

"Were you ever asked to buy alcohol or tobacco products for him?"

"Yes. Sometimes the pilots would have a list of refreshments for the plane. That was the pilots' responsibility, but the head pilot, Mr. Beck, didn't like to do it so I usually did it for him. I know a little shop that sells Cuban cigars. Max often had me pick up a box for him."

"Are you aware that it is illegal to import cigars into the U.S. from Cuba?"

Quentin smiled and laughed in that deep, soft tone that was so uniquely his own. "Well, these were legal. I have an old friend in Denver who is a Cuban refugee. He's been here twenty years and he rolls all the cigars he sells by hand. That's what makes them genuine Cuban cigars."

"Did Mr. Riley ever ask you to purchase Absinthe for him?"

"Yeah, a couple of times. But he didn't like the stuff I bought him. He said it was counterfeit. That the real stuff came from England."

"Have you ever tried Absinthe?"

"Yeah. One day Max poured me a glass while I was loading his bags onto the airplane. There's some weird way you're supposed to make the drink. You pour water or the Absinthe over a spoon with a sugar cube or something. Max seemed to enjoy showing me how to do it."

"How many times did you share an Absinthe cocktail with Mr. Riley?"

"Just once. I practically choked on it. I don't know how anyone can drink that shit. Oops, sorry. It tastes like black licorice mixed with engine fuel. But the boss, I mean Max, loved it. He told me that every time the plane took off, he saluted the end of the day with a few puffs of a good cigar and a glass of Absinthe. Me, I guess I'm more of a Bud Light kind of guy."

"How did Mr. Riley procure the Absinthe from England?"

"He told me a friend of his bought it on the Internet."

"Did he ever say who that friend was?"

"No. But he didn't have to. It was no secret and no big deal. Every couple of months, Leah Beaulay would give me a bottle to deliver to the airplane."

"Was there ever a note attached?"

"Always."

"Did you ever read the note?"

"Never."

"I notice that you refer to the head pilot as 'mister' but you call Max Riley, the president of GWC, by his first name. Why is that?"

"I call people whatever they want to be called. Mr. Beck liked being called 'mister' or 'sir'." No further explanation was required. Quentin's sneer and carefully raised eyebrow told the rest of the story. "Max, on the other hand, insisted that I not call him Mr. Riley. So I called him Max or Boss."

"Did you like Max Riley?"

"Very much. He was a regular guy. He never acted like he was better than anybody. He treated all the employees equally, no matter what their rank."

"Did you consider him a friend?"

"Yes, I did. I've driven lots of big wigs around and I've overheard many conversations, I guess they think I'm deaf. But for all the bad mouthing I've heard, never once have I heard a bad word spoken about Max behind his back. Everybody loved him."

Lanie asked Quentin if he knew Leah Beaulay and would he please point her out to the jury. He did. Leah smiled at Quentin but he did not reciprocate. Lanie asked about Max's last trip to Denver. Quentin spoke warmly about Trish and the Riley children going off on a skiing trip while Max worked. Referring to his daily log, he testified to the detour Max instructed him to make to the company condo. Lanie asked Quentin to speculate on why Max stopped off at the condo. Before Davis had a chance to object, Quentin answered.

"Don't know. Don't care. Didn't ask."

Still referring to his log, Quentin answered a list of questions about the day Max died. He ran through who he drove where and when. He detailed his last conversation with Max. His last orders from The Boss were to pick up Leah Beaulay and bring her to the Gulfstream.

"She had something important to deliver to him. I was told to pull up as close to the airplane's stairs as I could and wait for her. She was in there about ten minutes, I'd guess. As we were driving away, I saw the stairs go up and the door close."

"Do you know what the defendant delivered to Mr. Riley just before take off?"

"Nope. That's not my business. Don't know. Don't care. Didn't ask."

Chapter 77

The prosecution called pilot, Brad Wilson to the stand. Gene Knoll took up the questioning. From previous interviews, Gene was afraid that Brad might volunteer colorful testimony that was unasked for. Gene felt he could rein him in better than Lanie.

"Mr. Wilson, wasn't it one of the pilot's duties to prepare Max Riley's cigar and cocktail for the return trip to Omaha?"

"Yep."

"For the court reporter, I need to ask you to answer the questions with a yes or no, please."

"Oh, sorry. Yes, Max wanted the pilots to take care of the refreshments for the passengers, including his smokes and booze."

"Did you prepare an Absinthe cocktail for Mr. Riley the day he died?"

"Nope...er...No. No, I did not."

"If it was your responsibility, why not?"

"Max Riley had just fired me. He fired Jim Beck, too. I had to fly the plane safely back to Omaha. That's what good pilots do. And I'm a damn good pilot. But I wasn't about to do Max's grocery shopping and bartending after I'd been fired."

"Who terminated your employment."

"Max Riley, himself."

"He told the board of directors he was downsizing the pilot staff and selling some airplanes. Is that why you were laid off?"

"I wasn't laid off. I was fired. Fired. Not downsized or rightsized. Fired. I was fired because Beck and I walked into the company condo and discovered Max and Leah Beaulay doing the big nasty."

"Objection!"

The judge didn't wait to hear Davis' reason for the objection. He advised the jury to disregard Brad's last comment and admonished him. Brad apologized to the judge and quickly rubbed his hand under his nose to hide a smile. He was loving this and so was his audience.

"How were you notified of your termination?"

"When we walked in on Max, he told Beck and me to wait for him in the hallway outside the condominium. We thought we had just landed a big piece of job security. But when Max came out, he was all business. He told us we were being downsized and that we were expected to fly him back to Omaha after the board meeting, as planned. He told us that if we said anything disparaging about Great Western or 'anything we think we might have seen at the condo,' we would have to repay our very generous severance checks."

"Did you pilot the airplane on the return trip to Omaha?"

"Technically, I flew in the co-pilot seat. But yes, I flew."

"In addition to preparing Mr. Riley's cocktail, wasn't it your responsibility to see to it that the refreshments for the passengers were well stocked."

"Yes."

"Did you do that?"

"No, not on my final flight."

"Why not?"

"Why should I? I'd already been fired. We were pilots, not flight attendants. Stocking the plane with drinks and snacks should never have been our responsibility."

"Mr. Wilson, you testified that on that final flight, you did not prepare Mr. Riley's cocktail and cigar. Can you tell the jury who did?"

"No. I only know it wasn't me."

Davis Bunker asked Brad about his work history as a pilot. Brad recounted his time in the Air Force and his four years at GWC.

"At some point you were given the responsibility of developing a security plan for the flight department, is that correct?"

"Yes."

"Who gave you that assignment?"

"John Wellman was very concerned about the lack of security at the company hangar and on the plane so he asked James Beck to study it and develop an action plan. Beck passed the assignment onto me."

"Tell the jury what was in your proposal to Mr. Wellman."

"Well, there were no security procedures in place at all. Anyone could enter the plane when it was unlocked. There was no passenger manifest. Passengers did not have to show identification when boarding. My proposal suggested implementing formal security checks, taping the doors after the pilot locked the plane so he could inspect it before unlocking it to see if the doors had been tampered with, matching passenger security badges against a passenger manifest as they boarded the plane. Those were a few of the key points."

"When you presented the plan to Mr. Wellman, what was his response?"

"I reviewed my work with James Beck and he presented it to Wellman. Beck told me Wellman was impressed with the plan and gave him the go ahead to implement it."

"What parts of your plan were implemented?"

"None of it. It's my understanding that Beck took the credit for my plan and when Wellman pressed him to find out why he hadn't implemented it, he put the blame on me."

"Was the plane locked when it was in the company's hangar in Denver?"

"I locked it when we left the airport for the condominium."

"When was it next unlocked?"

"I believe James Beck unlocked it when he pulled it out on the tarmac in preparation for the return flight to Omaha."

"And what time was that?"

"I'm not sure. I think it was several hours before take off."

"Is the airplane ever left unlocked and unattended?"

"Yes. If the pilot pulls it out and leaves the plane, or even the airport for lunch or something, it is usually left unlocked."

"So anyone could walk onto the plane unnoticed."

"At times, yes."

"You didn't like Max Riley, did you?"

"He had a lot of charm—charisma. But I didn't like him. I thought he was a phony."

"Were you angry at him when he fired you?"

"No. I was surprised. But it didn't take me long to see what a blessing it was. I was more than ready to move on. And two years severance pay is unheard of in pilot circles. Within a week I had a much better job than the one I'd left at GWC."

"With Max dead, you weren't really fired, were you?"

"Riley called the severance orders into HR the day he fired us. I wanted to move on. Beck is still working for GWC, so I guess if I had wanted to stay on, I could have."

"Was James Beck also relieved to be terminated?"

"No. Beck was scared. Before we departed for Omaha, I heard him trying to get Max to reconsider his firing. He swore he'd keep his mouth shut, that he'd even sign legal papers to that effect. But Max told him it was already a done deal."

"How did Beck respond to Max? Was he angry?"

"No. He was a wimp."

Chapter 78

James Beck sat rod straight on the witness stand. His pin-stripped suit and bright white, heavily starched shirt made him look every inch the company man.

James gave a short bio of his piloting experience and history with Great Western. Then Lanie asked him to carefully recount what happened at the condominium.

"Brad Wilson and I had reserved the company condo for the week through the company's internal travel department. When we arrived, Leah Beaulay was in the bedroom and Max Riley was in the shower."

"That must have been uncomfortable for everyone."

"I know it was uncomfortable for me. Leah didn't seem too bothered."

"And Max Riley responded to the situation by firing you and Brad Wilson?"

"Well, I think it was a panicked reflex. I don't think the firing would have stuck. I never thought he really meant it. I think in a few days he would have backed off."

"Explain why Brad Wilson is no longer with GWC

and you are."

"After Max's death, the HR department, through Mr. Wellman's office, I believe, gave us the option of taking Max's severance offer, or staying with Great Western. I chose to stay. Brad decided to leave."

"What time did you arrive at Denver's Centennial Airport on January fifteenth?

"Around noon."

"Was Brad there when you arrived?"

"No. And that concerned me. He should have been there to stock the drinks and refreshments. I telephoned him on his cell phone but he didn't pick up. I quickly realized he had no intention of restocking the food and drinks. Brad was done. I worried he wouldn't even show up for the flight, but he did."

"When you checked the food and drink supply, did you check on the status of the Absinthe?"

"Not at that time. I left the airport to get some appetizers and complete some paperwork. When I returned, Brad was there. I wasn't going to give him the satisfaction of seeing me schlep in the groceries so I left them in the rental car and went in to prepare Max's cigar and Absinthe."

"What time was that?"

"About 4:00 pm."

"And what did you find when you went to prepare the Absinthe?"

"It had already been taken care of."

"And who did you think had 'taken care' of it?"

"Well, it was Brad's responsibility. I was a little surprised. But I assumed he must have decided to step up and act professionally and complete his assigned duties."

"Where were you when Quentin Saunders brought Leah Beaulay to the plane?"

"I was in the pilot's seat."

"Did you speak to her?"

"No. I watched her get on the plane from my window. The door between the pilots and Max Riley was shut. Max had a door installed to separate him from the rest of the passengers. That door was pulled closed as well. Quentin pulled up very close to the steps and Leah came and left without speaking to anyone but Max."

"Do you know why Leah paid a visit to Max before take off?"

"Max told me we needed to hold the plane until Quentin delivered some last minute reports to him."

"Was the defendant the courier of those reports?"

"That was the assumption. She was carrying a folder."

"How long did the defendant stay on-board?"

"Less than ten minutes."

"Did you hear any of their conversation."

"Yes, all of it."

Lanie made every effort to modulate her voice to sound calm and matter-of-fact when she asked the court to enter the tape recording of Leah and Max's conversation into evidence.

Davis quickly and passionately objected. The judge explained to the jury that there had been a pre-trial hearing to determine what evidence would be allowed and disallowed. He explained that Mr. Bunker had requested that the tape be ruled inadmissible. It was perfectly proper for Mr. Bunker to object to its admission here today. But the judge, as expected, overruled Davis and again allowed its admission.

Lanie asked James what the purpose of the tape was. James explained that he listened in on conversations for security purposes. If there was any threat to the passengers or aircraft, the eavesdropping could tip him off and the tapes could provide evidence.

The jury was anxious to hear the tape, but Davis didn't want it to be the last thing the jury heard that day. It was 4:25 pm on the third day of the trial and the press was hungry for some scandalous ink. Davis thought the judge owed him this much. He suggested that this might be a good place to break for the day. The judge understood what Davis was thinking and agreed to call it a day

Chapter 79

DAY FOUR

The courtroom was filled to capacity. The much anticipated audio tape would serve as a powerful witness for the prosecution and plenty of people wanted to hear it. Claudia and Ruth were seated in their usual spot.

"I'll save your seat for you if you want to leave the courtroom when the tape is played. I really don't think you want to remember Max this way— you don't want his final encounter with Leah on your hard drive," Claudia cautioned.

"I've come this far. I think I can take it."

James Beck was recalled to the stand and asked a few questions to help set up the recording. He explained that the humming the jury would hear in the background of the recording was the motor of the cooling system that ran while the plane was on the ground.

Leah sat at the defense table with her hands folded in her lap. As the recording played she kept her head down in a practiced look of shame.

Max: "Unbutton your blouse. Can you feel what's happening under that sweet ass of yours?"

Leah: "I want you in me."

Ruth gripped the edge of her chair with white knuckles. Her eyes bore holes in the back of Leah's head. Claudia rubbed Ruth's hand quickly as if to suggest she might leave. Ruth shook her head 'no'.

Max: "There's no time. Get on your knees and take care of me. You'd better start puffing, too. Your president needs a quick blow job."

Ruth picked up her purse and quietly exited the courtroom. For a full three minutes, the only sound on the recording was the distant hum of the Gulfstream's air conditioning motor. The jurors stared uncomfortably at the tape recorder as Leah continued to focus on her folded hands. The silence felt like listening to live porn with the lights on in a room filled with strangers. Leah's recorded voice finally broke the silence.

Leah: "I remember a time when pleasing me was at least as important to you as pleasing yourself. Now, everything you do is fast—detached. We don't even share a glass of wine or Absinthe anymore. (Pause) Let's finish our conversation about my move."

Max: "I've got a planeload of people waiting to take off. This isn't a good time."

Leah: "Let me get this straight. There's time for me to give you a blow job, but no time to discuss my future. People do desperate things when they're made to feel as powerless as you make me feel. I've about reached my breaking point."

Max: "Please, be patient. It will be months before I can pull the strings I need to get you to Denver. I know you love me enough to wait."

Leah: "You know I love *you* enough? What about you? Do you love me? Before you know it, months will be years. You think you can use me forever, but you're wrong. There's a limit to how long I'll put up with this. After all, I'm not Trish."

Max: "That's right. You're not Trish. She is the mother of my children and has more class in her little finger than you'll ever have. I don't ever want to hear you speak her name again. This conversation is over."

Two minutes and nine seconds of silence on the recording was interrupted by the sound of a knock on a door. A door opens, the jury hears the airplane's steps pull up and lock into place, the airplane door closes, and the engines fire up.

Chapter 80

L anie called Sumner Jackson to the stand. Leah may have been the last person alone with Max, but Sumner was the last person to speak to him. Sumner set the stage for what would be the final scene of Max's life. Max held a crystal tumbler in one hand and a cigar in the other. Sumner explained that smoking was forbidden on company property.

"I thought it was rather disingenuous for him to be openly smoking a cigar but, hey, Max did a lot of things that weren't by the book. He flew by the seat of his pants. He liked his reputation as a maverick but it wouldn't have hurt him to take a lesson from the Denver executives and study things more carefully before acting."

Sumner testified that he had witnessed Leah exiting the plane and getting into the car with Quentin. He testified that Max's mood had seemed upbeat—pretty typical. "He was full of his usual charm and bravado."

John Wellman took the stand. He appeared relaxed and confident in his black suit and red tie. As always, he looked the part of the elder statesman. Lanie questioned him about his relationship with Max.

"I was too old to be his brother and too young to be

a father figure to Max, and that's how it felt—a very close but hard to define friendship between two men."

Lanie asked John to recount the morning he confronted Max about his affair with Leah.

"I was angry and disappointed. My wife and I were, still are, close to Max's wife, Trish, and their children. Max had worked hard to build a good life for them and with them. I couldn't believe he would throw that all away."

"When you explained to Max that Leah would have to be transferred or fired, how did he respond? Was he upset?"

"Not at all. He was ashamed and relieved. He told me that he loved Trish but that Leah had some sort of emotional hold on him he could not break. He actually thanked me for taking this out of his hands. He wanted Leah out of Omaha and out of his life."

Davis Bunker couldn't have asked for a better set-up. Lanie may have thought John's testimony would help establish motive but Davis saw a much more complicated psychological case in the works.

"After Leah moved to Connecticut, how would you characterize the Riley marriage?" Davis asked John.

"I would say it was on the mend. They were often seen out together laughing and holding hands. The entire family seemed happier. Max was much more relaxed."

"Were you aware that Max was still involved with Leah?"

"Not at the time. I only found out after Max's death."

"You characterized your relationship with Max Riley as, 'very close,' yet you didn't know he was still involved in this other relationship. How well did you really know Max Riley?"

"To be accurate, I defined my relationship with Max as a very close but hard to define relationship between two men. We men aren't known to be very good at sharing our emotions with others. I knew Max as well as any man can know another man. Which may be to say that I didn't know him very well at all."

Chapter 81

Lanie called Larry Walton to the stand. She asked a series of questions designed to establish that he had received permission from Max's family and was not breaching the client/therapist expectation of privacy. He detailed how damaging Max's extramarital relationships had been on the Riley family and how dedicated Trish was to repairing their marriage.

"Dr. Walton, do you think Max Riley was honest with you?"

"As far as it went, yes."

"What do you mean, 'as far as it went'?"

"I don't think Max lied to me. I'm a pretty good judge of that. But I do think there was a lot he wasn't telling me—lying by omission."

"How would you characterize his relationship with

Leah Beaulay?"

"Complicated."

"You stated that Trish Riley has given you permission to speak candidly about your sessions with Max. Tell us about his relationship with Leah, how it began, what the progression was, what the status was at the end of his life."

"First, let me say that Trish was everything that Max, or any man, could ask for. She is intelligent, kind, passionate, beautiful, dedicated. There was nothing she could have done to stop Max from self-destructing. Max was having a crisis with his self-image. He felt his masculinity was on the wane. He needed affirmation from women other than Trish that he was still desirable so he embarked on a series of affairs. Each of those affairs was ended when Max decided to end them. Some of those women were hurt and wanted the relationship to continue but Max was very clear from the beginning that he would call the shots and that he would never leave his wife.

"But that all changed when he met Leah. He fell in love with her and was prepared to sacrifice everything for her. Before long, love turned into obsession and eventually addiction. Max was addicted to Leah."

"Did Max eventually end his relationship with Leah?"

"Yes. He was forced to. John Wellman told him it would cost him his job if he didn't end it, so he did. He told me that he was relieved that Wellman did for him what he could not do for himself. He told me that Leah was not going away quietly. She was making demands on him that he had not anticipated. That annoyed him, but he was also flattered. He was working very hard to rebuild his marriage, but Leah was making that difficult."

That was it. No further questions. Davis couldn't believe the defense was making this so easy for him. The prosecution set them up and he knocked them down.

"Did you ever suggest to Max that he might be depressed?" Davis began.

"Yes. I thought he suffered from mild to moderate depression."

"Did Max agree with your assessment?"

"Not at first. I remember him balking at the idea. He told me that he wasn't exactly curled up in the fetal position all day. I explained to him that, in men, the most common sign of depression is walking around being generally pissed off at everybody all day. Max laughed and admitted that sounded like him."

"Did he ever take anti-depressant drugs?"

"Yes, for a time. And Trish was pleased that the medication seemed to even out his moods. He wasn't snapping at her or the kids anymore."

"You said 'for a time.' Did Max stop taking the medication?"

"Yes. He thought it made him tired and diminished his sex drive."

"At the time of his death, was Max taking his medication?"

"No."

"At the time of Max's death, would you say he was depressed?

"No."

"Did Max tell you he was still in communication with Ms. Beaulay?

"No."

"Did he tell you he planned to have her transferred to Denver to resume their relationship?"

"No. He didn't lie to me about that, but he didn't volunteer the information, either."

"If Max told you he ended his relationship with Leah, but hadn't, then he lied to you, isn't that right?"

"I suppose so. Max was an addict. When addicts start using again, they lie."

Chapter 82

Dr. Mary Woods' physical appearance belied her twenty years experience as a forensic psychologist. She looked all of thirty-years-old, but was actually forty-five. Her blonde hair was choppy and short. She wore a hooded cashmere sweater and tweed skirt. Only the reading glasses that hung around her neck on a multi-colored cord hinted at her age.

She was the best in her field. And she was expensive. But Gene Knoll knew it would be worth the price so he hired her before the defense beat him to it. Dr. Woods learned everything she could about Leah Beaulay. She conducted six hours of interviews with her, at a cost to the county of three-hundred and fifty dollars an hour.

Dr. Woods testified that Leah had weathered many hardships in her life and that she had developed a coping mechanism to deal with difficult times: she shut down emotionally. Against Bunker's objections, Lanie was allowed to question Dr. Woods about the time Leah hit and killed a young boy.

"This is a good example of Leah's state of mind. The accident was unavoidable and certainly not her fault. Nevertheless, most of us would feel guilty, grief-stricken, deeply troubled at being a part of an event that ended a life. Leah did not exhibit any of those feelings—not now, not at the time of the accident. Leah does not take responsibility for the pain she causes others. She feels no remorse for hurting the wives of men she has been involved with. She feels no responsibility for the failure of her first marriage. She agreed that her two young children from that marriage would be better served if they lived with her ex-husband in another state. She sees them regularly but not frequently. She tells me they are happy and well-adjusted and that living with their father was a good decision. When she is away from her children, Leah does not long for them."

"She is grateful to have her current husband's support and has promised to be a faithful wife in the future. But she does not feel guilty for the affairs she has had during her marriages."

"What is your diagnosis of the defendant?"

"Leah is a narcissistic sociopath."

"Will you define for the jury what that means?"

"Yes. Leah worked very hard in a very focused way to escape the poverty of her birth. But somewhere, she crossed a line and became so self-focused that only her wants and needs mattered to her. The needs of others mean nothing to her. What separates sociopaths from the rest of society is their inability to feel empathy for others. Leah's lack of empathy for others, even her own children, is what defines her."

Davis knew that the cardinal rule for any criminal attorney is to never ask a witness a question unless you are certain you know what their answer will be. He had some questions he wasn't one-hundred percent certain of but he had to risk it. Dr. Woods had painted a picture of Leah as a cold, calculating, sociopath. He had some serious deconstructing to do.

Davis began by asking Dr. Woods questions about who was paying her fees and how much those fees were. He knew her hourly rate of three hundred and fifty dollars would not score points with the working class jurors. He made it clear that she was working for the prosecution and implied that because they were paying her, she was bound to paint a picture of Leah that served the prosecution's purposes.

"Dr. Woods, you interviewed my client on six different occasions. You testified that she was emotionally 'shut down'. Can you tell us what you mean by that?"

"Yes. Leah doesn't feel sadness, guilt, responsibility, empathy...there are no highs and no lows in her emotions. They are flat."

"If her emotions are flat, does that mean she doesn't feel rage?"

"That's correct."

"Did Leah exhibit hatred toward anyone? Jealousy? Envy? Anger?"

"No. She didn't show any of those emotions."

"Would you characterize Leah as a peaceable person?"

"Yes."

"Did you like Leah Beaulay? Would you say she is a likeable person?"

"Yes, I found her very likeable."

"I have no further questions."

Bunker turned his back on Dr. Woods. He was pleased with his work and could not conceal the smug look on his face.

Unasked, Dr. Woods added, "Most sociopaths are extremely likeable."

Chapter 83

Trish Riley walked quickly to the witness stand. She was wearing a white oxford shirt with button down collar and cuffs. It was tucked neatly into perfectly fitted black gabardine trousers that grazed her black leather Cole Haan loafers at precisely the right point. Despite the simplicity of her outfit, it was obviously expensive. Her only jewelry was her plain gold wedding band and Timex watch with the glow-in-the-dark feature she couldn't live without. Claudia had often remarked that, no matter how they dressed, rich people just looked different from the rest of us. And Trish Riley looked rich.

Trish took the stand and scanned the room for Ruth and Claudia. When she met her mother's eyes a look of comfort washed over her face. The jury turned to try to locate the onlooker who had made the connection. On the stand Trish looked fragile, almost canary-like. Claudia knew the jury would be surprised by her strength.

This would be the prosecution's final—and Lanie hoped—most powerful witness. A series of brief questions and answers established that the Riley's had been college sweethearts and had celebrated their twentieth wedding anniversary shortly before Max's death. Lanie then asked Trish to recount the last day she spent with Max.

"Max was flying to Denver for a board meeting. The children were out of school, and there were some empty seats on the company plane, so we went along. The kids and I left Max in Denver and went skiing. I would characterize it as a very happy family day. Max was in a great mood. We all were. The morning was hectic. Everyone was rushing around. When we got on the plane, Max and I snuggled together and read. Max massaged the back of my neck or held my hand for much of the flight."

"Besides you and Max, what family members flew to Denver with you that day?"

"My mother, Ruth O'Kiefe, came along. She visited

her sister in Denver while we skied. Our daughters Korey and Katy, and our son Tim also were on board."

"Were you or any of your family on the return flight to Omaha?"

"No. We knew all the Gulfstream seats would be spoken for, so we booked commercial flights back to Omaha."

"Where were you when the Gulfstream landed in Omaha?"

"We were at home. Our flight left Denver a day earlier."

"Mrs. Riley, how would you characterize your twenty-year marriage?"

"Like any long marriage, we had our ups and downs. I would go so far as to say that we had many excellent years and a few very difficult ones."

"Do you know the defendant, Leah Beaulay?"

"Yes."

"Will you point her out to the jury?"

Trish turned slightly in her chair and pointed towards Leah. Leah continued scratching with her pencil on the legal pad in front of her. She did not look up. But Trish continued to fix her gaze on Leah as she answered Lanie's questions. This was her opportunity to confront the woman who had so callously betrayed her.

"Tell the jury how you know Leah and what your relationship is with her."

"Leah was an employee at Great Western. I first met her at a company awards dinner We entertained company officers, up and coming employees, and board members in our home from time to time. Leah was frequently our invited guest. Because her position within the company was so much lower than most of those in attendance, I went out of my way to welcome Leah into my home and make her feel comfortable."

"Did you know Leah Beaulay was having an affair with your husband?"

"Not right away. But yes, eventually I confronted Max and he admitted that he was involved with Leah."

"What was the status of the affair on the day you flew to Denver?"

"Max told me it was over. He said that, with the help of John Wellman, he had transferred Leah to Connecticut. I fought hard to save our marriage and once Leah was out of the picture, I knew I had done the right thing. Max was grateful to have his wife and children happy again."

"Do you know how Leah responded when Max ended their affair?"

"No. Max didn't offer any details and I didn't ask. I was just happy to have my husband back. The last month of Max's life may have been his happiest. He told me that getting rid of Leah was a great relief to him and he swore he'd never put us through anything like that again."

"Were you aware that Max drank Absinthe and smoked Cuban cigars?"

"Yes, Leah brought that into his life."

"How did you feel about that?"

"I didn't like it. I found it very demeaning. Max

would smoke a cigar with Absinthe at the end of the day. He enjoyed it alone in his study. When he was done, he'd extinguish the cigar in the Absinthe glass and I'd have to clean it up the next day. I hated it because I knew it was something he shared with Leah, but not me. That may sound strange, but it just really hurt my feelings. He knew how I felt, but I didn't make a big deal out of it. I wanted Max to end his affair with Leah. Period. I wasn't going to ask for anything more."

Davis Bunker could have objected a number of times, but he elected not to. He didn't want to attack or intimidate the grieving widow. Trish had won the sympathy of the jury and Davis didn't want to come off as a bully. If he was going to turn this around, he would have to tread lightly.

As Davis approached Trish, Claudia had to remind herself that she was watching a skilled actor. Davis had hit on Claudia once at a party and she wondered if he even remembered her. He was one of those men you knew you should hate, but couldn't help but like. In that way, he was a lot like Max Riley.

Davis stroked his chin and looked first at the floor and then towards the jury.

As he walked closer to the witness stand, he smiled at Trish in a way that simultaneously communicated warmth and agony.

"Mrs. Riley, first let me extend my sympathies to you and your family. I apologize in advance for any pain my questioning might cause you. Please understand, we are all looking for the same thing, the truth. Did you hire your own private investigator to assist in the investigation of your husband's death?"

"Yes."

"Can you name that person and tell the jury why you decided to hire your own investigator?"

"We hired Claudia Sullivan, a close family friend and former Great Western employee. Claudia resigned from her position as public relations vice president to open her own private investigation agency. We have been friends for many years and know how bright and competent she is. She knows more people at Great Western, and more people in Omaha, then anyone I know. We knew that the resources of the police department were limited. We wanted justice for Max. Hiring Claudia meant every lead could be investigated. She interviewed anyone and everyone even remotely associated with Max. Claudia is incredibly thorough."

"Has Ms. Sullivan reached any conclusions?"

"No. We've given her the go ahead to continue her work."

"So, after months of investigation, Ms. Sullivan has not gathered enough evidence to confidently name a prime suspect?"

"We asked her to research and investigate. We didn't hire her to play an expensive game of Clue."

Davis turned and walked to the defense table. He appeared to review notes on his legal pad in preparation for his next line of questioning. Claudia pretended to stretch so she could get a look at the pad. It was blank. Davis removed his reading glasses and slowly walked back towards Trish.

"Again, I sincerely apologize in advance for what might sound like a terribly insensitive, even cruel line of questioning. You testified that you wanted to find justice for Max, is that correct?"

"Absolutely."

"We talk a lot about means, motive, and opportunity. To your knowledge, who knew how to prepare Max's Absinthe cocktail?"

"In addition to Leah Beaulay, the pilots all knew. I was curious about this secret ritual Leah had introduced Max to, so I looked it up on the Internet. I know how to prepare it, but I never have. I'm sure others know the process, but I couldn't name them."

"Didn't Max know how to prepare his own cocktail?"

"Oh yes, of course."

"Tell the jury, Mrs. Riley, to your knowledge, who knew that Max smoked a cigar with his Absinthe cocktail?"

"The same people. Leah Beaulay, the pilots, me."

"Isn't it possible that on January fifteenth, Max fixed his own cocktail for the flight back to Omaha?"

"Anything's possible. But that doesn't explain who added the liquid nicotine."

"In the year leading up to Max's death, was he ever depressed?"

"He was mildly depressed from time to time. Nothing extreme or unusual."

"Were anti-depressants ever prescribed for him?"

"Yes."

"Was Max taking anti-depressants at the time of his death?"

"No, but he wasn't depressed. In fact, he was extremely happy."

"What qualifies you to make that assessment? Are you a psychiatrist?"

"No. But I knew my husband. I was never in denial about his affairs, his drinking—any of his human failings. Max was not depressed when he died."

"Did Max ever mention suicide?"

"Never. Never."

"And you are relatively certain that if he had thoughts of suicide, you would have known about them?"

"I am absolutely certain."

Davis spread the fingers of both his hands and rubbed his fingertips up and down on his forehead. He took a deep breath, audible to the jury, and resumed questioning.

"Mrs. Riley, you testified that you and your family accompanied Max to Denver on the company jet, is that correct?"

"Yes."

"How old were your children on that day, January fifteenth?"

"Korey was nineteen, Katy was seventeen, and Tim," (the sound of his name caught in her throat and Trish visibly fought back tears.) "Tim was fifteen."

Trish's eyes welled up. She dug her nails into her thighs and took two deep breaths.

"I am so sorry," Davis said. "Would you like to take a break?"

"No."

"How old are your children today?"

"Korey is still nineteen, Katy is eighteen, and Tim has passed away."

There was movement in the jury box. Tim's death came as news to many of the jurors. Claudia leaned forward in her chair. She wasn't quite sure where this was going.

If Davis wanted to win the jurors' hearts, bringing Trish to tears over the death of her son surely wasn't going to get the job done.

"Again, forgive me. I appreciate how difficult this is for you. Please tell the jury how Tim died?"

"He took his own life."

"In hindsight, were there any warning signs?"

"None."

"Losing his dad must have been difficult for him. Do you think Max's death may have led to Tim's depression?"

"Tim wasn't depressed. He was very protective of me and he was very angry about Max's involvement with Leah. Max's death was almost a relief to Tim."

"Do you have any idea what led Tim to take his own life? Did he leave a note?"

"No. There was no note. I've gone over this in my mind a thousand times. I have no idea why it happened. Sometimes, absent a note, I wonder if Tim's death was accidental. I'm struggling to accept what I will never understand."

"Is it possible that Max took his own life?"

"No. That's ridiculous."

"The day before Tim's death, if I had asked you if he was suicidal, how would you have answered the question?"

"I would have told you that you were nuts."

"Again, is it possible that Max killed himself?"

"I suppose anything's possible."

"Please answer yes or no. Do you think it is possible that Max took his own life?"

"Yes. It's possible."

The prosecution huddled together at their table. Lanie wanted to redirect the witness but Gene Knoll wanted her dismissed. He felt this suggestion of suicide was better left until closing arguments. Trish looked at Ruth and Claudia as she left the courtroom. She smiled and shrugged. Ruth returned the gesture. The prosecution rested its case.

The judge adjourned for the day, admonishing the jury not to discuss the case or read any newspapers or watch coverage on television. The jury filed out and the spectators left quickly. Ruth and Claudia were the last to stand. As Davis and his team walked out, eager to meet the press, he abruptly turned to Claudia.

"What did you think of that?" Davis beamed.

"What do you mean?"

"What just happened in my cross-examination of Trish Riley?"

Claudia glared at him. Speechless. She didn't know where he was going with this but his gloating demeanor showed an appalling lack of respect for Ruth.

Davis beamed. "I'll tell you what just happened

here. Reasonable doubt just happened. Not only is there doubt that my client committed a crime, there's reasonable doubt that a crime was committed at all."

Claudia stood in disbelief. Davis couldn't possibly know who he was addressing.

"Davis, have you met my dear friend, Ruth O'Kiefe?" He extended his hand to Ruth. "Mrs. O'Kiefe is Trish Riley's mother."

Chapter 84

The media loved Davis, and Davis loved the media. Despite the judge's admonition, he knew at least some of the jurors might see him on television and the confidence he showed in his client could have an impact.

After answering reporters' questions, Davis and his team convened with Peter and Leah to talk strategy. Davis was rightfully proud of today's developments. He suggested that when the prosecution rested their case, the defense might be wise to do the same. He acknowledged it could be risky, but he felt it was a bold move worth taking. What could be more powerful than Max's widow suggesting that he may not have been murdered at all?

Peter and Leah were not comfortable with that approach. Potential character witnesses were waiting in the wings, eager to tell the jury what a wonderful person Leah was. Leah needed the jury to hear—no *she* needed to hear—that there was more to her than the callous adulterer the prosecution had painted. The only person in the room who needed to hear that more than Leah was Peter. He wanted the world to know what he knew, that Leah's beauty was far deeper than the eye could measure. Davis relented. All he could do was give his best advice. He couldn't force his client to take it.

"Okay. Let's all get a good night's sleep and we'll meet back in this room at 8:00 am," Davis concluded. He quickly packed up his briefcase hoping to make a break for the door before Leah raised the issue she had raised five times since the trial began. Davis was quick, but he wasn't quick enough.

"I want to take the stand," Leah said firmly. Davis shook his head in the negative and continued to shake it as Leah made her case. "I am innocent. I'm nothing like the person the prosecution claims I am. You know if I don't tell my story, the jury will think I have something to hide. I know they'll believe me. It's my decision. I want to testify."

Peter agreed with his wife. He had watched enough Court TV to know that despite a judge's explanation to a jury that it is a defendant's right not to testify, it is human nature to want to hear from the star of the show. Juries often conclude that if the defendant has nothing to hide, he or she would take the stand.

Davis tossed up one good legal argument after another to try to dissuade Leah from testifying. As fast as he lobbed them, Leah and Peter batted them down. As always, this trial was about much more than

Leah's guilt or innocence. It was a competition, a high stakes game that Davis didn't intend to lose. He had always treated Leah firmly, but with respect and genteel manners. But today, that wasn't cutting it.

"If you take the stand, you will go to jail for the rest of your life. I promise it. I have to shoot straight with you, Leah. Please listen to what I'm saying. That's what you're paying me for. Dr. Woods' assessment of you wasn't far off the mark. You have no concept of how others see you. Those who know you well, love you. But those who do not know you well, do not like you. If you get on the stand, you will not be able to charm your way into the jurors' hearts. They already think of you as a liar and a slut. They have been told that you are full of yourself and don't care about anyone else.

"Whatever you say on the stand, they will not want to believe you. I can try to chip away at the prosecution's portrayal of you in my closing argument, but if you take the stand, the jury won't change their opinion of you based on my words. If you take the stand, there is nothing the prosecution can't and won't ask you. So far, they've actually gone pretty easy on your past affairs. But if you take the stand, they'll eat you alive and there's not a damn thing I'll be able to do to stop them. You'll end up providing details of your extramarital affairs that will make you look worse than you already do. The prosecution will pull those words right out of *your* mouth. And that's what the jury will remember. It's up to you."

Leah Beaulay would not be taking the stand in her own defense.

Chapter 85

Day 5 - 8:30am

Claudia stood inside the courthouse lobby waiting for Ruth.

The thunder and lightning was impressive. Claudia had lived in the Midwest all her life but was still awestruck when a powerful storm blew through. The sky was darker than grey. It was almost black. The rain came down the enormous plate glass windows in sheets. Claudia wondered if Ruth might already be in the courtroom. In all their years of friendship, Ruth had never kept Claudia waiting. Should she be worried? Claudia turned to ask the security guard if he had seen an attractive, older woman come through security. He had not. When she turned back to the window, she saw Ruth under her bright red hooded rain slicker running across the slippery plaza.

Once inside, Ruth threw back her hood and shook her body like a waterlogged Spaniel. She raked her fingers through her short grey hair, fluffing it at the roots. She smiled broadly and laughed a deep, throaty laugh. Claudia smiled back at her. It had been months since she'd heard the sound of Ruth's robust laugh.

"Nothing makes me feel more alive than a good, ground-shaking thunderstorm!" Ruth laughed.

When they arrived at the fourth floor courtroom, they were intersected by Davis Bunker and Leah as they walked into a conference room. Leah looked at— through—Ruth before shooting a long hateful glare at Claudia. In response, Claudia smiled and shook her head as if to say, "You're pathetic."

Lanie explained to the judge that the State was ready to rest its case. Davis could now attempt to salvage the reputation of his client. A parade of character witnesses took the stand. Davis ran each of them through a similar list of questions. There was Lynn (Leah's best friend at Great Western), Leah's minister, former supervisors and co-workers. All swore that Leah was kind, caring, honest. At the end of each line of questioning, Davis asked the witnesses, "Would you characterize Leah Beaulay as a peaceable person?" Each answered that she was.

Claudia was struck by what an odd word choice 'peaceable' was. You could take the girl off the editing desk, but you couldn't take the editor out of the girl. Claudia felt doomed to a life of mentally editing every spoken word.

The prosecution declined the opportunity to cross examine Davis' witnesses. This was a murder trial, not a popularity contest.

Davis called Rick Johansson to the stand. Claudia sat up straight and strained to see Rick walk to the front of the courtroom. She understood that ninety-five percent of all communication was non-verbal and she wanted to catch any unspoken emotions. Rick sat down and adjusted the microphone. He looked over at Leah with an unmistakable look of affection. She did not look up.

"Please state your name and your relationship to the defendant," Davis began.

"My name is Richard Johansson. Leah Beaulay was my first wife."

"Did that marriage result in any children?"

"Yes, we have two children, a girl and a boy."

"What would you say was the cause of the break-up of your marriage?"

"I was having an 'early mid-life' crisis. I was in medical school at the time and decided to quit and pursue a career selling vacuum cleaners at Sears. This was not the life I had promised Leah. She referred to it as a classic bait and switch and she was correct."

"As your marriage was unraveling, did the arguments escalate?"

"No. We rarely argued."

"When you did argue, did Leah threaten you?"

"No. Never."

"Did she ever show any signs of rage?"

"None."

"What kind of mother is Leah?"

"She is very patient, loving."

"Did she spank the children?"

"She never spanked them. I have never heard her raise her voice to them, or to anyone, for that matter."

"Would you characterize Leah Beaulay as a peaceable person?"

"Yes."

Gene Knoll had a few questions for Rick—*mano y mano.*

"Rick, what is your current occupation?"

"I'm a physician."

"How long after your divorce from the defendant did you return to medical school?"

"About a year."

"Did that make Leah angry?"

"No, I don't think so."

"Did she show a renewed interest in you?"

"Yes, she did. But I knew her interest in me was only because of my future potential earning power. Besides, I had begun dating my current wife, Ruby."

"During your marriage to Leah, did she have any extra-marital affairs that you know of?"

"Yes."

"How many?"

"Three that I know of."

"Who has custody of your children?"

"I do."

"Is Leah a good, loving mother?"

"She tries. The children adore her and they get along well with Leah and Peter when they visit. Leah wasn't born with that maternal instinct—whatever that is. Nurturing doesn't come naturally to her."

"How contentious was your divorce?"

"Not contentious at all. Leah wanted a divorce and I agreed. We both thought the children would be better off with me."

The defense called Ruby Littlefoot Johansson to the stand. Claudia caught Ruby's eye as she walked to the front of the courtroom. Ruby smiled and waved. Her hair was wet from the rain and she was wearing just a trace of peach colored lipstick. Her hands were shaking and her olive skin was flush with nerves. Ruby gave her name and spelled it as she looked at Leah. Their eyes spoke to each other with sisterly love and devotion.

"Please tell the jury how it is you came to know Ms. Beaulay," Davis began.

"We met when we were freshmen at Haskell College in Lawrence, Kansas. We were roommates."

"That can be a tough relationship. How did the two of you get along?"

"Beautifully. We have never had an argument. We are best friends."

"Would you characterize Leah as a peaceable person?"

"Yes. She's nice to everyone. Everyone at Haskell loved her."

Lanie approached the witness. "Mrs. Johansson, what is your relationship to Rick Johansson?"

"I am his wife," Ruby beamed.

"Did you know your husband when he was married to Ms. Beaulay?"

"Yes. I was with Leah the day they met. We were new to Lawrence, Kansas, and stopped for lunch in a restaurant where Rick worked. I think it was love at first sight for Rick."

"Did you remain close to Leah while she was married to your husband?"

"Yes. I was friends with both of them."

"Did Leah ever tell you why the marriage deteriorated?"

"Yes. Leah wanted to be married to a doctor and when Rick, temporarily as it turned out, decided to quit medical school, Leah thought she'd been tricked and wanted out of the marriage. Her pregnancies came as a big surprise to her, and she said the kids made her nervous. I know that must sound terrible to you, but if you had any idea how poor she was growing up on an Indian Reservation, you'd understand."

"Did you grow up on an Indian Reservation?"

"Yes, I was very poor, too."

"But you didn't marry for money or leave your children in someone else's care for a more comfortable life, did you?"

"No. But I can understand why people do."

"Who are Ned and Lindsay Johansson?"

"They are my children."

"You gave birth to them?"

"No. Leah gave birth to them, I guess I should say I am their stepmother."

"What do they call Leah?"

Ruby paused. "You know, I guess I've never heard them call her anything."

"What do they call you?"

Ruby looked down so Leah would not be hurt by

her smile. "Mom. The children call me mom."

Davis leaned over to Leah and whispered in her ear, "This is exactly why I wanted to rest our case without putting on character witnesses."

Leah still couldn't understand what Davis meant. She was pleased with the glowing things Ruby and the others said about her. She heard herself described as kind, peaceable, rising above poverty, patient. She was oblivious to any suggestion that the jury may have heard other, unspoken words: adulterer, self-centered, gold digger, and worst of all, unfit mother.

Davis called his final witness. A short, round woman entered the courtroom and made her way to the stand. Her shiny black hair did not show even a trace of grey. As she took the stand, she looked at Leah and smiled warmly. For the first time since the trial began, Leah Beaulay showed emotion. She cried.

"Please state and spell your name."

Without taking her eyes off of Leah, the small woman with knitted brow and a soft, halting voice said, "My name is Fawn Beaulay, B-e-a-u-l-a-y."

"Please tell the jury how long you have known the defendant and what your relationship is to her."

"I have known Leah since before she was born. I am her mother."

"Tell us a little about the type of child Leah was."

"She was a very happy little girl. She was never fussy. She took good care of her little brothers and sister. We used to call her Little Mommy."

"How about her teenage years? No teenager is

perfect. What kind of trouble did she get into?"

"No trouble at all. And I'm not just saying that because I'm her mother. If you asked me that question about my other children, I would have a very different answer. Leah obeyed our rules, came home on time, did not drink or smoke—she was a good girl. I don't remember ever having a cross word with her."

"Well, she must have fought with her brothers and sisters."

"Never. I know that's hard to believe, but it's true."

"Would you characterize Leah as a peaceable person?"

"Oh my, yes."

Lanie declined the opportunity to cross examine Fawn Beaulay. Anything she asked this heartbroken mother would sound like badgering. Even Ruth O'Kiefe was visibly moved. The pain of a mother's love is a universal emotion. If it's true that a mother is only as happy as her unhappiest child, then Fawn Beaulay was very unhappy today.

The defense rested. Closing arguments would have to wait until tomorrow.

Chapter 86

Day 6

Ruth and Claudia arrived at the courthouse at 8:00 am, a full hour before closing arguments were scheduled to begin. Claudia knew the courtroom would be packed for the closing fireworks. One of the points of law she could not grasp was the fact that attorneys had the right to say pretty much anything they wanted in their opening and closing statements. This point, coupled with the potentially superior presentation skills of one lawyer over another, often meant that theatrics could overshadow the facts, especially in a case laden with scientific details.

Gene Knoll was unaware of the chairs filling up behind him. He obsessively checked and rechecked the slide projector, life-sized crime scene photographs, and bagged physical evidence for what would be the most important closing argument of his career. By 8:30, the courtroom was packed. The room felt close with the smell of over-fragranced shampoos and the smoke-stained clothing of the press section. Claudia breathed a sigh of relief when Gene cracked open two large windows. As Gene passed the defense table Davis Bunker smiled and joked, "Good idea. Get a little fresh air in here so you don't put the jury to sleep." Gene gave a good natured nod to his nemesis, but it bothered him. He recognized that form over substance was responsible for many an undeserved "not guilty" verdict.

Gene picked up his retractable silver pointer and walked over to the jury.

"Good morning," he said somberly. Everything in Gene Knoll's voice, face, and aura communicated one thing: sincerity. "The prosecution has asked you to listen carefully and consider the facts of this case. In our attempt to be thorough, we sometimes become tedious. We have facts and truth on our side. Don't be fooled by the razzmatazz of the defense. Just consider the facts.

"I'd like to briefly review some of those facts, if you'll allow me. I will walk you through the facts of what led up to the day of Max Riley's death. As you consider these facts, keep in mind three things: means, motive, opportunity. Detective Platt and his team interviewed eighty-three people who may have had a motive to kill Mr. Riley. My staff interviewed dozens more. Despite Leah Beaulay's adulterous affair with Max Riley, Trish Riley, Max Riley's wife did not want anyone to be wrongly accused of his murder, so she hired her own private investigator who has logged hundreds of hours working this case. Above all, Trish Riley wants justice. Every lead—no matter how small—was investigated. I've been Douglas County Attorney for twenty years, and I have never worked on a case that was so thoroughly investigated. But all roads kept leading to the same place. They led to Max Riley's jilted, adulterous lover, Leah Beaulay." Gene turned and pointed at Leah. She did not flinch.

He walked to the photo board leaning against the

witness stand. He picked it up and took a full 180-degree turn so the spectators could see it before placing it in front of the jury. It was a life-sized photo of Max Riley slumped dead in his airplane seat. The greenish brown vomit at the corner of his mouth and on his chin showed up well against the grayish white skin of a man dead several hours.

"You've seen a smaller version of this photograph. It is Max Riley as he was found shortly after his last encounter with Leah Beaulay. No one saw what happened during their final minutes alone. But they heard it—you heard it. You heard Leah Beaulay tell Max Riley that she had reached her breaking point with him."

Gene turned to the cardboard box on the table behind him and removed a bagged drinking glass and the bagged bottle of Old Spice aftershave.

"Absinthe is not a common drink. Until this trial, most of us were unfamiliar with the proper preparation of the drink using a sugar cube and teaspoon. But Leah Beaulay knew how to prepare an Absinthe cocktail. She introduced Max to the forbidden liquor and prepared it for him many times. Few people knew of the end-of-day ritual Max had of smoking a cigar and extinguishing it in the last of his Absinthe cocktail. But the defendant knew. If few knew about the Absinthe, fewer still knew that when Max Riley had a sexual encounter with someone other than his wife, it was his habit to wipe his genitals with a washcloth and lemon water and then pat his skin with a generous splash of Old Spice aftershave lotion.

You heard testimony to that effect from one of Max's former lovers.

"The motive for this murder is as old as time—a love affair gone wrong. Max Riley dumped Leah Beaulay, ending her dreams of marrying him and attaining wealth and respect in the world of big business. The means, as the forensic scientists demonstrated, was nicotine poisoning ingested by Max through his Absinthe cocktail and absorbed through the pores of his hands and genitals when he applied the nicotine laced aftershave.

"This took planning and forethought. You heard testimony that to leach the nicotine from the cigars, the killer had to soak them over a period of days. Leah Beaulay had time to soak the cigars and she also had time to reconsider her plan. An overdose of a narcotic or a traditional poison would have been much easier for most killers to administer. But not for Leah Beaulay. Absinthe, cigar tobacco, and aftershave were the tools of her trade. And doesn't that send a very personal message to the man who used her up and discarded her? The one man she could not control but who controlled her? Yes, Leah Beaulay had motive, and she certainly had the means to commit this murder.

"Opportunity. You heard testimony about the whirlwind that was the last week of Max Riley's life. Group dinners, lunches, board meetings-—he was rarely alone. Only one person spent time alone with Max Riley in Denver—Leah Beaulay. She was alone with Max at the company condominium, and she was alone with him on the company jet. In fact, Leah Beaulay was the last person alone with Max Riley prior to his death. Opportunity? Leah Beaulay had opportunity that no one else had.

"The defense introduced you to a few people who had motive. We interviewed those people, too. But those people lacked the means or the opportunity to murder Max. Every one of them had an alibi. They could all account for their whereabouts while in Denver. Only one person possessed the means, the motive, and the opportunity to murder Max Riley." Gene Knoll turned and looked at the defense table. Leah Beaulay continued to study her folded hands.

"And that person is Leah Beaulay."

Chapter 87

The judge suggested that they take their mid-morning break. Davis asked that the visuals used by the prosecution be removed entirely from the courtroom. He wanted the room empty of anything that might be mistaken as evidence against his client. He wanted the space cleared of everything, especially the photo of Max's lifeless body. Even with it turned against the wall, the energy of what was on the other side could impact the jury.

For the first time since testifying, Trish Riley entered the courtroom. She chose not to be present during the prosecution's closing statement. She had no desire to, again, hear the lurid details of Max's affair. But she was determined to hold her head high in the presence of Leah and the jury. Seeing Max's killer brought to justice was the final act of devotion from a loving and faithful wife.

Gene Knoll looked relaxed as he reentered the room. He walked over to Davis and smiled. "Would you like me to close the windows?" Davis did not return the smile or acknowledge the question.

Leah Beaulay was dressed in an outfit borrowed from and selected by Davis Bunker's legal assistant, Mary Nathan. The boxy white turtleneck sweater and pleated grey flannel trousers could not disguise Leah's trim, shapely figure. But the cut of the clothing, coupled with the flat ballet slipper style shoes, did give Leah the appearance of being even smaller than she was. It was an attempt to make her look harmless, vulnerable, and hopefully innocent.

Davis and Mary had coached Leah well and she had proven to be a good student. As directed, she never gave in to her urge to look Gene Knoll in the eye when he addressed her. During Davis' closing arguments she would make eye contact with him and the jury as rehearsed. Davis spoke slowly and deliberately.

"Max Riley is dead. We do not dispute that. He died as a result of nicotine poisoning. We do not dispute that." Davis stroked his chin and sighed. He looked at the three prosecuting attorneys and shook his head.

"But those are the only facts that are not in

dispute. You have listened to six days of testimony but none of it ties Leah Beaulay to the death of Max Riley. The prosecution made much of Ms. Beaulay's relationship with Max. We all do things in life we are not proud of. Leah Beaulay was engaged in an extramarital affair with Mr. Riley. Of that she is guilty. But she's not on trial for adultery. She's on trial for a murder that she did not commit. In fact, there is reasonable doubt that Max Riley was murdered at all. What evidence do we have that Max did not end his own life? The answer is we have no evidence at all.

"Detective Platt admitted to you that Leah Beaulay was a suspect from the very start of his investigation. He may have interviewed eighty-three 'persons of interest', but his mind was made up from the beginning.

"Much has been made of the audio recording of Leah and Max on the airplane. As the judge explained, I unsuccessfully fought to have that recording suppressed. An audio recording without the accompanying video, is worse than meaningless, it's deceptive. And you know who agrees with that? Homicide Detective Charlie Platt. He said so himself on this very stand. Do you recall what his testimony was when I asked him why he didn't audiotape all his interviews with my client? He responded that only five-percent of communication is verbal and that ninety-five percent of all communication is non-verbal—body language, touch, smell. Charlie Platt thought any audiotape of his conversations with my client would be meaningless. And he is correct. But that also renders the airplane audiotape—an unauthorized, secret, and illegal audiotape by the way, meaningless. We couldn't see the expressions on Max and Leah's faces as they spoke. We don't know if they were being playful or sarcastic. Without being present at the time of the conversation, we don't really know what we heard.

"One minute the prosecution would have you believe that Leah Beaulay plotted and devised a complicated plan to murder a man she loved. The next minute, they portray her as a simple woman of limited intellect. Well, which is it? If Max was murdered—and that's still a big if—by extracting nicotine and spiking his cocktail and aftershave, it would have required a very intelligent, complex mind. That does not describe Leah Beaulay. The prosecution accused my client of getting ahead by using her good looks and feminine wiles alone. If Max was murdered, he was murdered by someone who was highly intelligent. Did the prosecution ever demonstrate that Leah is highly intelligent or a complex thinker? Quite the opposite.

"Leah Beaulay had no reason to want Max Riley dead. He had not ended their affair. He was making plans to move the company to Denver and relocate Leah to Denver, as well. She had everything to gain by Max's continued success. She had everything to lose by his death.

"Leah Beaulay did not have the means to kill Max Riley. You heard the head pilot, James Beck, testify that he checked and found the Absinthe cocktail prepared and in place *before* Leah Beaulay delivered the package to the plane. Leah didn't rent a car while she was in Denver. There is no record of her taking a cab to the airport. But you know who did have opportunity? Shall I tell you who could have slipped into the company hangar and onto the plane when it was unattended? Anyone and everyone! There was no security. Zero. James Beck pulled out the airplane, unlocked it, and left it unattended while he went to purchase refreshments for the return flight to Omaha.

"The prosecution has asked you to focus on means, motive, and opportunity. I ask that you do the same. Leah Beaulay did not have the means, she had absolutely no motive, and she had no opportunity to commit murder.

"Finally, I ask you to consider the testimony of people who have known Leah Beaulay for most of her life. One might expect her ex-husband to attack Leah's character, but he didn't. He testified that he has never heard her raise her voice or seen her do anything physical when angry. He characterized her as peaceable.

"Ruby Johansson has known Leah since they were freshmen at Haskell Indian College. She is married to Leah's ex-husband. You'd think she'd have lots of reasons to dislike my client, but she doesn't. She considers Leah her best friend. She has never seen Leah angry. Never. She testified that she has always known Leah to be a peaceable person.

"Trish Riley, the dead man's wife, conceded that it

was possible that Max committed suicide. Ladies and gentlemen of the jury, there is reasonable doubt that a murder was committed at all. Leah Beaulay is guilty of being a lousy wife. She is guilty of trying to battle her way out of poverty by tying her dreams to powerful men. That was stupid. That was wrong. But if every person who has ever had an affair was thrown into prison, the jails would be full and neighborhoods would be empty. The prosecution wants you to convict my client for murder because she had an affair. Don't fall for that."

Davis walked to the defense table and stood behind Leah. He put his hands on her shoulders as she looked doe-eyed at the jury. "Leah Beaulay has never physically hurt another human being. She did not kill Max Riley. Leah Beaulay is innocent and you must find her not guilty of the charges."

The judge turned to Gene Knoll and asked if he wanted to re-address the jury. *"Oh, yes. Oh my, yes."*

Chapter 88

S moke and mirrors," Gene said to the jury. "Smoke and mirrors. I warned you to watch out for that kind of trickery. Max Riley plotted and chose a painful means to kill himself at the peak of his career? Please. That is an outrageous, irresponsible claim.

"What did the defense's case consist of? A few character witnesses testifying that the defendant is a 'peaceable' person. I'm not even sure what that means and none of the witnesses were asked to elaborate. But I'll tell you something. I was impressed by every one of those character witnesses. I would suggest that their testimony told us a lot more about their character than it did Leah Beaulay's.

"She was unfaithful to her first husband, elected not to seek custody of her children, left them to their father and her childhood friend, Ruby, to raise and yet they testified that she is a patient woman who doesn't raise her voice or strike her children. I admire their ability to forgive and not lose sight of the fact that she is the mother of two innocent children. Good for them. But their testimony was irrelevant. Prisons are filled with mothers who claim to love their children, yet they kill them. There are women there who have never raised a hand to anyone, until the day they commit murder. We are all capable of committing heinous acts. Defining someone as 'peaceable' is meaningless. It's opinion, not fact.

"The judge is going to ask you to consider the facts of this case. And the facts are that Leah Beaulay was sleeping her way up the corporate ladder when she landed the big prize—Max Riley. He had more money, more power, more social standing then she could ever have dreamed of.

"Max asked her to be patient and he would leave his wife and children and marry her. But John

Wellman stepped in to save Max from himself. Leah was given a choice, move to Connecticut or be fired. So Leah took the transfer. But she was fed up with Max and his unfulfilled promises. She warned him. And then she killed him.

"The way Leah murdered Max was very telling. She took the very vices she introduced him to and turned them against him. It took thought. It took planning. She had plenty of time to change her mind but she chose not to.

"Leah Beaulay has established a pattern of putting herself first at the expense of wives and children. When it became clear to her that Max Riley wasn't going to keep his word, she told him he couldn't get away with that. She threatened him. You heard her threaten him. Unfortunately, Max didn't take her threats seriously. Sometimes when people feel powerless, they push back. Leah Beaulay committed the ultimate act of pushing back. With great thought and careful planning, Leah Beaulay murdered Max Riley. Don't let her get away with it."

Claudia, Ruth, and Trish all leaned forward in perfect symmetry. They strained to hear the judge's instructions to the jury. His rapid monotone reminded them of a priest leading his parishioners in recitation of the rosary. This was required verbiage the judge had rattled off hundreds of times. Trish was particularly bothered by the delivery. It felt to her like the judge was on auto pilot and not taking his responsibility seriously. At the end of his monologue, he said something that made the three women stare at each other in disbelief: "If you cannot agree on a verdict of murder in the first degree, you may consider the lesser charge of murder in the second degree."

The jury filed out of the courtroom followed by the spectators. Claudia, Trish, and Ruth stayed behind to thank Lanie and Gene for their hard work. Lanie explained to them that the judge's style of instructing the jury was pretty standard. Offering the option to find a defendant guilty of second degree murder is part of the uniform instructions the judge is required to read verbatim.

"So much work went into establishing the premeditated nature of this crime, how can second degree even be an option?" Claudia asked.

"Sometimes, a jury knows a defendant is guilty of first degree murder but for other reasons doesn't want to send them to prison for life. The second degree option can mean the difference between a guilty verdict and a hung jury," Lanie explained.

Trish hugged Gene Knoll and thanked him for his dedication. "What's your best guess, Gene? If you were a gambling man, where would you put your money? What's the verdict going to be?"

"If I was a gambling man, I'd leave this bet alone. You can never second guess what a jury will do. I firmly believe Leah Beaulay is guilty or I wouldn't have filed charges against her. But you never know what a jury will do."

Chapter 89

Claudia stopped by the grocery store and picked up a bottle of Penfold's Rawson's Retreat and a block of horseradish cheese. Korey and Katy were sitting at the kitchen table with their mother and grandmother when Claudia arrived at the Riley home. Katy jumped up and gave Claudia a long bear hug. Despite all that had happened to Trish Riley, Claudia envied her for the loving family she had built.

Katy took the grocery sack and released Claudia. "Korey, get over here and give your old friend some sugar," Claudia demanded.

Korey was the antithesis of Katy. As soft and physically affectionate as Katy was, Korey was bones and muscle and always felt cold to Claudia's touch. Hugging Katy felt like hugging Max. Korey took after her Grandma Ruth.

After the girls left the kitchen, Ruth poured Claudia a glass of wine and said, "Well?"

"Well what?"

"Well what is the verdict going to be? As always, I trust you'll be honest with me."

"Gene Knoll is right. Juries do goofy things. I don't want to predict what they'll do. But I'll tell you this, both sides did a heck of a job of lawyering. I know way too much about the case, but if I forget all I know and consider only what the jury heard, I'd have to say that Davis Bunker did a good job of establishing reasonable doubt. He was right when he told the jury that it was never proven that Leah administered the poison. This is still a whodunit."

"So you think Leah's going to get off?"

"No. I didn't say that. If I was on the jury, I'd vote not guilty. But I think Leah will be found guilty not so much for murder but for being a self-centered adulterer who abandoned her children. I think the jury will want her to pay for that behavior. Every time Davis reminded the jury that Leah was not on trial for adultery I wanted to scream, 'wanna bet?'"

Chapter 90

It took the jurors three days to reach a verdict. The judge cautioned everyone in the courtroom to hold their emotions in check. Everyone complied. The foreman read, "We the jury, find the defendant, Leah Beaulay, guilty of murder in the second degree." Leah was handcuffed on the spot and taken to jail. Sentencing was scheduled to take place in four weeks.

Leah was in a state of shock. For the first time in her adult life, she would have to pay the price for her behavior. There was no way out. Nothing, not her good looks, sex appeal, hard work, conniving...nothing was going to return her to the life of privilege she had worked herself into. She felt numb and hopeless.

Peter Anderson sat two rows in front of Claudia, as he had every day of his wife's trial. His feet were planted in a wide stance, his elbows were on his thighs and the fingertips of both hands pressed into his forehead. He did not raise his head until Leah had been escorted out of the room.

Claudia touched him on the back. "I'm so sorry for all the pain you've been through. You're a good man..." Claudia was suddenly at a loss for words. "I'm sorry," she repeated. "I'll keep you in my thoughts."

Ruth and Claudia stayed out of the camera lights that flooded the hallway outside the courtroom. Davis Bunker was finishing his comments to the press, "My client has always maintained her innocence. She feels terrible for the Riley family, but she can't apologize for something she did not do. We will appeal. Of course. Right now I'm still reeling from the verdict. There was no evidence that tied Ms. Beaulay to the poisoning of Max Riley because she simply did not do it."

The cameras turned to Gene Knoll and Trish Riley. Gene thanked the jury for their hard work and explained that what had transpired in the last months should serve as a model for how the system should work. "The police worked their tails off on this case. My staff, Lanie Reynolds in particular, worked round the clock to see justice was served. The case was filled with technicalities and scientific detail and we didn't want the jury to get tripped up on any of it."

The pushy blonde court reporter from Channel 3 cut Gene off to ask Trish, "Are you satisfied with the verdict, Mrs. Riley? Were you disappointed the jury didn't find Beaulay guilty of first degree murder?"

"I don't know if satisfied is the right word. I'm glad

it's over. Second degree murder is fine with me. Either way, a life was ended and three great kids had their dad taken from them."

"Does the verdict bring closure?" The blonde with the Brenda Starr complex shouted.

Trish gave her a steely glare that went right over her head. "There is no such thing as closure. Energy never ends, not even in death. That is one thing Stephen Hawking and the Dalai Lama agree on. Leah Beaulay brought a lot of misery into my life. There will never be closure. You should strike that word from your vocabulary."

Another reporter shouted, "Do you have anything you'd like to say to Ms. Beaulay?"

"Yes. Not that she's asked, but I'd like her to know that I forgive her."

Chapter 91

8:17 am

Claudia was in a deep almost trancelike sleep when the phone rang. She wanted Jake to answer it but couldn't make her mouth form the words. Four rings, five, Claudia's eyes sprang open and she rolled across the empty bed and answered without thinking, "Hello."

"Claudia? It's Joe, did I wake you?"

"No, no, I just couldn't get to the phone," she lied.

"I just got off the phone with Ruth O'Kiefe. She's asked me to submit a final bill and tie up the investigation. She'd like to meet with you this afternoon so you can review your findings and turn over your files."

It was time. Claudia was happy to hear Joe's instructions. "Of course, I'll give Ruth a call."

"No need. She wants to meet with you first and then have the two of you sit down with Trish. I think she's still trying to protect Trish from the ugly details. Probably wants to brief you on that. Can you be at the Riley house at 4:00, today?"

"Yep, I'll be there. Joe, if I haven't said so, thank you for all you've done. I now know that the nicest thing a friend can do for someone starting out is to throw them a piece of business. This means a lot to me."

Claudia hung up the phone and headed to the shower. A sticky note on the bathroom mirror read: "I wanted to take you to breakfast but you were snoring so loud I decided you needed your sleep. Dinner tonight? A roll in the hay? Call me. Love, Jake."

3:15 pm

Claudia arrived at the Riley house forty-five minutes ahead of schedule. She wanted to soak in the glory of the day while she reviewed her summary presentation. Despite their friendship, Claudia wanted to give Trish and Ruth the same formal presentation she would have given any other client. Three file boxes of notes were neatly arranged in her trunk. Claudia hoped she could convince Trish to destroy them. She would hate for the children to read them someday.

With all the windows down, Claudia could hear the rustle of the wind in the spring leaves of the old elm tree. The sound and feel of the wind in the elm was gift enough on this perfect day. The fragrance of newly blooming lilacs was a bonus. Claudia put down her notes and soaked up the moment and the day. She closed her eyes and tried to breathe through the thick feeling in her throat and chest. Everything was going so well. Why was she overtaken by a sense of impending doom? The sound of the ancient tree reminded her of a story Ruth once shared. Claudia had wondered how the old elm had managed to escape the Dutch elm disease that swept through Omaha and claimed nearly every elm in its path.

"Don't underestimate the individual strength of one crusty old bird to beat the odds. It's true of any species," Ruth said. "When my mother was eighty-three, she suffered a terrible stroke. She was so completely out of it that the doctor felt safe discussing her condition with us as though she wasn't there. In those days, you never discussed the possibility or probability of death with the patient. Anyway, the doctor told us that she had no more than a five percent chance of survival.

"Turns out, mother heard every word of our conversation. She not only survived, but she went on to make a full recovery. She later told me that she had heard every word of the doctor's conversation. Hearing that she only stood a five percent chance of survival didn't faze her in the least. She told me, 'somebody had to be a part of that five percent, I figured it might as well be me. I didn't give it a moment's worry.' Today, mother is ninety-eight-years-old, lives in her own apartment, and is the most independent, positive person I know. She just *knew* that she'd be okay. I've got that same survival intuition. Every time I look at this old elm, I say a little prayer of gratitude for all of us who have beat life's odds."

Chapter 92

3:45 pm

Trish's Volvo station wagon turned into her driveway. Dressed in the navy blazers and plaid skirts that comprised the uniforms of the neighborhood Catholic school, six of her nieces and nephews (some of Ruth's other grandchildren) piled out of the car as they continued to sing along with the song blaring over the classic rock radio station: "War, good God now, what is it good for? Absolutely nothing!"

Claudia smiled at the sight of little children of privilege singing such a grown up serious song with such conviction.

Trish closed the doors and the children scattered. Finally, Ruth grabbed onto the door jam, rocked herself and stepped out. Standing next to the Volvo, she steadied herself for a split second before closing the car door and walking with a slow but steady gait to the front porch. She sat down in the white wicker rocking chair and sighed. Ruth O'Kiefe was slowing down. On the rare occasion that Claudia caught a glimpse of Ruth or her own mother showing their seventy years, it made her sad.

Ruth picked up the evening *Omaha World Herald* and began to read. Mallory and Sally, began to kick the soccer ball around the front yard, Ruth looked up. How she wished competitive sports had been around for girls when she was young. Watching her granddaughters' fluid movements was mesmerizing. Living life was so much richer than reading about it, Ruth thought as she set aside the newspaper.

Claudia heard the car before she saw it come barreling over the crest of the hill. The reverberating rap music meant high school was out for the day. Mallory slid fearlessly into the ball but missed it. Sally leapt over her and single-mindedly ran after the ball as it rolled into the street. Claudia saw the tragedy unfolding but could not move. She sat frozen in her seat.

Ruth fueled by Adrenalin and love, without hesitation, bolted out of the rocker and across the yard with the grace and speed of a cheetah. Sally's eyes were fixed on the ball, Ruth's were fixed on Sally. Neither looked up at the Jeep bearing down on them. Without breaking her stride, Ruth swept Sally up from the street and kept running until they were safely on the other side.

The Jeep screeched to a halt. The terrified boy behind the wheel looked into Ruth's panicked eyes and squealed off. The pulsing base of the Jeep's radio was drowned out by the pounding in Claudia's chest, her throat, her ears, her brain.

Ruth and Sally sat entwined in grateful embrace. When Ruth looked up, she saw Claudia for the first time, still sitting behind the wheel, strapped in her seatbelt. They both nodded in acknowledgment of what had just transpired. What Claudia had suspected for months could no longer be denied.

Sally sat dazed, both by the physical force of her grandmother's adrenaline-driven speed and by the shock of the experience. Claudia was now standing over the two, her eyes still locked with Ruth's. Finally, Ruth spoke. "My darling, darling Sally," Ruth started in a steady tone, "If anything ever happened to you, I would quite literally die. I mean that. I could not go on. And your mother would die, too. Do you want that?"

"Of course not. Grandma, I am so, so sorry."

"I can fix almost anything. I can live through anything. But I can not live with the death of another one of my children or grandchildren. Not again."

Ruth kissed Sally on the lips, both cheeks, the forehead and chin. Then again on the lips. Hard.

Sally stood and looked up and down the street before she ran across to the Riley yard. Claudia extended her hands to help Ruth up. She groaned as her knees cracked and she wobbled into an upright position.

"How long have you known?" Ruth asked.

"I've suspected it all along but I wouldn't allow myself to go there. But now there's no denying it. I never doubted you'd die for your family. I just didn't want to let myself believe you'd kill for them."

The power of love—not just romantic love—can force people to make powerful, even deadly, decisions.

Chapter 93

"Shall we take a walk?" Ruth asked.

"No. I think this deserves a face-to-face conversation, don't you? Get in my car. We'll go to Elmwood."

The drive to Elmwood Park took less than ten minutes but it felt like an hour. Not a single word was spoken. 99.9 Classic Rock was playing on Claudia's radio. It was British oldies: "Mrs. Brown You've Got a Lovely Daughter," Mick Jagger singing "Satisfaction" and finally John Lennon singing Claudia's favorite Beatles song, "In My Life".

Ruth turned up the radio. A look of serenity sat comfortably on her face. Despite the sick feeling in her stomach, Claudia was struck by how beautiful Ruth looked and by how much she loved her. To Claudia's surprise, Ruth joined Lennon in perfect pitch:

There are places I remember ...

Claudia waited for John Lennon to finish before she turned off the car. Without a word, the women walked fifty yards to an empty picnic table near the ravine. They sat across from each other in awkward silence. Finally, Claudia spoke. "Okay. Spill it."

"Are you familiar with the term inviolability? It means that anything I say to you is sacred. It's a sacred trust protected by law. You can never breach the trust of what I say. It's a fancy word for lawyer/client privilege. I hired Joe Duprey. He is my attorney and he hired you. The checks you receive for your excellent investigative work come from the law firm—not from me. They bill me, along with a healthy commission for the firm, I trust, then they issue you a check. The attorney/client privilege of confidentiality extends to anyone who works for a client's lawyer, anyone on Joe's legal team, right down to the clerk who runs the copy machine. And you, my dear, work for Joe. Everything you learned in your investigation and everything I share with you today and in the future is strictly confidential. That's the law. Talk to anyone else about what you know—like the police or your husband, for instance—and you will be breaking the law.

"I always knew you'd figure this out. Only you. To everyone else, I was invisible. I was never considered a suspect. I believe in you. I knew that, sooner or later, you would see what had to be seen—not what you wanted to see. I knew you'd figure it out. So *I*, not Trish as everyone assumes, asked Joe to hire you. I pay my lawyer and my lawyer pays you.

"Now that you understand that you are obligated under the law to keep this conversation confidential, what would you like to know?"

"I want you to start at the beginning—no, before the beginning. When did you first hatch the idea of killing Max? Why? Did you ever think about backing out? How did you pull it off and not get caught? Who else knows about this? You know me. I want every detail."

Ruth took a deep breath. "You planted the seed of the idea in my head."

"Me?! What are you talking about?"

"Remember that miserable Christmas party at the house where the kids were walking around like zombies? They had been through the wringer living in an unhappy household knowing that Max was leaving them for Leah. Remember what you said? You said they looked 'dead behind the eyes'. And you were right. Max and Leah were killing Trish and the kids. They just hadn't disposed of the bodies. Trish didn't have the strength to leave him so I made him leave her in a way that would bring them all back to life.

"If you could save the lives of your children and grandchildren, you would. That's exactly what I did. I brought them back to life. It was easy to rationalize that this was an act of self-defense. I had to save my family. I was blinded by grief. I couldn't bear to see Trish and the kids suffer any longer. And it worked. After Max died, the life force returned to all of them.

"Do you remember the Buddhist speaker we went to hear at the Unitarian Church? Do you recall his explanation about what life is? That stuck with me. I remember he said that he did not believe in aging. That who we are is what we are thinking, our experiences, our emotions. Our bodies are simply containers, packaging. Who we are is what's inside the packaging. That helped me rationalize my plan. I wasn't murdering Max, I was getting rid of the packaging. He and Leah were the murderers. They were sucking the souls out of everyone they touched."

Claudia couldn't let this pass.

"That's your rationale? Don't you feel the least little bit guilty?"

Ruth laughed. "You already know the answer to that. I'm Catholic. You're Lutheran. We live in the guilt. It's like breathing to us. There is never good rationale for killing. I know what I did was wrong. I can explain why I did it, but it was wrong and I should not have done it. My religion not only makes me feel guilt, it also makes me feel hopeful. I have sincerely asked God to forgive me and I know he has. So I don't allow myself to wallow in it. That would be a waste of my life and a waste of the energy I should be using for good. I refuse to let guilt get in the way of living in the moment, so I chose to let go of it. What good would punishment do me? I'm not a threat to anyone.

"Speaking of Catholic guilt, Trish used it as an excuse for staying married to Max but religion wasn't the real reason. She honestly believed that she wasn't worthy of Max and that she was lucky to have him. There was no debating the issue with her. I convinced myself there was no other way. Every now and then, I'd come to my senses and then Max would do something so sadistic that I'd remember why I had to kill him.

"I'll give you an example. Max's cigar and Absinthe ritual was all the more enjoyable to him because it was so demeaning to Trish. She hated that damn cigar smoke. Every night, he'd snuff out his cigar in the last of the Absinthe. Trish knew that Leah introduced him to this evening ritual so of course that made it all the more painful. He'd leave the dirty glass in his study and expect Trish to clean up after him the next morning. When Trish was out of the house, Leah would sneak over and join him. They didn't even try to hide it. Trish was expected to clean up after Leah, too.

"I remember a morning when Trish had returned from one of her trips to the Indian reservation to find that Leah had joined Max the night before in his study. There were two empty glasses, one with a Cuban cigar butt extinguished in about an inch of alcohol. For once, Trish showed an ounce of pride and declined to clean up the mess. Instead of feeling ashamed or relieved, Max lit into Trish when he got home that night. I'll never forget it. I could hear his tirade all the way in the carriage house. He just went on a rant: 'What do you do all day? It's your job to keep my study clean. It's the only place I can get away from you and the kids. If I did my job as poorly as you do yours, I'd be fired.' Well, that was the last time Trish refused to clean up after Max and his whore. I couldn't bear it. I told her I had heard the argument and insisted that I would start cleaning up after Max.

"It got worse. After the guests left the Christmas

party and Trish and the kids had gone to bed, I watched Leah slip into Max's study. While she waited for him to join her, she poured him his Absinthe and opened a bottle of Trish's favorite wine for herself. She poured the wine into her Absinthe glass and lit a cigar for Max. Max had become so cruel. I think he enjoyed the idea of getting caught. After they finished their drinks, Leah took the cigar from his mouth and snuffed it in the Absinthe.

"I was outside letting the dog pee and watched the whole thing. Want to know what's really sick? I'm sure they knew I was watching and decided to really put on a show for me. Anyway, after they finished their drinks, Leah walked Max to the window, leaned over the sill and lifted up the back of her skirt. Max unzipped his pants and, well, you get the picture. I swear they were looking straight at me. They got some twisted thrill knowing that this old lady—Max's mother-in-law for God's sake—was watching them.

"The next morning, I retrieved Max's Absinthe glass and took it back to my house. I was careful not to disturb Leah's fingerprints though it turned out I didn't need them. After that night, every time I cleaned up Max's mess, I would add the cigar and Absinthe to the glass I had back at my house. Over the months that followed, the irony that Max and Leah were concocting his own deadly drink, was not lost on me. It all began to feel like some sort of cosmic justice.

"I knew that nicotine could be lethal in concentrated form because when I was doing volunteer work at the Humane Society we tried to get some sicko prosecuted for giving his dog Kool Aid that he'd been soaking cigarettes in. He knew it would kill the poor thing. He was just curious to see how long it took and if it seemed painful."

This was a lot for Claudia to digest. But she found it all sickly fascinating. "So that explains your means and your motive, but how did you pull it off? Where was the opportunity?"

Chapter 94

I possess a super power," Ruth continued. "All women of a certain age do. I am invisible without even trying. That gave me all the opportunity I needed. You'll become invisible too, someday. It begins when you turn forty. You walk into a restaurant and a man might look up at you and go back to his meal. He won't take a second look. By the time you're fifty, he won't even give you a first look. Neither will his female companion."

"By the time you're my age, forget about it. You're completely invisible. You'll walk into the department store and the clerk will ask if you need help. Five minutes later, she won't remember you and she'll act like she's asking if you need help for the first time. Nobody is interested in your opinions or defines you as attractive in any way. People you know and run into in the grocery store pretend they don't see you because

God forbid they might have to exchange a few words with you. I could never have pulled this off without my power of invisibility.

"It was even more useful during the police investigation. They testified at the trial that they looked carefully at all the family members. I guess they didn't consider me family. The police didn't suspect me because they never even noticed me. They never asked me where I was the day Max died or when I returned to Omaha. Nothing. I had my answers all rehearsed, but they never asked.

"For weeks after I'd concentrated the nicotine, I had no idea how I would get it to Max. I didn't want Trish or the kids to find his body at home and I was afraid if I set things up at one of his little out-of-town love nests, someone else might accidentally drink it. Then, one day I hitched a ride to Portland on the company jet and I overheard one of the pilots complaining about all the work he had put into an aircraft security plan. The pilot was really ticked. He said that kiss-up, James Beck, took full credit for his plan and that Max even gave him a cash bonus for it. He said Beck took the money and the credit but never implemented the plan. This pilot genuinely seemed more upset that the plan had not been put in place than he did about not receiving credit. I heard him say that thanks to Beck's incompetence and lazy ass, anybody and everybody could do damage to Great Western planes and hangars.

"I drove to the company's Centennial hangar in my rented car about an hour before it was scheduled for boarding. Nobody was there but the plane was unlocked. At any point, I could have been scared away from following through with this, but there was no one there to stop me."

"I walked onto the plane like I owned it. Everything was wide open. Nothing was locked. I switched Max's on-board bottle of Absinthe with the one I had 'fixed'. I poured some into the glass I'd brought along and placed it on the shelf. I had plenty of time to do some snooping so I took a handkerchief from my purse and started opening doors and drawers. That's when I found the aftershave. It didn't take a genius to figure out why Max kept that handy, so I poured some of the nicotine spiked Absinthe into the aftershave.

"As I drove down the empty stretch of road away from the airport, I passed Beck driving to the gate. Instinctively, I waved at him. He did not wave back. He looked right through me. Being invisible has its advantages."

"How did you know that Leah would visit the airplane before it took off? How did you know James Beck would be the pilot that day?" Claudia interrupted.

"I didn't. I did very little planning and, truth be told, I was pretty sloppy. So much of what happened was just dumb luck, or coincidence. I never dreamed Leah would be arrested or that they could make a case against her. None of that was due to any planning or expertise on my part. Leah's arrest and conviction— now that's cosmic icing on the cake. One 'serial killer' of the spirit is dead and the other 'serial killer' goes to jail where she can't kill any more families. Karma."

Chapter 95

R uth and Claudia walked into the Riley house as Trish was placing glasses of iced tea on the tray she had inherited from her grandmother. The tray had bright lime green flowers imprinted under a high gloss heavy resin finish, giving it an authentic 'sixties' look. Trish loved the ugly thing. She used to play cards—Gin and I Doubt It—with her paternal grandmother on that tray when she was a little girl and that made it precious to her.

"Let's hear your report so we can put a period at the end of this horrible sentence," Trish blurted out in the no nonsense style she inherited from Ruth.

They spent the next hour discussing the possible events in various suspects' lives that changed their character. They speculated about how two people placed in the same situation, can make very different choices and have very different outcomes.

"What turns a person like Leah into a conniving, gold digger yet her best friend, Ruby, grows up under similar circumstances and is the very picture of humility and goodness?" Claudia asked.

"Just another one of life's mysteries," Trish said. "Life is full of things we're forced to accept without understanding."

As Trish cleared the table, Claudia voiced her concerns about the boxes of files locked in the trunk of her car. Trish agreed they could cause more unnecessary pain for her children and asked Claudia to shred them.

Trish and Ruth walked Claudia to her car. As Claudia buckled herself in, Trish handed her a small sack. "I want you to have this," Trish said. Inside the sack was the chipped coffee cup Tim had made. Tears flashed in her eyes.

"I will treasure this more than you can imagine." Claudia got out of her car and hugged Trish long and hard.

Chapter 96

6:30 pm

Claudia flipped open her cell phone as she rounded the corner away from the Riley house. Three missed messages:

"Hey Claudia, it's Joe. How did it go with the Riley's? Give me a call."

BEEP

"Call your mamma."

BEEP

"Hello, wife. I'm still at work. Don't wait dinner for me. I'll find something when I get home. Shouldn't be too late. Maybe 7:00. Love ya."

As Claudia entered the crowded parking lot of Julio's Restaurant, a sense of peace washed over her. She couldn't wait to get home to Jake, make love and with it perhaps a baby. Things were falling into place. Closing the investigation marked the end of an important chapter in her life. The timing seemed right to start a new chapter, a new life.

Richard Wolf, owner of Julio's and Claudia's friend, greeted her at the door with his signature bear hug. Richard was glad he'd never met Jake. "Knowing your husband might ruin you as my Number One fantasy," he teased. "The usual?" Richard laughed. "Somebody's gonna get lucky tonight."

Claudia's usual was Julio's Super Nacho Platter. There was something about pulling apart the messy, cheesy pile of guacamole, ground beef, and peppers that she found very erotic. Claudia couldn't imagine why anyone would order dinner when this appetizer could easily be a complete meal for four. "Easy," Richard smiled. "We call it 'the super nacho rule.' We train waitresses never to deliver super nachos to the table until the dinner order has been turned into the kitchen."

The dimly lit restaurant was a favorite for upwardly mobile twenty and thirty-somethings. The perimeter was lined with tall, dark oak booths. The high back-to-back booths also ran down the center of the bar area. Richard quietly pointed to one of the coveted center booths as four young men in suits prepared to leave. She grabbed the booth and ordered a Pepsi while she waited for her nachos. Finally, a few minutes to work on some long overdue checkbook balancing.

As she worked her way through the check register, she heard a familiar voice from the booth on the other side of hers. She slid to the inside so she could hear the conversation. The room was noisy but the coy voice and phony tone came through loud and clear. She pressed one ear against the common wall of the booth and plugged the other. She was eavesdropping on FBI agent, Nan Levine at her flirtatious best.

Claudia strained to hear Nan's end of a hot, almost pornographic, conversation. "What's that bulge between your legs, Big Guy?" (So much for Jake's theory about Nan's sexuality.)

"Correct me if I'm wrong, but didn't I just take care of that thing? Unzip your pants and whip it out. My toes are good, but they don't do zippers. That's better."

Claudia' couldn't stop smiling. She couldn't believe her ears. Nan Levine was helping some guy get off in a booth at Julio's!

Claudia wondered how long the waitress had been standing there before she placed the foam box of nachos on the table. She silently mouthed the words, "thank you," and handed her a twenty.

In one fell swoop, Claudia scooped her calculator, pencil, and check register back into her purse. She was going to enjoy "bumping" into Nan. She spun around to the booth on the other side, prepared to act surprised. Nan's cell phone and purse were on the table, but no

Nan. She was underneath, finishing off her date.

In an instant, Claudia found herself frozen in an out of body experience. She saw movement from under the table. Her alter-ego somehow took over and she heard herself say to her wide-eyed husband seated alone in the booth, "That's quite a blow job you're getting from The Lesbian."

Chapter 97

Claudia dropped the box of nachos onto the table in front of Jake and hurried to the parking lot leaving Jake speechless.

Claudia strapped herself into the driver's seat and, somehow, drove herself home. Safely in her driveway, she wondered how she had gotten herself there. She couldn't recall a single stoplight or consciously making a turn. Without thinking, she walked into the house and to the telephone to call her old friend in Santa Barbara. Jane answered the phone on the first ring. The sound of a kind voice made Claudia choke up.

"Damn it, Jane. Why did you have to move half way across the country? I need you." Claudia found she could only choke out one word responses. So Jane took over.

"Is it Jake?"

"Yes."

"What? Is he sick? Has he been hurt?"

"No."

"Crap. I know where this is going. You are to drive straight to the airport and get on the 10:00 pm flight to Santa Barbara. I'll meet you at the airport on this end. You are not to say a word to Jake. Claudia, do you understand what I'm saying? Call me from Eppley before you get on the plane. You're going to stay in our guesthouse and we're going to figure this out. I love you and I'm on your side. Now get going."

Claudia hung up the phone and started throwing things into her gym bag.

Makeup and toiletries would have to wait until California. She did not want to be at home when Jake finally showed up. As she pulled out of the driveway, she looked at her watch. It was 7:35. It had been forty-five minutes since her world had exploded. The drive home from Julio's took all of fifteen minutes, so where was he? Was he that big a coward? Was he at Nan's house? Were they trying to get their stories straight or did they even care if they had a story?

Worst of all, the nagging question she could not get out of her mind: *Is Jake in love with Nan?*

Claudia was met at the ticket counter by the agent. Jane had arranged everything and purchased a first class ticket for her. Jane knew how to take charge and it was just what Claudia needed at the moment. Once in the boarding area, Claudia picked up her cell phone to return her mother's call.

"Hi, Mom."

"How are you? What's new?'

"Oh, I'm not so bad. What have you been up to?"

"I played bridge with Vi and Evelyn and Betty today. I won fifty-five cents."

"Wow, high stakes gambling, as always." Claudia could not bring herself to tell her mother about Jake but she didn't want her calling the house or worrying.

"Mom, I'm at the airport. I'm going to visit Jane in California. I'll call you tomorrow."

"Give me Jane's phone number."

Claudia complied. She could hear the worry in her mother's silence more than in her voice. Dorothy was the strongest woman Claudia had ever met. She had never seen her mother cry, not even at her father's funeral. She had also never heard her mother say, "I love you." But she used other words that meant much more. And all of Dorothy's children knew they were loved.

"Come on, Claudia, what gives?"

"I just can't, Mom. Don't worry. Nobody's sick or dying. I've just hit a very big rut in the marital road. And don't say anything nice to me. If you do, I'll cry. Neither one of us wants that."

"Okay. Have a safe trip. I wish you'd talk to me. But, I'm glad you have Jane."

Claudia took a deep breath and closed her eyes. She could imagine the pained look on her mother's face as she said goodbye.

"God bless you, honey. God bless you."

There it was. The three words that meant so much more from her mother than "I love you" ever could.

Claudia closed her phone and took off for the ladies room. Once she safely ensconced herself in a locked stall she indulged herself in a good, loud cry.

After a few minutes, the sobs ended as quickly as they had begun. She washed her hands and wiped the mascara away from under her lower lashes. The flood of tears washed away what was left of her day old makeup. Oddly, nothing made Claudia look more beautiful than a good cry. The tears made her watery blue eyes pop with the color of the Caribbean. As she exited the restroom, she heard a man's voice call her name. It was Peter Anderson.

"Claudia, I thought that was you. Are you all right?"

"Not really, what about you? How are you doing?"

"To tell you the truth, I'm better than I've been in years," Peter smiled. "I finally got sick of playing the schmuck and filed for divorce. I'm on my way to Hawaii for three weeks of sun, surf, and exercise. I'm going to purge myself of all the toxic waste that has become my life. What about you? Where are you headed?"

"I'm running away. I just discovered my husband is having an affair so I'm going to visit a friend in Santa Barbara and figure out what to do with my life." Claudia cocked her head and smiled through pursed lips.

Peter took both of Claudia's hands into his own and said, "Welcome to the club. I'm sorry the dues are so high. May I pass on some advice I wish someone had given me?"

"Please."

"Our marriage counselor told me that nothing had to happen quickly and that I should not rush into anything. Problem is, the longer you wait, the harder it is to pull the plug. I was helping my mom prepare yams for Christmas and I had a rare moment of clarity. As mother slowly and repeatedly scooped the insides of the boiled yams away from their skins, I realized that was what was happening to me. I had allowed my insides to be slowly and carefully removed until I had become nothing more than a beat up, empty shell. That was the moment I decided to reclaim my life.

"I waited far too long to call it quits. I hate like hell to quote Dr. Phil, but he preaches that we teach people how to treat us. And he's right. I taught Leah that she could have affairs again and again and I'd stand by her. Now that you've caught your husband cheating, if you take him back it will only teach him that he can have his cake and eat it too. And he'll do it again and again. I'm speaking from experience. He may be okay for someone else, but he'll never stay faithful to you.

"So here's my advice: *Don't wait too long to pull the plug. If you do, it will suck the life right out of you.*"

Acknowledgments

Special thanks go to:

Daughters Mallory and Sally Car who gave me time and space to write and encouragement and nagging to persevere.

John Car who was my go-to-guy for police procedure and aviation questions—not to mention the personal and practical support.

Erin Jennings who has been more like a daughter than a niece and is always on my side.

David Mack for his friendship and superior editing skills.

Early readers and friends who encouraged and corrected me along the way, Trish Billotte and Marilou Woodard.

The best models a writer/photographer could ask for, Ava and Tommy Steele.

Sharon Kava and Deb Carlin for encouraging me to keep writing and see this through to publication—*and then making it happen.*

And for all the unnamed friends I am so blessed to have in my life. You have helped me through the rough patches and shared my joys.

About the Author

Brock Car grew up in Omaha, Nebraska, and graduated from the University of Kansas School of Journalism. After a long career in corporate communications, she established her own advertising and public relations firm and wrote for magazines and literary journals. Car lives on North Hutchinson Island, Florida, and in Omaha. This is her first novel.

To learn more about Brock Car, visit her website www.BrockCar.com, find her on Facebook and on Twitter at BrockCar_Author

Lightning Source UK Ltd.
Milton Keynes UK
UKOW05f1810150617

303414UK00001B/145/P

9 780983 676164